The

Progeny

Assassin

A Tarnished Lands Story

P.A. WIKOFF

This book is a work of fiction. Character names, places and events are products of the author's imagination. Any resemblance to characters (living or dead), incidents or settings is entirely coincidental.

Visit the author's blog pawikoff.wordpress.com

Patreon.com/pawikoff

Follow @pawikoff on twitter and Instagram

Facebook.com/pawikoff

Edited by Crystal Wikoff. Copyedited by Cheryl Wikoff.

Cover art by Levon Jihanian

Visit Levonjihanian.com

ISBN: 9780999005835
ISBN-13: 978-0-9990058-3-5

Be sure and check out my other stories in the
Tarnished Lands series.

The Forgotten Woods Saga
The Harrowed Half-Breed – Book 1
The Progeny Assassin – Book 2
The Mad Wizard – Book 3

Contents

The Hunt 1

Mistakes are Made 14

Trapped 33

Yes, Master 45

All by Myself 64

The First Night 77

Growing Up 90

Sacrifice 104

A Dance, a Debt, and a Deception 124

The Edge of the World 138

One Side of a Thought 147

Frozen in Time 159

First and Last 173

Call to Action 184

Eastern Bound 200

A Grave Memory 229

The Leftovers 240

Onward 250

Work or Play 262

Exploring the Tide 271

Land of Humans 279

Village of Broken Dreams 297

A Fight to the Death 325

Reunion 342

About Time 358

The Immortal 371

Parting Ways 399

Epilogue 407

Tarnished Lands

In the aftermath of the utopian regime that ruled for over a millennium, famine, chaos, murder and deceit reign in lieu of balance. The pendulum now swings in favor of disorder. The fierce strong-arm the weak, cowards lurk in the shadows like rats, and the wicked take everything that's left over. This is no longer a place for good intentions; this is a place of survival.

The Hunt

The lake is a dry, decimated wasteland with deep cracks and fissures marring the once enchanted waterscape. Vibrant shells are left behind by the decayed acting as a reminder of a lush, majestic time that has long since passed. What used to be a spectacular oasis filled with pink sparkling water is now an empty dream, nearly forgotten by all. Time has taken its splendor from this world and the memories from those who were fortunate enough to witness this once serene spot. Its beauty has been stripped away like a skinned unicorn left for dead. Now it only lives on the pages of outdated maps, hidden under stacks of tattered documents, withering away with time.

A young adolescent girl sifts through a decorative trove—not for something girlish or pleasing to the eye, but rather anything deadly sharp. Never one for vanity, her desires are that of a different nature, especially by the standards of other girls around her age. She didn't come here for the silky, rippling waves, as there haven't been any for even longer than the long-lifers can recall. One would expect that only the reckless or unhinged would venture to such a place of peril and punishment. Yet here she sits, knees tucked into her chest as her little fingers do the busy work of the day's find like an eager crustacean bottom-feeding off the discarded.

She appears to be at play, fixated on her task without a care for the drought that surrounds her feet, the scorching air that sits above her pressing down upon her like a weight, or the dryness in her joints—a gift from her dehydration. There is no question about it, this is not a place for a youth, or anyone for that matter.

But this is no ordinary young girl. Her skin has been hardened by the grueling ways of her ancestry, and her slim, agile body is a result of living off only one meal a day. None of this seems to faze her one bit. It's just another day in paradise...if evil had sucked all that is good and pure out of it.

The ridge surrounding the lakebed is covered by burnt foliage, serving as a cemetery of the catastrophe that had rampaged through these parts. The roaring flames came in hot and fast and left just as quickly—never staying long enough for an explanation of why, or for the trees to be reduced to dust—leaving the leaves and bark seared and charred.

The soot casts its own darkness upon the land, an unforgiving scar. Ash normally turns grey as it transitions from ember to residue but not in this anathematized place. Here, the ash is black as coal and cold to the touch. The penetrating effect from the fire has had the same effect on the dirt, leaving everything dark and unfertile.

There is only one plant that grows naturally off this rancid earth—the butterfly kiss. Don't let its name and frail-looking stems fool you. It is highly poisonous to ingest and quite corrosive to the touch. If that isn't bad enough, during the spring season it releases pollen that will burn you from the inside out if you happen to catch a whiff of it. The real cruelty is that the pollen has an aromatic fragrance that is to die for, literally.

It's muggy with nowhere to find relief from the scorching sun. The clouds no longer cast their shadows this far out. Even the sun's rays don't want any part of the blighted earth, and you can feel its unforgiving heat just as strong as it reflects off the ground—misery attacking you from all angles.

This forest was once a lifeline for many humanoid and animal species. Scattered around the blackened forest are the occasional signs of trees that had reached temperatures so high, they exploded from the inside out, and on even more rare occasions, evidence of lifeforms dying in the same fashion.

Hidden deep inside the evidence of death, broken tools, pottery, and even clothes are scattered everywhere—signs of the past occupancy. Unfortunately, they all have been kissed by the fire and are brittle, if not completely in ruin.

The smart ones ran away with their lives, leaving their fears behind. Others had no choice—trapped like a wolf in a snare forced to eat itself alive. Lara is neither. She came to be long after the near extinction of her kind—the feathered-folk. She spends her days reading the emotion of the land, and it tells a tale of hardship and disaster. It says, "Everyone dies when everything is death."

She often wonders why anyone brought her into this dismal place to suffer alongside the aftermath. To most, nothingness seems more appealing than living in famine and poverty, but for her this is all there is, all there ever will be. Her own story is one of the many mysteries to be solved. She has become numb to the questions that she once racked her brain over during countless sleepless nights.

"The past never thinks about you. Why should you show it such importance?" Lara says in a mocking voice, recounting one of the many unsolicited pieces of advice that her master forces upon her constantly. If Lara weren't so micromanaged and lectured all the time, she might not be out here today to find comfort in the brutal silence.

Her soot-covered body blends perfectly with the charredscape, hiding her tough bark-like skin against the wicked wreckage. Her kind walks and talks like humans do, only with a particularly distinguishing characteristic—delicate feathers that sprout from her body instead of hair. Though she has no way of hiding her violet eyes, her soft silver feathers blend nicely with her dark disguise. This feature gives the feathered-folk an almost symphonic sound when a breeze travels through the forest, like a meadow of foxtails brushing up against each other on a spring afternoon, although Lara has never known the swishing sound or the feeling it evokes. It died alongside the trees when the forest lost its breath.

Her people used to believe that the wind would cleanse the nightmares that tainted their souls. However, her master says that the wind never took away the fears, but rather, brought everyone else's to them to play out its cruelty. Lara doesn't know what to believe, but in either case, the breeze no longer blows here since the leaves stopped growing to cheer on its presence with their rustling applause. Movements are difficult to hide in a place so still. Like hearing moaning in a graveyard, it puts you on edge. If it weren't for the sun's crusade in the sky, one might think that time had perished alongside everything else.

Closing her eyes tightly, Lara brings the blistering air to her face, mimicking nature's embrace—trying to trick herself into believing in a better time, one that is filled with hope and...something, anything. Feeling the hot air crash upon her face unlocks emotions she has never known—love, pride, compassion, just to name a few. She is almost intoxicated with the sensation, though still in her adolescence, she has never experienced adult libations.

Lara longs to indulge in these emotions forever, like a gluttonous snake in a pit filled with mice, where each bite entices the next. It's a stolen feeling that gives her solace in this wretched land now known as the dead forest. It used to have a name—a great one—but similar to people, when forests die, they are long since forgotten inside their unmarked graves. Lara and her master are the last of their kind, acting like worms feasting on what is left of a cadaver.

Her eyes almost pop out of her head as she snaps out of the false euphoria that sedated her curious mind. She senses that something is terribly wrong. She knows this feeling well.

Lara sinks her fingertips into the soft residue on the ground, heeding nature's call. She senses movement to the east, and suddenly she is seeing through the shadow of another. It is faint, but it's undoubtedly there, far beyond the limits of her sight. Her vision is blurry, like looking through dark water, as she uses this trespasser's own darkness as a betrayal. To some, the scenery behind him may look like more of the same—burnt-out trees, rotted old stumps that have long since been severed—but Lara knows exactly where to go and where he is going to be next. She has plotted her domain all too well, and now it is time to reap the benefits of her iron-clad memory.

The forest, its ghost, haunts her bones when trouble is afoot, and currently it's trampling on her moment. No one ventures out this far for sightseeing or a brisk hike, as there is no food, water or animals to observe. From experience, Lara knows that no good can come from outsiders, and she must act before the bad makes things much worse.

Lara stashes the shells she has scavenged inside her satchel, avoiding the sharp spirals that could easily cut her tough skin. She proceeds to climb out of the dry lakebed hopping from boulder to boulder. Each step is memorized from past excavations—this is her playground, and she knows it well. Every boulder, tree and rolling hill is imprinted in her young mind. Rarely is anything out of place, and when it is, she takes notice and updates the map she has internalized. New discoveries can only be found underground or outside of her territory, though the latter is a forbidden act. Like anywhere, rules are rules, and breaking them can have horrifying consequences.

Although Lara wishes she could spend the entire day inside the lakebed, she reluctantly follows the aching feeling inside her, like a homing pigeon, where home is death.

While she skips, Lara wipes all her tracks away with a bristle sweeper she has invented to make erasing her steps much faster. It mimics the natural ripples of the dead forest, leaving no trace of her whereabouts for curious eyes that may be lurking.

She is quite proud of her accomplishment, but sharing her ingenuity with her master would result in more work and less time for leisure. So it is withheld, like many aspects of Lara's day-to-day operations. She doesn't see this as a betrayal, by any means. It's exactly what her master preaches more than anything else—survival.

Her stomach tightens the closer she gets to the culprit, as if she were starving. Though no food could tranquilize this feeling.

This is the part of her daily activities that she dreads—her real work. She prefers the openness and freedom of discovery, not the rigid routine of the task ahead of her. It must be done by her master's strict instructions, and there is never room for improvisation.

Her ashen body glides low against the uneven ground, like a shadow escaping its owner. Only the birds would know the truth, if there were any soaring above.

Approaching the last garden, and only place to grow anything that isn't a butterfly kiss, Lara is nearly upon the source of her discomfort. She hears the intruding footsteps. *Crunch, crunch, crunch.* She cringes at every step, which inspires her feet to quicken as she carefully dodges between the rows of small crops, showing more tact than the intruder. He is ruining everything, trudging through nearly a year of hardship and dedication. Water is scarce and extremely laborious to acquire. Each plant and sprout has been carefully nurtured and looked after, more so than a spoiled prince or princess.

She creeps in fast, without warning, acting on her master's will. It's orphan-making work, and Lara just began her shift. She catches the invader's foot midair, before it crushes another seedling—a variegated bristle thorn that Lara has spent months trying to grow in this rotten and unforgiving soil. The fragile growth is weak now, but she hopes that it will grow into a mighty thorn-producing shrub, much against her master's warning...*this field is strictly for consumable vegetation. Remove that thing immediately! You cannot eat thorns.*

Lara has no intention of eating the thorns. That would be ridiculous. What she has in mind is much more exciting, and lethal. Luckily, she was able to apprehend this person's foot before he unknowingly carried out her master's wishes.

The invader wobbles, caught off guard by her actions. He never expected to find another living creature out so far, let alone a youngster.

Looking at the two-leaved sprout that has been spared, Lara lets out a sigh of relief and allows a smile to brighten up her dark face. It only lasts a moment, as her grind begins.

Lara pushes against the invader's standing leg, causing his ligaments to tear. Her countless hours of study have taught her that this injury hurts just as much as breaking a bone and takes longer to recover from. It also requires less strength to inflict upon someone, which is something she has been trying to solve for a while now.

The invader starts to squawk out in pain like a dying bird, but Lara's little hand is already silencing his mouth. She is quick, that's for sure. The man didn't even see her change positions. For a moment, he thinks there might be more than one of her, though he is wrong. She is merely an army of one. He would fare much better if her talents were split among many different people.

"You entered the wrong garden," Lara whispers, slithering her arm around his neck like a constricting snake.

The utter disbelief in his eyes is replaced by terror as he tries to break free from the much smaller girl. He hobbles and flails, trying to reach his belt, but it's no use. She shifts and rotates her position on him without relinquishing the pressure on his neck. The young girl is much too sly for him to lay a hand on her, or anything else to aid in his struggle.

Lara rides him like a bull, steering his limping body out of the small garden, lessening the destruction his leather boots are causing.

He cries out again, this time in frustration. "What is happening?"

She ignores his strife and shifts her body. The extra pressure causes his sprained leg to buckle, bringing him to his knees. She then uses his weight to assist in her chokehold. It is only a matter of time now.

To Lara, this is a boring, predictable, and often menial task. To others, this is murder.

Mistakes are Made

*L*ara lets out a long yawn as the invader writhes between her dainty arms. This is how it must be—no cuts, no weapons—just slow, uneventful execution.

In order to make the experience slightly more enjoyable for herself, she imagines how exciting it would be if there had been multiple intruders. Then she would have to do something clever. Maybe she could separate them with a diversion, or perhaps lure one into some brush where she would be lying in wait. Her mouth unknowingly moves as she acts out the battle inside her head, complete with swooshing and crunching sounds, like a child playing with figures.

What if I had to fight them both at the same time? That thought gives new life to her eyes.

This method is clean, tried and true…and most of all, safe. She doesn't like safe. It's far too predictable. Accepting reality, her excitement is replaced by rolling eyes and a drab expression.

Instead of asking the invader what business he has in these parts, she makes up her own story inside her head. It isn't really going to matter in a couple of moments, but it sure is a good way to pass the time. *He's a renegade of the royal throne, seeking refuge by befriending simple people in the region and murdering them in their sleep. Just like a no-good coward, he takes more than he is given but only what he can carry, as his treachery brings him to the next home to plunder. Nameless, he is known simply by his actions—the destroyer of families, or more succinctly, as "the divorcer." Today is different, however. He doesn't expect to find a feathered-folk in these parts, as they are said to be extinct. If only he were that lucky. His evil red eyes grow tired as the ironic truth sets in—he will die in his sleep today, and her mighty arms are the things putting him to bed.*

Then something catches Lara's eye, breaking her out of her internal dialogue. It's a sparkling light reflecting off the intruder's belt. It's the thing he was struggling to get ahold of, the very thing she is also after—a weapon. Not a shell or a thorn but an honest-to-goodness implement of war.

Suddenly, all her regimented instruction and training disappear like a corpse at a cannibal dinner party. Lara quickly releases her hold on the intruder, relinquishing the upper hand she had over him. This is careless. If Lara had any patience, she would have waited for him to perish before giving in to her curiosity. This is not part of the plan. This is the reckless behavior her master is always scolding her for. But her master isn't here, and her master won't find out...or so she believes.

The man gasps and wheezes as air returns to his lungs. "That really...hurt," he says, underestimating how close to death he really was. He has a human-made weapon, one that is not rusted beyond repair. It has a jeweled hilt and great potential. With her arms outstretched and her body low, Lara gives the human an opportunity to arm himself so that she can give him a fighting chance before liberating him of

16

his weapon and cutting his throat with it. She imagines herself as a proper hunter, allowing the rabbit a head start before giving into the chase. She is always honorable inside the fantasy of her active mind.

The human stands up. He holds his neck while making puke-like faces. A horrid croaking sound escapes his throat. He will live.

She slowly bites her lower lip. Her enthusiasm makes her almost appear to glow, though he doesn't pay her any mind.

The human staggers, forgetting about his lame leg. "Ouch."

Looking closely at the unshaven man with greasy hair, Lara wonders how someone can be so self-involved as to not give her the proper acclaim for such a beautifully executed assault. She was proud of it until this very moment. Overthinking the whole situation, Lara starts to wonder if she isn't as deadly as she thinks. She quickly shakes off the notion. *It will all be over soon.* "Go on, then," Lara says, staring at the sheathed blade, raising her feathered eyebrows in an encouraging sort of way.

This could be the fight she has been pining over for a very long time—the moment she often calls "The One." She isn't referring to a person of romantic interest. "The one" is something far more special to her. Just the mere idea of "the one" keeps her up at night and under her covers on the morning that it infiltrates her dreams. "The one," the only one, the fight of her life, the worthy adversary worth dying for and giving her life meaning. It's best described as a battle where losing could actually be an outcome. That, above all else, is what excites her—a challenge, a fight to the death, to witness the power of unmatched skill. Had "the one" finally come to claim her attention and test every aspect of her discipline? This question has her full attention as she waits impatiently for the human to ready his bejeweled weaponry.

"Get out of here, you filthy folk, before I find your parents," the man says, straightening out his fine leather vest and leggings. He seems almost...civilized. Not at all like a divorcer of life. Not like an evil with a profound pain threshold. Not like the bringer of "the one."

She notices that his attire has no signs of battle or wear, and his face shares a similar quality. It is almost like he was newly born but with unkempt hair and stubble. To her, the only reasonable answer is that the weapon he possesses is quite spectacular, far exceeding her wildest expectations.

One thought leads to another until she is lost inside herself again. Lara wonders how this human identified her species by name, which contradicts the lore she had been taught about her kind. Old questions, dismissed during yesteryear's fights with her master, start to attack her memory.

So many questions she can ask him—ones that she desperately needs answers to. *What do you know of the feathered-folk? Are there more of us? If so, where are they? How did you come to acquire such an exquisite weapon? How many humans are there? Why have they been coming more often?* And the list goes on and on.

Was she really not above consorting with the enemy? She shrugs off that idea. Her only hesitation is trying to figure out which question she should ask first.

Like all good things, her master's words weigh on her conscience. *Never trust a human, except with treachery and deceit.* With that thought overshadowing the others in her mind, Lara dismisses the whole concept and is back in the fight. "Arm yourself before I cut both of yours off, renegade."

"Renegade? Who are you talking to?" The human turns his head, wondering if there is someone else around. "Don't you dare threaten me, girl. I am not in the mood." The man limps back toward the garden, looking directly at the scorching sun for direction. Despite her talents, she is but a child to him—weak and insignificant.

"It isn't good for you to look directly at it." Not that she cares the slightest about his well-being or anything, she just doesn't want any excuses when she beats him to a pulp.

"You are one deranged child, you know that."

"A child? I am not a child." Lara had beaten him. She can't understand how he can still look down upon her after she overpowered him with such ease. "Humans." The word escapes her lips, and she quickly covers her own mouth, hoping he didn't notice her blatant racism.

He flashes a smug look in her general direction, which would have really set her on edge if it weren't for him staring off into empty space. Undoubtedly, a result of the sunspots in his vision. "Really? How old are you, then?"

She doesn't know why she is compelled to justify herself to the likes of him. Lara stops to think about her life in order to prove her maturity to this undeserving human, but it is another one of those mysterious questions that she has no answer to. *I've done so much, lived so long, fought so many. Why are the easiest questions the hardest for me to answer?* "I...don't think I know."

"Well, you look like a child to me. Know this, it's not beyond me to strike a child who doesn't know their place."

"My *place*?"

"Yes, which is as far away from me as possible. Begone." With a wave of his hand, the man turns his back to Lara, not fearing her one bit.

Oh, really? Lara is determined to show him exactly where her "place" is, through pain. Mouthing obscenities, she pulls out one of the sharp shells that she found earlier. Squinting one eye, she takes aim. She intends to get his attention the only way humans know—with violence. Her thinking is that if he finds out she is armed, maybe he will give this fight the importance it deserves, or at least find her mildly threatening.

"Respect must be demanded through fear," she says quietly.

Ignoring her, the human keeps turning his

map every which way, trying to find his bearings. "Hey, do you know the most direct route to The Deep?" He jars his body around to look at the girl as the shell whistles through the air and slices him directly in the throat. Blood dribbles down his neck and onto his chest.

"Oopsie, a child's mistake," Lara says, half joking. Due to her anger, she didn't hold back her throw as much as she had planned. A part of her feels bad for her miscalculation, another part is happy to watch him die.

The human collapses to the ground as he reaches for his blade.

"I guess this is more like a zero than 'the one.'" Her plan has proven to be a little too successful. "Now I've done it." Lara rushes over to him and pulls off his hard-helm. His hair is damp with a moistness that covers his whole body, and he is secreting a musky smell. She gags as it hits her senses. "Stupid, man. You weren't supposed to turn around. Why did you have your back to me anyway? Never lose eye contact. That is a very basic rule. I guess you don't have a master to control you. Well, not anymore, that's for sure."

He spits and sputters. Blood is bubbling out of his neck like a crimson geyser right before an eruption. She positions the wound over his headpiece trying desperately to collect every single drop. "Stop moving. Why do you have to die so easily?" Instantly, regret swallows her pride.

The man slowly raises the dagger behind Lara, with a convulsing hand. She is too distracted to even notice or care. It's no use. Most of a human's blood is stored inside their heavy heads, and this one already leaked most of his all over himself. His hand drops the dagger as he slumps over. A look of horror still scars his face.

"Don't look at me like that. It's your fault." She isn't exactly sure what to do. Blood is smelly, traceable...and quite messy. Too bad too, because it really is everywhere. "Master is going to kill me for killing you all wrong." Feeling nothing for her victim, Lara lays him down and kicks dust over his body hoping to absorb the moisture into the black sand.

"Well, I did my best. What else could she want from me?" Lara says to herself, though she knows full well that this is nothing close to her "best."

Spying the dagger still inches away from his limp hand, she is quick to collect her reward.

Under closer inspection, she fears that it might be more decorative than deadly. The blade is made from soft metal. Her small hands easily bend its dull edge. The shell she threw was far sharper. The glamorous hilt must have been made to intimidate an opponent into submission before a fight even broke out, or so she tries to convince herself. Unfortunately, Lara isn't human and doesn't understand their logic one bit. This seems almost plausible to her. She wonders if she can find a use for the thing, as hurting someone with it is out of the question.

One of the jewels pops out of its casing just from her rubbing it, proving that the gem itself is a fake. "Isn't that just great? Too good to be true. Is there anything in this world real enough to live up to its legend?" Her excitement quickly fades from existence, like a child opening an unwanted gift.

"Typical. It's all a mirage. Master was right for once. They really are tricky, deceitful buggers." Even though deep down she knows the value in her master's lessons, on the surface everything is black and white to Lara. Especially when it comes to following orders that don't align with her objectives.

She mulls over her options, none of which

seem very good. "I had no choice." She puts up her hands, rolling her eyes at the whole scene. There is a lot of grueling work ahead of her—messy, sticky, backbreaking work that she wants no part of.

She goes through the human's belongings and finds some worthless coins, a bloody map, and an empty water pouch. "Empty? I could have just let him walk himself to death. What a waste." The only thing of value is a small paper filled with starchy crackers. Without smelling them for traces of poison, she shoves one in her mouth. It is flaky and dry. Munching on the human food, she desperately tries to think of something clever to clean up the mess she made.

"These taste like his smell." Pacing back and forth, Lara makes sure the pouch really is empty. She really wishes she had something to wash down these crackers. "It had to be one of those kinds of days, didn't it?" she says, flaky bits falling out of her mouth.

She knows that no one would believe this to be suicide or an accident, not with that poor blade. Plus, Lara is a horrible liar. If she knows her master at all, she knows she'll see through any deception. It is settled. She will have to be honest about her defiance, or at least honest about the parts her master grills her on.

She grabs her stomach, as a sharp pain is making her uneasy. It feels as if something is trying to claw its way out of her. She isn't sure if it's the human food, or if the forest's warning hasn't faded for some reason. Normally, after an intruder is killed, the forest's cry quickly subsides. Maybe she has something else to do, which just adds to her aggravation. "Why won't this day just cooperate?"

She dips her fingertips into the topsoil, like she did to pinpoint the location of the intruder, only this time it isn't giving her anything. Frustrated, she wipes her fingers, which are covered in human filth. She tries again, and it just smears the mess wider. It isn't coming off that easily.

Another crisis catches her attention. It is a calamitous day, as far as gardening goes, with a long trail of devastating footprints. The garden is nearly destroyed. Spitting on their roots, she gives up some of her moisture as penance for not stopping him before he reached the garden. She carefully replants any seedlings she can salvage. Repairing the garden is a delicate task that takes love and care, and those two things can eat time faster than a hibernating bear.

Over and over again, she apologizes for the harm that has come to the plants. She shows them more respect than the corpse that's growing stiff only a couple of feet away. If only she hadn't gone down to the lake today. She would have been much closer to the garden, and none of this would have happened. What's done is done, but *she* is done for, if her master finds out.

After tending to the garden's needs, Lara transfers the human blood out of the helmet and into the empty water pouch. She places the headpiece back upon the human's crown. She looks into his dead-eyed expression. "What a way to be cast into the afterlife, like a total idiot." She takes a moment to add his image to her internal catalog. The ridiculous faces that people make right before dying never cease to amaze her. "You're the idiot, child," she says, lowering her voice to match his timbre.

Using his belt as a rope, she ties it around his wrist. "It's now or never." She proceeds to drag the heavy corpse through the hot wasteland. Even without his liquid, he's more than twice her weight.

All she can do to keep herself moving is

think about how much of a nuisance intruders are. They always interrupt a good day with troublesome extermination. She doesn't value human life the way the humans do, because to Lara, death is a near-daily task. If she had her way, there would be signs graphically depicting human murder all around their perimeter as a deterrent. Even making traps would allow her freedom to express herself without direction. She would much rather spend her time on crafting weapons than murder. Alas, her inventions must be hidden. What's the point of creating something deadly if you never get to use it? Even more so, living, if no one knows you're alive?

Humans are soft and squishy. No wonder they wear thick apparel to protect themselves from virtually everything—bugs, twigs, rocks, thorns. It's baffling to her how they've survived this long. It only took that one shell to end him so effortlessly. *It isn't my fault that they're so fragile,* she tells herself.

Tugging and pulling the lifeless human through the harsh terrain is exhausting. Lara continuously changes her stance, giving different sets of muscles a rest every few minutes. If only she had asphyxiated him and stashed him in their underground chest like she was in-structed to, then she wouldn't have to do this manual labor.

Noticing the cresting sun, she knows it is too late for regret. Blood is in the air, and the night killers will be out soon enough.

While dragging her kill like a sack of pota-toes, she spies something out of the ordinary—two more sets of footprints leading perpendic-ular to her travels. These prints are most certainly new. One heavy set of boots and a pair of bare feet are the cause. This must be why the feeling inside her hasn't gone away, even as she is currently disposing of his body.

She catches her breath like a hunter catches its prey—focused and refined. Lara is already in a heap of trouble. She can't idly let some intrud-ers go by. She diverts from her path, following the new tracks. One set is heavy footed with a big stride, and it appears to be dragging some-thing in the dirt, maybe a stick. She hopes it's a sword or staff, though she knows the odds of that being true are slim to none. What with the last weapon she found being a total bust.

The other tracks portray a different, meeker personality—one that keeps turning around, as if looking for something. Lara finds her own

29

paranoia manifesting as she also looks behind herself. Following the tracks, she can only assume where they are heading—in the direction of the edge of the world. If they have reached the edge, they're already dead. But the feeling...it never lies, it never needs to.

"I better make sure they've left," she says, trying to convince herself that this has nothing to do with her own curiosity about their destination.

She isn't sure if she's imagining it or not, but something else seems to be out there. Something out of sight that doesn't want to be seen. It is stalking something...hungrily. Her master doesn't allow her to venture out this far. Maybe she is someone else's intruder now.

More regret weighs on her. If only she hadn't spent so much time looking for shells, she might have been prepared for two encounters back to back. Never has even one intruder gotten past their perimeter before. *Two of them...hmmm.* Lara wants to find joy in this situation, but time is running thin. Perhaps tomorrow she might care about "the one." Today she is over it and no longer in the mood.

The terrain is unknown—harsh and wild. Who knows what is out here or up ahead. She doesn't appear to be gaining on the tracks, due to all this dead weight she has. With time running short, she finds some hidden strength to move her cargo at an expedited rate.

She knows something is gaining on *her,* however, and it's kicking up dirt behind it. She lost all her advantage when she decided to drag this baggage through the charred forest.

Snap!

The corpse suddenly comes to a dead-stop causing Lara to whip to the ground. She rolls to her feet and into a defensive stance. The low sun is creating a glaring cover by piercing her eyes. She is vulnerable, and she cannot help but snarl defiantly.

Something is just over the ridge behind her. She hears it getting closer. The sound of rope tightening gets louder and louder still. Whatever is chasing her must have smelled the blood like perfume. Does it want to eat the corpse, or something fresh? Either way, Lara is ready for anything, even if it's cold death.

She looks at the corpse to see what has snagged it. A metal-jawed clamp is attached to its foot, with a chain disappearing into the soft ash. The contraption almost looks like it's smiling as it takes a bite out of her victim. Lara begins to piece all the clues together.

This is no intruder. This is an ambush.

Trapped

This never would have happened if only Lara
had stayed inside the perimeter that her
master confined her to. Like a domestic bird released from its cage, she knows nothing of the
outskirts, but she has been feeling trapped for
far too long.

Being caught unaware is something she is
not accustomed to. Normally she is in complete
control over every situation, or at least she
thinks so. Secretly, she hates making decisions
and deflects blame outward when things go
wrong, to save herself the inward deprecation.
Lara had brought herself on this journey. She
had wanted something different—a challenge.
There is no fun in succeeding all the time—

enjoyment comes from the struggle. Change is inevitable.

Lara stares intently at the ridge where some unknown lifeform is about to descend upon her. A sense of anxiety envelops her. Fighting isn't an option at this juncture. She can't drag two, or possibly more, corpses back to her cleft. One is proving barely manageable for her strength. Plus, the smell of death has already ruined her day as it is.

I can never make an off day on again, no matter how hard I try.

Her feet are sinking into the thick layers of ash. The cursed ground here is softer than what she is used to. It's almost powdery.

A shadow creeps up the hillside, painting a humanoid shape out of darkness. So far, there appears to be only one silhouette. Slightly re-lieved, Lara still has no tactical advantage in this encounter. Her body is beat. She will have to rely on her mind for a solution.

The shadow beast descends upon the folk-princess with the intent of kidnapping her shadow. Not that she's a kid, not anymore. It's just an expression. Though what the wretch doesn't know will most certainly be its down-fall in the end. This princess doesn't have a

run-of-the-mill shadow. It is that of an assas-
sin—stolen from her prince's killer long ago...

"What am I doing? I don't have time for this," Lara says under her breath, putting an end to the playtime inside her head. Having an active mind can be a crutch used to disconnect from reality, and like most bad habits, this one is difficult for her to break. Only now, her mind is blank, and she is lost for solutions. If only she *were* a folk-princess, then she might have a wealth of magic at her disposal.

Unless provoked, she has no reason to engage in this fight, and doing so would result in a world of anger from her master. Instead of taking a stand, she decides to show some restraint. She is in enough trouble as it is.

Lara takes a deep breath and conceals herself in the soft ash, hoping a better plan arises. It is much deeper in parts than she had expected. She is almost swimming in it—the ash well over her head. She wiggles back and forth to smooth out her deception. It's not perfect, but it will have to do for now.

From underground, Lara feels the heavy foot of the stalker as it draws near. Each step is slow and precise. It then stops right on top of her. It knows.

She will have to hold her breath until the whole encounter is over. Luckily, she has trained for this situation. Well, not this "exact" situation, but expanding her lung capacity for a prolonged amount of time is part of her discipline. She never thought the exercise would come in handy, what with there being no lakes, rivers, oceans or streams to contend with.

There she waits, listening to the unique sound of a rope tightening. It reminds her of how she always imagined riding in a boat would be, the mast swaying back and forth against the invisible force of the wind—relentless and beautiful, neither one yielding as they push and pull against each other in their rivalry.

"Something..." the oscillating voice starts to say. Without warning, an object is thrust into the ash a couple of feet away from her.

Lara nearly flinches, but she manages to calm her system to avoid giving away her hiding place.

The weapon stirs around in the ground. He missed...for now.

"...is here." With another thrust, the weapon enters the dirt swiftly. This time, a little closer to where Lara is lying in wait.

"This is, by far, the laziest plan you've come

up with yet." She hears her master's voice as a figment of her imagination. *Must you ruin everything for me?* She closes her eyes even tighter, hoping to shut out her subconscious as well as the gritty dirt. Deep down, she knows this isn't one of her finer moments. Especially since this is the exact excitement she had just been longing for. Only now that it's here, she doesn't want to partake in the gift that the dead forest has so graciously given her. No doubt about it, her age is showing in her ungratefulness.

As the figure scans the ground for his target, Lara hears something out of the ordinary— bones click and grind loudly against each other; lungs fight against the air as they wheeze. Each wrenching sound plays off the other like a chorus of decay. Whatever he/she/it is, they are gross. Not only by young-girl standards, either.

She has no control over this situation. It's both dangerous and terrifying, and she loves every moment of it. She plans what she will do if the culprit manages to get a lucky strike on her. *First, I will roll on my side, trapping its weapon between my mighty legs. Next, I will use everything I have to launch at it. Upon seeing the whites of my eyes, it will tremble at my skill and aptitude. Throwing a flying punch will cause it to block, if it has any training at all. Well, it has to be experienced to have survived this far out in the nothingness. Anyway, it will never guess what I'll do next. This is the best part. I will bite out its eye. Oh, yes, I can almost taste the horror.*

Finally, while it reverts to dealing with its pain like a child, I will dominate the situation, entangling myself between its limbs like a spider taking down an inferior fly. And that's when I'll snap its neck in two. Wait, no. Last time, I failed master's neck-snapping trial. I could have had it, if she'd just stopped barking orders at me. I guess I will have to squeeze the life out of this thing, slowly. It takes everything Lara has to not let out a sigh.

"Tsk, tsk." A third thrust of the weapon stabs right next to Lara's head.

Now she's quite relieved that she didn't exhale. Any movement would have resulted in her downfall. As it is, that hit was way too close for her comfort. If it were a little to the left, she might not be able to devastate him the way she imagined. She thinks about executing her plan but sticks to the cue—getting hit.

Never give away your position unless you

are left with no other possible option, she re-members her master's teachings once again. *Get out of my head and just leave me alone already.*

Another strike pierces the dust, this time near her arm. She can almost grab whatever it is—most likely a spear of some sort. It has the reach of one.

Her eager finger twitches. *Being patient is painful, but so is getting murdered. There is no high reward without an even higher risk.* Remembering more of her master's words nearly causes her eyes to roll underneath her closed lids. It is not until now that she comes to a great conclusion—her master talks an awful lot. Even when she tries desperately to tune her out, the information haunts her so. It must be the curse of her own overachievement. Like the last encounter, she suddenly takes great interest in the spear thingy that is viciously searching for her skin. The weapon slowly retracts from the black earth. It is doing what it was forged to do, and that excites her—even if it is at her own expense.

How can he miss so many attacks in a row? It has to be more than just dumb luck, because I'm not that lucky.

Lara realizes this creature knows exactly where she is and is enjoying this little game of hide and seek. What he doesn't know is that the feeling is mutual.

Lara tries to distract her body from the lack of oxygen. All her senses focus on the creature looming over her. She feels the change in temperature as its shadow casts over her hiding spot. Drawing its movements in her mind, she senses its head scanning for another spot to poke. Its movements are unnatural and cold.

Another strike stabs through the dirt, this time farther than the last couple. It's still searching for her, like a pin to a cushion. The spearman kneels low, and the ash shifts. "I can taste you."

She focuses on the wetness of its salivating mouth. Maybe it doesn't know where she is after all. It is only a matter of time before it finds what it desires, and she does, too.

Like a stone, she doesn't budge, no matter how much she wants to.

"There you are." It readies the long weapon high above its head. This time she can envision him using both hands for a critical amount of damage. Right before it thrusts the weapon upon her, there's a low, rumbling growl, almost like thunder. It's unlike anything she has ever heard.

There's a lot of movement back and forth causing the sand to shift.

Everything turns quiet.

The familiar sound of the intruder returns, just as lackluster as before—slow and laborious. She hears a high-pitched snapping sound. Based on the change of weight above her, she is sure that this thing just threw the human corpse over its shoulder as though it's weightless. Lara wishes to one day have strength like that. Envy is not a new feeling for her. Talent is something that she wants to have without having to earn it. This is no exception.

"I'll be back for the main course. Don't you move." The figure puckers its lips and lets loose an unattractive kissing sound.

Lara wants desperately to breathe, but she knows it is still too early. She waits. Her willpower is stronger than her instincts. All involuntary systems heed to her command. She can hold her breath until she perishes, if she so desires.

She studies its walk. Each ghastly step is followed by the dragging sound of its heavy cloak. *Damn thing is really taking its time. It moved a lot quicker when it was hungry and coming right for me.*

Then, there is nothing. Lara launches out of the ash and shakes her body like a wet dog, before treating herself to air—to life. What could have caused it to leave before stabbing her through? Nevertheless, the thing is gone, and she is no longer burdened with having to carry that heavy load.

Much to Lara's surprise, its cloak has cleanly swept all its tracks away. She is quite jealous of such a useful coat. Rubbing her aching back, she spies her sweeping tool. It suddenly doesn't seem as great as it did before. Though it's blistering out as it is—even the thought of wearing one more article of clothing causes her to melt. The old ways will have to do, as they always do.

The sky is growing dark. She must abandon her scenic route to the edge of the world for the time being. As she takes one last look around, her assumption proves to be correct—the human corpse is long gone. At least she still has its pilfered equipment. And there is something else. The metal claw is still lying on the ground where it took a bite out of the corpse's leg. Only now the chain is cut clean in half, and the jaws look bent and mangled.

She knows that there is no way she could have snapped that chain, not without some tools and leverage. That thing was unnaturally strong. Lara feels a pang of sadness for not attacking the foe, even though attacking it under these circumstances would have been suicide. Though in actuality, she is happy with her decision. She doesn't want to add any more pitfalls to the streak she is currently on.

"To break a trend, you must always inherently change yourself before your luck will obey." It was the right decision, and her master's words are to thank, though she would never tell her, as her pride is loyal to her defiance.

She contemplates covering her footprints, along with the miles of drag marks leading from the garden. Quickly, she dismisses that idea as she realizes there isn't time for such tasks. The sun is already low, much too low. The longer she waits, the larger the risk of her not making it back before dark. No, she must deal with the other intruders tomorrow, and this time she will be more than prepared. That idea gives her the hope that ignites her stride.

Lara's body is wrecked from pulling that

corpse all over the wasteland. If she had never stopped to hide, her body wouldn't have lost momentum. She only has one option—push through the pain and make her way home.

Racing the light, she runs, breathing between each step in perfect rhythm. Launching off boulders, dodging through burnt shrubbery, she is lightning fast with her little steps, shattering burnt branches onto the burnt ground. Her theory is the less tracks you make, the less work you rake.

She isn't going to make it. The sun is almost completely gone as she gives her legs everything she has left. Focusing her energy for the active muscles, Lara's eyelids droop. Her hands flop against her sides. Her goofy stride isn't elegant, or even warrior-like, but it's effective for its purpose.

Just when she thinks she can't sustain anymore, Lara reaches her master's gaze, which is angrily awaiting her arrival.

Yes, Master

The young feathered-folk meekly approaches her master like a puppy who got into something it shouldn't have while its master was away. This isn't so far from the truth. Coy shoulders and cute looks won't get her out of trouble this time.

Her master stands outside their underground abode, arms crossed like a statue...a very judgmental statue. Looming high above her cowering pupil, it takes all her restraint to not scream out her frustration. There is danger in her vicious look.

Illuminated salts glow from atop a staff next to her. Accentuating the small scars from more than a lifetime of hard living, the dim light of the crystalized reaction makes her face seem even more fearsome, almost demonic.

When it comes right down to it, Lara knows the importance of having the first word. Saying the wrong thing can dramatically change how the events will unfold. It is a delicate balance, teetering on the edge of truth and deception. She has it all worked out in her head, and it will work, as long as she can properly set the stage of events. First, she will lead with the good news, which will put a crack in this hardened exterior her master has already built up. Compliments won't work—they never do with her master. She wants facts, and nothing coated with sweetness to soften the inevitable blow of disappointment. Then she will hit her fast and hard with solutions before presenting the problem. That way she can sneak in the problem more as an afterthought.

Lara is now ready to put her plan in motion. She opens her mouth to speak, but before she can explain, her master talks loudly over her.

"You failed me, again."

The lecture quickly fades in Lara's deaf ears. Her master is quite masterful at many things—fighting, strategy, foraging—but reprimands aren't one of them. In all the countless years they have kept each other company, Lara has already heard it all. There are only so many ways to say "you let me down." And her master doesn't beat around the bush with flowery analogies or extensive vocabulary. She is as direct as possible so that there is no room for interpretation.

Lara catches a snippet of the verbal rampage her master is settling into.

"Do you think I like having these conversations all the time?"

With exhausted eyes, Lara looks up at her. Eyes on eyes, she doesn't dare blink. If only she can explain what she went through, maybe her master won't be so cross. She quickly dismisses the idea and replaces it with the opposite assumption—she will be even more disappointed. Internally debating with herself as to which fairy tale will be more believable—the shadow stealer or the renegade—but then settling on telling the whole truth, Lara tries to speak again, though her heavy panting blocks her words.

"You know why you're so tired? It's because you lost five minutes of your life today. Nothing you can say will draw forgiveness out of me. Don't even try it. Now get inside before it's six minutes," her master demands.

Wait, what was that last part? This is something new in her arsenal of insults.

The muscles in Lara's legs shake and feel weak. The extent of her running has caught up with her. Lara lingers, catching a glimpse of the evening mist rising out of the cracks on the desolated ground.

Every night this happens precisely at sunset. Though, to her, it seems unreal—pure and majestic—like a fantasy she is forbidden to ever witness. In the past, she has only ever smelled the fog release from the confines of her underground dwelling. It has a cool, fresh scent to it. This is her first time witnessing the event with her own eyes.

Once, in passing, her master had told her that the mist is the forest's ghost releasing itself into the moonlight.

The young girl still doesn't understand what a moon is, how it got in the night sky, or why it collects spirits—nor is she brash enough to ask for clarification. What she does know is that it's the sun's bride. They don't speak anymore, only pass each other twice daily. A marriage that used to be hot with passion. Only now the nights grow cold with forgotten affection. They both still love each other, though they're careful not to show it. They've grown too stubborn to forget the past. This is the story Lara invented. It's the only way she can forgive the sun for taking its pain out on her daily. What else besides a broken heart could cause such scorn?

Fact or fiction, it feels true deep inside her. A feeling is much more convincing than a thought. You can change your thoughts easily enough when new information comes to light. Feelings, on the other hand, they defy your command and ignore all forms of reason. This is why she always butts heads with her master. While her master is analytical, Lara acts on feelings alone. Without facts, Lara has no choice but to come up with her own wild conclusions.

There is a long list of questions built up inside her head. Most of them are about the old days and the history of this broken place. She knows that her master remembers everything, though she never speaks of it. She is certain that one time she caught her master thinking about the days past while going through their storage. Her whole demeanor had changed. Behind her watery eyes she had looked almost like a different person entirely, though she was quick to wipe away the feeling.

Chitchat isn't her master's forte—lecturing is. If she ever happens to offer up any information, Lara accepts whatever it is with hidden gratitude.

Like an archeologist, Lara searches for the truth-treasures veiled inside her master's anecdotes. Mostly her preaching is geared toward making herself right and her pupil wrong.

Lara's eyes are still lingering on the magnificent swirls of fog, like she's in a trance of sorts. The vapor flirts with the air as it dances around, like oil in water.

"I've had enough of you today! Don't make me tell you twice," her master threatens, anger now marring her face.

The girl's aching bones remember what that means all too well. The first warning is vocal, the second is physical, and who knows what a third would entail. Feeling the immortality of youth, Lara has no reason to fear the afterlife. Still, Lara doesn't enjoy pain, though her tolerance has been getting better with each mistake.

Heeding her master's words, Lara disappears down the obscured hole leading into the drab underground—the clefts. This is the place she has called home since...always.

She thought about what her master said a minute ago. *Did I really lose time off my life? And if so, why? How come she can walk freely around the surface after dark without any negative effect? It's not fair. Maybe I'm the one who is abnormal, or worse. It could be harming her too, and she's careless on the matter. That would be something she would do.* Her mind is whirling around with more questions that she will never find answers to.

Until tonight, there was but one rule she never broke—venturing outside after dark. Ruling through fear was her master's go-to. Lara chalked it up as just another scare tactic and not reality. True or not, the stories about what dwells in the darkness were too much for her to brave. She liked control, and you cannot control what you cannot see hiding in the darkness. Though now, seeing the seriousness in her master's face, Lara is starting to believe there is truth in her warning.

As far back as she can remember, her master told her bedtime tales of the evils in the darkness. The night killers were among the most terrifying. Sure, her master mentioned other terrible afflictions that would be a direct result of any disobedience, but with a name like "night killers," she wouldn't take any chances, especially as an impressionable little girl. Even though she isn't that small anymore, the feeling is just the same.

Lara sizes herself up and pinches her own cheeks. "I don't feel any less alive." She wonders if the creature she encountered before was a night killer. Then she quickly dismisses the idea, remembering that it was clearly daytime when they met. She isn't afraid of any "day killer." She has gone up against burglars, ruffians, thieves and rogues, and they were all easily disposed of. Perhaps she fears the "night" more than the "killer" part of the bogyman.

Before she can come to any definitive conclusions, her master jumps down the hole with a violent thud—her frustrations showing within her deep breathing. "Where were you?"

"I...uh...was dealing with an intruder, like a good girl." Lara lets a smile out as a white flag to stop the war that is about to wage between them.

"Then what took you so long?" her master takes the first shot, using her words as a weapon.

"Look, it was hot out there today." Lara side-stepped the attack.

"Fair enough. I will cut you a little slack there. Is that it, the weather? Nothing else went on?"

"Yup." Lara's tongue signs the scroll of surrender, under false pretenses.

Her master's body slouches as she starts to relax. "I was just worried. You can't keep cutting things so close. You have to get things done right away and not wait until the last minute. The risk is much too great."

"I didn't mean to. I got caught up."

"Things will always come up, get in the way...change. You have to anticipate for this in your time management."

"What, like you do?"

"Hold your tongue."

"I'm just saying...maybe you should have anticipated me putting things off and compensated for it."

"This isn't about me. I got all of my duties done with enough time to stand around and worry about you."

"Maybe that is your problem. You have too much time on your hands to micromanage my life. I can do things on my own."

"Oh, now I'm the one with the problem?" her master says, restraining her rage.

"Better you than me."

"How is that better for anyone? How about we fix the situation so that no one has any problems or blame, and things just go smoothly for once?"

"I didn't mean to be late." Lara pouts, staring at a vase with all her intensity, hoping to shatter it with her mind...though she possesses no such power.

"No one means to be late, but life happens. You have to anticipate it, then it won't ruin your whole day."

"Is that what I'm doing? Ruining your life?"

"Look, I didn't say that. I just...you know what? Never mind. Did you dispose of the human properly this time? I'm assuming 'yes'?" The stiffness returns to her master's body the more agitated she grows.

"I did you one better." Lara pulls out the water pouch filled with human blood. She is quite pleased with herself.

"That doesn't look better. That looks worse. Much, much worse. What did you do this time?"

"I drained it for you. See, I am helping."

Her master raises one of her stump hands and motions like she is scratching her head, though no contact is made.

Lara wants to laugh at her phantom itch, though never in a thousand years would that be appropriate.

"That's not how we do things. You know that. If you really wanted to help, you would listen to me for once."

"See? I can't do anything right. I had no choice. He was feisty," Lara says, making a tight fist to further sell the lie.

"This is what I'm talking about."

"Look, I took care of it. I don't see the problem."

"That's because it's behind your eyes."

"Me?"

"What have I been training you all this time for? Your skills would be unmatched if you would only follow my teachings. Skill doesn't matter if you're dead before the fight even starts." Her master's feet stomp the ground harder as she grows more heated. "Where is the rest of him? Do you have a larger bottle hidden somewhere?"

Darn. She's quick. Lara was trying to sprinkle in a little truth along with her deception. She had high hopes that her master wouldn't investigate the little details she purposely left out. "Someone stole it. But before you get upset, let me assure you that I can get it back."

Her master looks around, trying to understand where she could possibly find a human-sized bottle. "You can't expect me to believe you bottled up a human like a fermented grape..."

"No, of course not. There was never a bottle. I am talking about the body."

"You said it was stolen? Who stole it? Another invader? Were you seen? Did they follow you?" Her questions came so fast that they were jumbled together like gibberish.

"Yes. I don't know. Maybe. Uh, no?"

"So, you're sure they were human? Was there more than one? Of course, you would have mutilated any single enemy in combat. But what would a human want with a corpse? Unless those wretched cannibals returned. Nonsense, they would starve faster than we are out here," her master debates with herself, ignoring her student.

Taking notice of her master's distraction, Lara tries to slink away into the background.

"Not so fast. You have a lot more explaining to do."

The excitement of her escape thwarted, Lara hangs her head low. Her body goes slack. "For the record, there might have been three of them. Or maybe one...I am not sure exactly."

"I don't understand. Did they look different than adventuring humans? Did they have bone weapons, stitched-up faces and white and red war paint?"

"You mean, did they look like cannibals?"

"Are you seriously giving me attitude, after what you just pulled?"

Lara's stone-cold gaze is fixated at the wall, with a slight pout to it. "No, not a human. Someone else," she says emotionless.

"Who else could it be, then?"

"I already said it was someone else. If I knew what it was, I would have told you, 'Hey, I saw a red-eared dwarf stealing my corpse.'"

"Dwarves are not real."

"I know that!"

Her master squints her face tightly, trying to control her anger. "Wait, you didn't get a look at them? Didn't you scout them out first?"

"I wasn't able to. It got the drop on me."

"It? Don't you mean 'they'? I thought you said there were more of them."

"Look. I didn't see it, or them, okay? I was outside of my element and I just hid."

"Outside of your element? Wait a minute.

57

Did you venture out past our perimeter again?"

"The trail was leading there, and..." Lara starts to say, her expression instantly changing.

"No! You promised that if I expanded our territory, you would stop exploring by yourself. That was our deal, and I kept to my end. How can I count on you to not get us both killed?"

"It wasn't my fault. The tracks..."

"You have to learn to take responsibility for your own actions. You can't just walk through life without consequences."

"Why not? You do."

Without warning, one of her master's stump hands soars at Lara's face.

Lara catches it in the palm of her hand, inches from her nose. "See, I can take care of myself. Nothing bad will happen to me. Why won't you trust me?"

Her master pushes against Lara's palm with great force, causing Lara's own hand to crash into her face. Her master continues to smash Lara's hand into her face repeatedly until Lara releases the grip on her stump.

"Ouch. Cut it out!"

"We all have a weakness and yours is your strength, or lack thereof." Her master pulls herself off Lara and can't help but flex her bicep tauntingly. "Among other things," she says, glancing over at the human soup.

"I don't want to fight with you anymore. Can I have just one day where I'm not a complete mess-up?"

"I don't know. That's completely up to you."

Lara picks up a ceramic bowl and looks for a place to throw it in frustration.

"You're going to have to clean that up, you know," her master warns.

"I don't care," Lara gently places the pottery down and tries to shake her anger out through her fingers.

"Go cleanse the blood before it spoils."

"Why do *I* have to?"

Her master's fierce look freezes Lara's rebellious mouth right quick.

"Because..." Her master takes a couple deep breaths. She doesn't want to start an argument she doesn't have time to finish. "Just make sure you're done before I get back."

"Master, why are so mad at me for this?" Lara says, holding up the pouch.

"How many times have I told you—no weapons, no exception! Don't play stupid with me."

"I'm not playing."

"Then don't *be* stupid."

Lara stares at her master's shaking stump as she scolds her. She was once a deadly fighter, only now both her hands have been severed from her limbs. Thus, she is adamant about Lara never relying on weaponry, as it can become a crutch. A rule that Lara broke today by throwing the sharp shell.

"It wasn't a weapon," Lara lies.

"The intruder didn't just hand you its blood in a water container, did it? You cut him, which I strictly forbade you to do...and for good reason."

Lara looks down at her fingernails, wondering if she could use their sharpness as an alibi. *Nope, they're too short and jagged.* "I know, but he drew his weapon first. I had to defend myself," Lara says, hanging her head, looking at her own wiggling toes.

"You should have been faster and apprehended him before he even knew you were there."

"But..."

"I've taught you how to disarm an opponent, but you wanted more. You wanted to play with it first. Greedy child."

"I did my job. I stopped him."

Her master walks up to the blood-filled

waterskin instantly noticing it is not one of theirs. "Where?"

"Where what?" Lara says brashly.

"Where did you spill his blood?"

"Uh...the garden."

"What were you doing that was so important that you let him get so far?"

Lara reluctantly pulls out the sack of shells that she had scavenged and holds them out. "I was at the dry lake."

Her master reaches back to smack the sack out of her hand, but refrains. "That wasn't...you weren't...did...You know what? Never mind. I just can't seem to get through to you." Her master fumbles and knocks objects around as she thrashes about trying to get herself equipped to venture topside, all the while uttering disciplinary lectures to herself in a hushed tone.

"Where are you going?" Lara throws the shells against the cleft wall herself. "Just punish me like always. Don't go out there."

"Don't look at me right now."

"What's wrong? I did my best."

"You have never done your best, not once, not even close. What you *did* do is leave tracks leading straight for us. You are careless, immature and reckless."

"I can fix it, tomorrow at dawn."

"We will both be dead by dawn."

"I'm sorry."

"I haven't spent years grooming you so that you can be sorry." She puts her arm through an emergency bag pre-packed with all the essentials to leave in a hurry.

"What do you want from me?"

"I want you to listen to my words and not get us both killed. Everything is balancing on that one principle. Why you keep messing up is beyond me."

Lara watches her master struggle to get on her custom-made shell armor. She wants to offer to help, but it will only result in making matters worse. "What are you going to do, master?"

"Clean up your mess."

"What if you need my help?"

"Then you will have to clean up my mess."

"Let me go with you. I can help."

"Never. We've been over this repeatedly. I can't risk everything we've worked for. I'll take care of it and be back by morning." Her master is a prideful person and never asks for assistance, even when it's necessary.

Even without hands, her master is cunning,

dexterous and deadly. Lara wonders what the big deal is, what is out there that's frightening her master so much? Could it be the spirit fog, the night killers or something entirely new?

Without a smile, or a heartfelt goodbye, her master is gone—off into the murderous night to remedy another one of Lara's mistakes.

Only she doesn't return by morning...

All by Myself

Without her master's interjections, Lara is lost in her morning routine. Normally, while she carefully applies her dark camouflage from a piece of burnt wood, her master complains about how poorly she is blending the soot. After accepting her help, Lara would roll her eyes at the idea of needing assistance at all. For the first time, Lara misses the help that she previously found to be unfounded. No longer having a crutch forces Lara to evolve, if only for the moment.

Breakfast is a whole ordeal within itself. There is no prepared food for her to eat, no pots to boil water in, only empty dishes and unwashed utensils. Thousands of times before, she has witnessed her master preparing the meals but never paid close enough attention to retain any useful information. It was an opportunity for betterment that was overlooked.

"How does she do it?"

Deep in a cubbyhole, Lara finds some salted meat and attempts to flavor it with unmarked dust vials she acquires from the pantry—not to be confused with the collection of poisonous powders that are located in a pile near the den.

"I hope none of these are misplaced or labeled wrong."

Lara remembers, when she was younger, she would mix up edible tinctures from the non-edible embalming fluid while cutting corners tidying up. Her master is a tricky wicket, and hiding poison among the spices seems like the sort of gift she would leave for an intruder. This thought makes Lara feel unsafe—an outsider inside her own home.

She sets a place for her master, optimistically awaiting her late return.

Cooking is an art form, and it's not her medium. Her master only ever taught combat, anatomy, strategies of war and weapons study. She suddenly notices how one-sided her training has been thus far. It appears that she can only be trusted to kill, like some sort of knuckle-dragger incapable of rational thought. Or perhaps she is accurate in her assumption.

Being inexperienced, she uses too much of the savory spices. The result is quite repulsive.

"I have to eat something."

She has no choice but to punish her taste buds with her mistake. With the long-lasting famine in these parts, being wasteful means being dead. Not even a corpse will go to waste in these parts, as Lara learned firsthand during yesterday's travels.

Each bite of her failed experiment wrinkles her face in disgust as the pungent taste murders her tongue buds. Now she wishes that she had mistakenly seasoned the meat with poison to end the torture. The only way she can get any of it down is by sticking out her tongue, holding her breath, pinching a morsel and shoving it directly down her throat. She chokes and gags on every bite, but it is better than the alternative.

After cleaning up breakfast, Lara is quick to do her mind battles. This is an hour of meditation where she visualizes different fights. She instructs her muscles to flex with each imagined movement, though not actually carry out the attack. The concept is that if your mind is practiced, your body will follow suit.

She can't help but construct a scene using the corpse thief in this imaginary fight. Her mind draws a perfect representation of its insides as she tears it apart mentally. Even inside her meditation, she is defiant to her master's instruction. No wonder things never work out the way her master desires.

During her mind exercises, she never mentally does what her master instructs. Not being a mind reader, there is no real way for her to ever get caught, either. Or so she thought. Through her actions, however, the proof is evident.

"No. This time I will do what I'm supposed to," Lara says to herself, as if trying to reason with a child. She knows that how she practices is directly tied to how she performs. Perhaps if she conditions her mind to follow orders, her muscles will follow suit. It's such an easy, yet complicated, concept.

Despite all the hardship the human invader gave her, she feels nothing for hurting it—not sadness nor happiness, just numb and bored. It is all too easy. She replays the scene again, this time by her master's rules—choking him out and placing him deep inside one of their trapdoor graves in the ground, for safekeeping. Now, this is unbearable to think of.

Since no one is watching, she finishes her practice with something epic and unattainable. Excitement gives life to her meditating face, twitching and smirking, as she creates a scene of a gruesome battle where she hacks a wizard's head clean out of his pointy hat. If only such things existed outside of her fantasies.

After her meditation, she moves on to her physical workout routine. This is something she never misses but equally never gains from. Out of all the years she can remember, she never could lift a new level of weight, or punch past the same point where her arms always give out. She already peaked way too early in life. This is frustrating for her. It's something she cannot overcome. Her body will not improve, no matter what she does to it. She has tried nutrition, extra sleep, potions and tonics. Even once she prayed to a human god. All her efforts are for naught.

Only, today is different somehow—she feels it before even starting—like she can overcome anything in her path. Maybe it's knowing that her master is out there in the unknown, or something entirely unrelated, but in any case, she manages to complete three more sets of each routine—punches, kicks, elbows, etc. Amazed by this development, she tests out her strength and finds that she can now lift two more pounds.

"Maybe I was purposely holding myself back somehow."

She jumps around the training room, excitement filling every pore. For years, she watched her master increase her skill each month, even if it was slight. Mostly she noticed because her master was always pointing out her own gains, much to Lara's frustration.

Now it is her turn to share her subtle brag. She looks around, but there is no one to congratulate her on overcoming this long-standing obstacle. That is when the loneliness sinks in.

"What is the point of doing anything if you can't share it with anyone?" She exhales slowly.

More questions that she doesn't dare try to answer herself. She has stuff to do, and sitting around wallowing in self-pity will only make things worse.

Continuing on with the day, Lara switches to her studies. She reads through her material faster than ever. A resurgence of excitement comes over her as she remembers the gains in her strength.

"What if I'm smarter somehow?"

Her master always says that her brain is the weakest of all her muscles. Lara's retort is always to squint her eyes tightly and try to execute some sort of psychic assault. It is the one attack she wouldn't be able to counter.

Just for fun, Lara tests her psychic ability again. This time she wants to try and establish a mental connection with her master instead of turning her brains into mush. Flexing her whole body, she focuses on her master's essence. Repeatedly, she fixates on a single word, "master?"

Her whole body shakes. It feels as though her brain is sharing in the sensation. This distracts her slightly. *It's not weak.* With that intrusive thought, she gives up. It's no use, she is not mentally gifted—not now, not ever.

"I can't have everything."

Even though, deep down, she wants to be the best at everything, her downfall is that she cannot dedicate herself to only one task to perfect. As a result, she leads a dilettante's life. Truth be told, her standard for "average" is higher than most humans' best efforts. It is the overachiever's plight.

Distracted, she starts to imagine what neat things she could do if she did happen to have such mental prowess.

"Stop it. You have work to do," she reminds herself, sounding like her master, in her absence.

She returns to her studies, grabbing the thickest piece of literature. From the human book, she memorizes the chapter on polearm weaponry. It was only yesterday that she had firsthand experience with the armament, and it feels like destiny. The chapter covers how adventitious lances are on horse mount and how effective spears are when accompanied by a shield. If only she had access to such things. Lara thinks about herself on top of a mighty steed, carelessly tearing through the cursed lands fast and fierce, never hiding her presence from the world. She can almost feel the air valiantly blowing her soft silver feathers.

Within these books, humans often talk about their riding animals, but never had she seen one firsthand. Something of that size would eat her out of her winter supplies by week's end. Her endless desire to own a beast keeps her mind busy for the better part of an hour.

Study time is by far the most exciting part of her daily chores. Inside this particular book, she notices that there are two pages torn out of it, which is far less than usual. She never understood why her master censored her from the texts. She always hung on to every word, and it seems like a waste to get rid of them—especially after someone went to all the effort to write them down. Her master must have had her reasons, but like most of the things her master does, it is never discussed or explained.

Each moon, her master supplies her with a new stack of reading material, mostly human in origin. Other times, they're from the sky people of the North or the beast trainers to the south.

Even though Lara has never met any of the authors, she feels like she knows them through the stories they provide. Artistic taste can teach you a lot about a person, both emotionally and mentally. Similarly, you can judge someone by what they eat. Do they care about being fit, or do they overindulge in their cravings and become portly?

Lara burps and briefly tastes her horrendous breakfast. She wonders what that meal tells about her character, but she knows the answer. "I would make a horrible wife."

Pushing thoughts of old maidhood out of her mind, she now has something bigger to contend with. Being alone has unforeseen consequences for Lara. She no longer has anyone to rebel against, and she can't exactly rebel against herself. As a result, her obedience is in perfect form. It is barely midday and she's already done with her chores, all while adding her master's jobs to her list.

"Maybe she's right about me. I don't apply myself fully. Whatever, she raised me that way. It's her own fault."

Her words don't hold the same sting when her master isn't within earshot of them.

Her master is supposed to be the warden of the forest, the protector of their kind from extinction. Except her recent action seems to have reduced the feathered-folk's numbers by fifty percent—from two to one.

This is the first time Lara takes her patrol seriously and doesn't get distracted. In the past, every one of her obedient steps was forced. There was always something else she would rather be doing, tinkering inside one of her stashes, foraging for treasure or setting up outposts. Now, she finds herself taking the task seriously. The responsibility is actually quite gratifying.

It would be a better than average day if her stomach didn't still ache from yesterday's intruder, but now it feels more like indigestion. She debates dipping her fingertips into the earth for answers, but that will excite her curiosity, which will most likely lead to more unwanted trouble.

"Why is she taking so long?"

Lara pictures her master chasing after some humans mounted on top of giant jackrabbits. Even though that may seem impossible to some, to Lara it is quite reasonable that people would ride something with such a speedy reputation. She has never seen a rabbit in the flesh, only in pictures. In her mind, they are much larger than in reality.

Lara makes it back to where her first mistake took place—the sacred garden. Everything appears exactly how she left it, her tracks still scattered around. She clears them away, along with the huge drag mark the corpse made.

Looking at her past self with new eyes, she says, "This is a total mess. What was I thinking?"

Personal growth often happens quickly. For her, it was in the course of a day. Even the saplings she replanted were done so in a rushed manner. She props them up, using old twigs to brace them.

"She said she would take care of this. Now who's unreliable?" Lara ponders aloud, getting worried about her master's whereabouts.

If her master isn't cleaning up her mess like she so boisterously announced, what is she doing exactly? That thought brings tingles to her skin. Lara's mind starts to wander again.

The armless assassin stalks the two invaders who walk funny. They travel deep into the barren wasteland. Their mouths are dry like the desert beneath their feet. But the master assassin has a thirst that cannot be quenched by any liquid. What she needs is the satisfaction of killing a man in cold blood. She stalks them, shrouded by their own shadows, mimicking their movements. It is a tactic she is a master of. She is so close that she can smell their stink and taste their fear, which are both plentiful.

Her capable pupil can take care of their castle while she's gone, so time isn't an issue. Killing them now will only yield the assassin a long walk back to her homeland empty-handed. Though if she follows them to their treasure, the walk will be justified with riches beyond her greatest imagination. What the assassin is after is the gold at the end of the rainbow. For these two invaders have a map that only they can decipher. Each step is jotted down, counting pace-for-pace with great diligence. Even one false calculation can render their efforts completely worthless. She plans on taking everything, leaving nothing but their begging tears behind.

Mostly inside her fantasies, Lara spends the rest of the daylight on patrol, cleaning her tracks all the way up to the spot where she left the perimeter. She doesn't dare cross that threshold again, not unless she gets the okay from her master who is still nowhere to be found. She was perfect at hiding her direction, a little too perfect for Lara's liking.

The night comes in swiftly, and Lara takes to the underground comfort of her cleft long before the moon's nightly rebirth. As she has a false sense of security, she did not set up the protective barrier that keeps the evil at bay. It's a task her master bore all on her own, and Lara was never privy to its importance. Tonight is the first night without her master's protection, and it's about to get ugly.

The First Night

The darkness seems blacker tonight, dense, almost solid. The hours feel longer and more daunting. Lara activates every crystalized salt torch at her disposal. Her aim is to brightly illuminate every curve and alcove of the underground, leaving no crack for darkness to hide in. This is a failed attempt to make her feel less alone. The faint crackle from the salt's chemical reaction makes the silence appear louder somehow.

Loneliness is a sensation the feathered one didn't predict having in a million moons. Her master normally spends the nights topside, leaving Lara alone with her slumber. Never had she felt the slightest bit afraid, but something is different about tonight because she knows that there's no one up there watching over her. Or if there is, it isn't from a place of kindness. It is from a sinister eye, looking for terror.

She has heard the folklore—the evils that humans are capable of, the treachery they're famous for, and the chaos they live for. Their worst appetite is, by far, their lust. Like a disease, they multiply without affection, need or probable cause. The moment she closes her eyes, she lets down her guard. Someone could slit her throat before she even wakes up. That is what she would do if she were a folk-killing human.

To some, dying in your sleep might seem like a very normal, and suitable, way to go—quietly inside yourself—quick and easy. Lara is not at all normal, and she would rather be outmatched and tortured by a great gladiator than die a boring death. Every time she gets hurt doing some piddly task for her master, the regretful feeling hurts far more than when she gets injured on one of her discovery escapades.

"If you die doing the thing you love, it's a sign that you really lived instead of wasting away inside the comfort of never trying." True or not, Lara likes that concept. She read it in a book during her younger years. Back then she didn't know what it meant, but luckily for her, she is able to reflect on it later in life. She spends quite a lot of time scanning through her memories, looking for any forgotten treasures. Sometimes it feels as though she went back so far that life is repeating. Like catching the end of a book before reading it.

The tiny feather-fuzz that covers her body stands up on end as goosepimply bumps appear out of nowhere. They're alerting her to something lurking in the shadows or to something completely constructed inside her own paranoia. Either way, it feels very real and quite terrifying.

Not being able to go outside leaves Lara feeling as though the walls are moving, shrinking around her, almost pulsating, like a mouse trapped inside the belly of a snake. She gets the sense that the end is coming for her, and it's taking its sweet time in order to make the experience more memorable. Feeling disoriented, she places her hands over her face—though one eye is peering out from between her fingers.

"This is not happening. It's all in your head. Just think about something happy." Lara imagines herself wearing golden human-made armor, on top of a snow-covered peak—a scene that seems out of this world to her. The sunlight glistens off the armor's polished metal, nearly blinding anyone who dares look upon her with a challenging eye.

A dark journey awaits her. The wind blasts her face, as if it's fleeing for its life. She smells smoke, death, fear, and it ignites her thirst for combat. She reaches out her empty hand, eagerly awaiting her squire.

She imagines a young, greenish boy who meekly approaches her with a sack more than twice the size of himself. "What are you craving today, miss?" The little man says with a lisp that makes him appear reptilian, even though he is not.

Lara smacks her lips loudly, looks to the heavens, and contemplates her craving. "What do you suggest?"

"Oh, the special is quite magnificent. It's called Eagle Eyes." The green boy proceeds to rummage through the sack. He pulls out a black bow and a handful of arrows. With a flick of his wrist, he spreads the arrows out like a fan and displays them over his forearm gracefully. If anything, this green guy knows his presentation. "This blackened bow has been forged from the hellfire's kiln. The arrows have been carved out of dragon's nail and coated with a demon blood sauce that really cuts through the air with perfection. Each feather was hand-plucked from a sleeping phoenix during the summer solstice, when the feathers are said to be the longest. With this exquisite combination, one shot can hit over six vital organs. It also pairs nicely with plate mail-armored foes."

Lara's eyes seem to grow as big as her smile while she imagines indulging in its sweetness. "As good as that sounds, the wind is a little bitey today. Besides, I'm feeling a wee bit stabby."

"Might I interest you in a Flaming Starkiller?" The man drops the bow and arrows on the ground, no longer showing them the care they deserve. He again reaches deep inside his sack.

"No, thank you. I'll just take the usual."

"Wonderful choice as always, miss. Any starters?"

"How about a potion of striking?"

"Coming right up!"

Small plumes of smoke billow out of the slightly bulbous glass container as he carefully pours the contents of several vials into it. After salting the rim, he hands her the mixture with a look only a connoisseur of fine weaponry could perfect.

The sweet smell of honey hits her nose as she brings the glass to her face. It invigorates her muscles with every sip. Lara looks valiantly onward, towards the burning village ahead of her.

The green humanoid goes back to his cart to gather "the usual" crystal axe that she has grown a taste for. It has a modified handle, making it almost the length of a lance. He places the legendary weapon delicately inside her outstretched hand while she continues to marvel at the destruction ahead.

"Dinner is served," he says with a bow, drizzling gourmet poison chocolate on the axe blade.

"Good thing too, because I'm starving." The weapon feels comfortable in her hand, as if it's in tune with her very soul. She charges forward, yelling a battle cry that would make a grown man soil his pants.

The squire sheds a tear from merely observing the greatness she exudes.

Lara is so immersed inside this fantasy that she doesn't notice the creeping shadow that is dancing across the floor of her cleft. With all the active salts about, there is no place for a shadow. Yet here it is, alive and well.

A faint clanging sound finds her ears and jolts her back into reality. It's coming from the other room.

"What was that?" Her eyes are glued to the entrance of the kitchen nook. The sound suddenly turns eerily silent.

One step at a time, she slowly slinks closer to the cause. The loudest sound is coming from her own exhaling breath as it stutters out of her unsteady lips. She wants to be fearless. In reality, she is acting the complete opposite of how she just imagined herself mere seconds ago. She can't help it, as much as she wants to help it.

"Hello? Is anyone there? Master?"

Fear is a dangerous beast—its strength comes from the unknown, as it feeds on imagination. The more imaginative one is, the more powerful it becomes. In Lara's case, it's unstoppable. Even though her fighting prowess has never been bested, it's the possibility of danger that gives her anxiety—even though she regularly wishes for such occasions to present themselves.

"Don't be alarmed. I'm coming in," Lara

says. Her echo repeats the words back to her, causing her to jump slightly. If there wasn't a chance that this could be her master returning, Lara wouldn't have given up the element of surprise.

She enters the kitchen nook in parts. First, she turns her eyes, then her neck and torso soon follow, and finally she jumps into the room—planting both her feet wide. "Aha!" Her hands are balled up into fists, but nothing is there for her to swing them at.

"Damn." Her fright is momentarily replaced by giddy excitement upon hearing her own vulgarities. "I mean...darn," she says slowly.

Her master never lets her use such language. She always told her that the trees judge her on every aspect of her life, and judgment comes faster than anyone expects.

Though the trees are all gone, aren't they— burnt to a crisp, she rationalizes her swear words.

It takes her the good part of a moment, but she manages to think of the worst possible phrase she can utter, now that she is free from admonishment. Even though she is alone, the words still linger on the edge of her mouth, the air building behind them. "Fundle snop!" she blurts out loudly, her mouth stuck open in awe. She said it—the naughtiest phrase she knows. She doesn't know the meaning of "fundle" nor "snop," but either way, it sounds insulting enough.

If the sound she heard earlier was truly made by her master's return, that phrase would have brought her out of hiding for a serious lecture, or possibly a vicious beating. Now she knows that she is very much alone, and only the walls heard her secret phrase. Knowing that makes her smile brightly.

There is more work that needs to be done before she will be comfortable enough to turn in for the night. After stacking all of their stone-carved furniture against the opening to the cleft, Lara doesn't feel any more at ease. In fact, the more she caters to her fear, the more it presents itself to her.

As the hours drift towards daybreak, Lara is more on edge than before. The night is biting cold, and seeing her own breath brings about quick movements. Even though she turned everything upside down, nothing appears to be around. She doesn't feel alone at all. She arms herself with anything that can serve as an improvised weapon.

The truth starts to sink in. Her master isn't coming back tonight, if ever again. This is her life now—living in fear and hiding from her own shadow. She feels like a human, or more simply put, a coward. The lack of sleep is wearing on her sanity. Everything seems to be out to get her, but not if she gets it first.

"Come out and get me. I dare you!" she says to the air, though nothing comes to accept her challenge. She drops her arms limply, exhaustion getting the best of her.

Both eating and song have proved to calm her nerves in the past. Quite desperate, she opts to do both at the same time. Humming a happy tune, she crunches on some raw vegetables. Time appears to be stretching out and so does her once upbeat song. There is something about the dead of night that adds an ambient tone to any sound, giving it a hollow, morbid feeling. Inadvertently, she hums it slower and in a lower key. Her once joyous melody has now turned into a murder ballad. It sounds like a nursery rhyme that humans use to scare kids into never leaving their beds, let alone looking under them. A shiver crawls up her spine and she covers her mouth, silencing the source of her torment—herself.

"This is making me sick." She spits the half-eaten carrot into her hand and tosses it against the back wall. It's wilted, the result of her forgetting to tend to it in the morning light.

"I'm going to be useless tomorrow if I don't get some sleep," Lara says, hoping that hearing herself talk might act as a substitute for company. She decides that slumber is going to be her only escape from the living nightmare she is in.

Upon leaving the room, she places coverings over the salt lamps, extinguishing their glow. Then, she quickly races to the next alcove to repeat the process. As each room grows darker, her feet become swifter.

She wishes that she could leave them all on. You see, to her, it is a practical use for the rare salts, though her master doesn't share this logic one bit. If she were here, she would berate Lara for reverting back to childhood. The truth is, perhaps, that she never really left. She puts up a brave front, puffing up her feathers, because her only friend is a serious adult that happened to witness the destruction of the entire civilization.

Like all types of life, Lara has to evolve—beat the beast without finding a loop-hole or cheating. That is the only way to earn your reward—through making it out the other side, no matter what scars you get along the way. To humans, scars are imperfections that detract from one's purity and beauty. To the feathered-folk, scars are a form of evolution. They show how much one has endured throughout one's life. The more marks, the more respect is earned from their peers. Lara had no scars to marvel upon, only wounds that have healed up in a forgotten sort of way. Though she remembers them—the pain, the anguish, watching the healing process while hoping for a not-so-great recovery. She is fortunate by human standards, but not so much by hers.

How can she forget what her master went through? It is apparent from every time she tries to carry something to when she scolds her, waving a ghost finger. None of that matters now. She is alone, and she might remain that way forever.

While turning off the second-to-last salt crystal, she notices that morning dew is already starting to make an appearance on a crack on the atrium wall. It is much later than she had predicted. If she wants to get any sleep before the sunrise, she has to act quickly.

Lara makes it to her sleeping quarters and debates leaving this last one on for the remaining hour or so of darkness.

"Stop being such a fundle snop," she tells herself, pointing her finger at her nose.

In one fluid motion, she tosses the covering above the lamp and jumps into her cot, as it feathers down on top of it. She pulls her woven blanket over her head while closing her eyes tightly. Once the sizzling sound coming from the lamp fades, she slowly pulls the blanket off her head. Though silly, this routine is the only way for her to transition from the light to the darkness. Her room is pitch black, and she doesn't dare open her eyes to confirm what she already knows as truth—it's scary out there.

As her mind wanders through her imaginative dreamland, the darkness conceals the shadow of the invisible creature that is scurrying around inside her cleft—unseen and uninterrupted...

Growing Up

*I*nside her quiet dreams, she is plagued with unsettling mysteries that never seem to add up—life, existence, her master's reason for giving no answers. After a couple hours of tossing and turning, Lara wakes up late for her daily routine. Her body is sore, as if she has been trampled on all night long. Her head feels like a walnut being cracked open by a vise. She is having trouble adjusting to the light. Stress can really disrupt the physical and mental wellbeing of any creature, and Lara is feeling it, hard. There is no way she is ready for the daily grind, or anything for that matter.

After eating another gut-murdering breakfast, she throws her utensil against the wall. A splatter of food, if you could call it that, is left as a reminder of where it hit.

Questions dance around her like a swarm of bees—where the truth's sting could easily kill her. Why was her master so determined to keep her sheltered? Why are they the last of their kind? But most of all, what was so important within those human books to warrant tearing the pages out?

As if it weren't already a mess, Lara turns the whole cleft upside down, tossing articles and supplies up in the air as she ravages through her home. She knows that at least some pages have to be around. When you already live in hell, there's nowhere else for bad things to go. Without access to fire, she couldn't have burnt them, Lara knows.

Over and over again, she looks inside every crack, every piece of pottery, in every unseen spot, but it's no use. There is no sign of the papers. Only last week her master brought back a new batch of books. She recalls her ripping out quite a few pages—each tearing sound made her cringe, as it always does. But with this particular batch, it seemed to last for the better part of an hour. She was surprised to find that there were any pages still left to read.

"They have to be around here, but where?" she mutters to herself.

Then an idea comes to her out of nowhere, like a mysterious gift or a stolen thought from an unseen entity.

"She wouldn't. Would she?"

After making some last-minute preparations, Lara storms into the lowest point of their dwelling, the last cavern she didn't dare investigate—the latrine.

***

They had to bury their waste in the deepest part of the cleft, without any air vents leading topside. Her master said that any escaping smells could give away their location. She would much rather forget this place and make a new, fresh hole every time nature calls.

Her nostrils burn the closer she gets to the putrid pile. Lacking worms, maggots and other filthy insects to consume their feces, all waste is left perfectly preserved in the same state it was in when it left their insides—timelessly disgusting. This is the place Lara despises the most, and her master absolutely knows this fact. This is the reason why it makes the perfect hiding place for the stolen pages. It has to be it. There is no other place it could be.

Lara has a habit of waiting as long as possible to use the facilities, hoping that she can avoid the place altogether. This is not one of those times. This is business. She wraps the mint-soaked rag that she prepared around her face. It doesn't block everything, but anything is better than nothing.

With a long stick in hand—which doesn't seem long enough—she descends down to the rank pile. This is not her idea of freedom; forcing yourself to do something repugnant. She always thought that if she were left to her own devices, it would be a party of a good time. Her curiosity, however, is not so easily swayed.

Cringing, with an outstretched arm, she proceeds to scrape off the dry topsoil. This is taking forever, she knows. Changing tactics, she confronts it with a slightly less submissive approach—jamming and stabbing at the pile almost angrily.

Greenish gasses escape in a cloud as she sloshes through the pit of waste, mixing it up into a cocktail of horrendousness.

Even Lara's mint mask can't shelter her from the truly putrid smell, which she imagines could melt the soft flesh off a human's bones.

While splattering the waste around, Lara thinks about how she is in too deep, literally. Partially, she hopes there is nothing here to find and that this is all part of another one of her "bad ideas," as her master puts it. But that would also mean that her master is right about her. To Lara, all of her ideas are well thought out and unique. It is the other variables that mess everything up. Things that are out of her control. Unfortunately, she knows that the longer she comes up empty-handed, the deeper she is going to dig. That means reaching the really soupy stuff, as liquid tends to pool at the bottom. If she could only find some sign to give her an excuse to leave, but that would mean her master didn't have a secret—or at least something to hide—and that would mean that Lara is wrong. She is never wrong, just slightly incorrect.

Just as she is thinking that this is the worst possible idea she has ever had—it isn't.

Against the cavern wall, looking more like skin or an animal hide, she spies something faded, crumpled and wet. It is positively paper. She found it, or so she hopes.

Extending her hand as far as she can with

the stick, she still comes up short. It is just out of her reach. She climbs a little further, on a precarious ledge, hoping this will get her just close enough. Again, she extends herself as far as her body is willing to go. She feels her joints stretch and pop. The tip of the staff is tickling the paper.

Still not close enough. Crap.

Frustrated, she removes the slipping handkerchief from her face and tosses it to the safety of the ledge. Just then, the stone ledge that her hand is gripping decides to play a cruel trick on her—it crumbles, causing her to lose her balance. The stick gets the reach she needs and stabs the paper. With one foot on the wall and the stick on the opposing wall, she hangs there as if on a tightrope, the deep waste pile lurking below, with no leverage to reach either side safely.

As hot gas hits her face, she can't help but gag. However, any movement, no matter how slight, could cause the stick to shift, and she would fall to the filth below. Her only option is to stop breathing altogether until she can come up with an escape plan. She closes her eyes tight, like a clam trying to hold on to its valuables. Her face turns pale and impassive, no longer accepting air into her body. She has used this skill now twice in the past three days.

She would rather die of asphyxiation than fall into the pit below. Plus, were she to fall in the poopy pit, she wouldn't get to reach that page before her system shuts down. And she *needs* to read that page, even if it is the last thing she ever does—which it very well might be. The worst of both worlds would be her body giving out before her spirt fully leaves. Plunging into the dark pudding, Lara would be left with the grossest last experience as she transitioned from this life to the next.

Her master told her that it is important to die with your head up and with honor. In doing so, you will be granted a better position in the next life. If she ends her life face-down in a latrine, what punishment will she get in her rebirth?

If I clear my mind, a solution will come.

In her meditative state, her imagination goes wild.

The brave heroine has the magical scroll well within her grasp, though the sleeping dragon below threatens her whole burglary. The scorching steam that billows from its scaly nostrils could burn a mere man's insides out.

Lucky for our champion, her armor is heat-resistant, and breathing is reserved for the lesser breeds of humanoids.

Waking the beast below means sudden death, and fleeing without the scroll means defeat—a word the brave mistress doesn't want to learn the meaning of. There is only one remaining option...

Lara's eyes open wide with great determination, grasping a new plan of action.

The young champion pulls out her mighty dragon-slaying spear and thrusts down, letting the magical scroll feather down above her.

Her stick still stuck in the crap-caked paper, Lara flips the pages high in the air as she descends toward the poop pit below.

Our heroine screams out a fierce battle cry that wakes the beast from its hundred-year slumber. It lets out a roar of its own. The ferocity is so intense that it suspends her in the air, floating in place like a humming bird.

Lara twists and turns in the air, maneuvering and contorting her body like a dancer.

The brave heroine dives head-first towards the dragon's mouth, pressing her hands at her sides like an arrowhead, creating as little resistance as possible, while the beast prepares its deadly fire-breath attack.

Lara has the ball of her foot positioned on the pole and pushes down with all her might.

Deep within the beast's throat, the power of a newborn sun starts to form, creating a molten eruption inside. The ancient myths about these creatures are real and so are the fables and songs about our heroine. This is where myth meets legend. With her dragon-lance in hand, she hurls it with the power of a giant. It stabs the creature directly in its thrashing tongue.

The stick digs into the sloshy ground. She bounces off it and against the adjacent wall, propelling herself upward. She climbs by dashing back and forth continuously against the slippery surface of the walls.

The power of the dragon-lance poisons the beast inside its bloodstream, turning each scale into stone. This doesn't kill the dragon, however, only petrifies it—still alive .

The beast's irate eyes shift back and forth. If intense looks could kill, this one would be a serial killer. Standing victoriously on the stone dragon's nose, our champion catches the magical scroll, which lands softly in her open palm.

This is what it feels like to be unstoppable.

Lara arrives at edge of the latrine safely. She reaches her hand outward with a smug look on her face. Escaping the pits gives her a feeling which mirrors that of her imagined persona. Her confidence is short-lived, though, as the wet paper lands not soft and gently in her hand, like in the dragon-slaying fantasy, but directly on her forehead—splattering congealed liquid all over her body.

She wants to die in this moment. No, wait. She wants to die the moment *before* this one. She doesn't die, cry, scream, or break down completely. None of those options are going to change what she currently has on her face. Instead, she stands there frozen in place, with a look of horror enveloping her completely.

A drop of viscous excrement slowly runs down her nose, right towards her open mouth.

"That's it!" She jumps into the pile of dirt that is used to cover each layer of waste after every visit. Bathing in the dry dirt, Lara rolls around more than enough to remove the latrine juice. Like a witch's curse, there is nothing she can do to make herself feel clean again. The friction of the granular rock leaves her skin feeling raw, almost rubbed to the point of a wound.

Finally, she decides that this insanity has to stop. Facts are facts. She is, now and forever, tainted.

Her stick slowly sinks into the disgusting pile of bubbling ooze. Watching it descend relaxes her, and her breathing returns to normal, despite the bad smell. Soon the long stick disappears completely as if some unseen creature is nibbling at it from below.

Using her mint-soaked handkerchief as a glove, she dries the page the same way she did herself, only with less frantic, overzealousness.

Before reading the words that are nearly rubbed off, she goes back to her library to find the exact book in which it got torn out of—not wanting to take anything out of context. She spends hours tossing book after book off the comfort of their shelves. The page number starts at CXIV, and she is looking for the corresponding rip. It is a huge undertaking, what with all the years of reading she has endured. This was the only room she hasn't already completely destroyed from either her fearful night or searching for her master's secrets. This is her most beloved room, only now it looks like a tornado hit it. Impulsive and irrational, she can't help but give in to her insatiable want, even if it means ruining a dear part of her.

It takes the better part of the afternoon, but Lara finally finds the missing link. She cautiously slides the page into place. Each tear lines up perfectly with the piece still in the binding. The book is titled, "The 5th King," a tale she remembers reading a couple months prior. It is a story of how horrendous humans can be—rife with torture, misconduct and deceit. Turning to the beginning of the chapter, she starts to read. Her focus is pure, hanging on every word clearly without missing any meaning or making any mistakes. Intrigue pushes her eyes to scroll rigorously until she reaches the secret page.

Her excitement slowly fades with each word she says aloud. It appears to harbor no significance, no evil plot or magical spell. It is almost...sweet and endearing. The human protagonist, who virtually destroyed everyone that cared for him, explains in poetic verse his motive for such heinous acts. It was in order to complete his destiny—for the good of the many, despite his love for his compatriots. She learns the virtue of being human—compassion. The story reads like fiction but feels real enough to have existed. If found true, it would mean that humans have feelings similar to her own race. Which also means that maybe she shouldn't regard them as the lowest forms of life—ones who don't even deserve a life to live.

Her tears drip on the page, as the beauty touches her. "He was a hero...not a villain," she whispers. This is the very reason this page was cut out of existence. It shows empathy and humanity for the humans. It is censorship to serve her master's own propaganda. But why? Why would it make a difference for Lara to see this side of the humans? She could have learned from this, exploited this weakness to the fullest of her ability. The only rational explanation is that her master wants total control over Lara's thoughts and opinions to shape her to her will.

Lara suddenly feels like an object—a sword to be used at her master's disposal and discarded when her point gets too dull. Being manipulated, tricked, and deceived hurts. There has to be a something more than this new role she has been forced into playing. She wants more out of existence—to be more like how she sees herself deep within her fantasies, weapon caddy and all.

So what if the garden dies or the perimeter gets breached? Who cares if the humans trample all over the cracked lakebed? Maybe my time would be better spent putting this cursed land to bed and ending its misery. What have we been sacrificing all these years to protect? Blackened earth? Burnt-out trees? Dew drops?

To live by another's decree means nothing but self-inflicted slavery. Freedom is the ability to choose. Even if she is making a huge mistake, she is entitled to the opportunity to make it. All she wants are some answers, and her master is the only one who can provide them. So much of her has been taken for granted, and she is not ready for another night alone in this place. Enough is enough. She decides right then and there to venture out into the unknown and look for her *beloved* master...and that means going on an adventure.

Sacrifice

Before starting on her journey topside, Lara checks on the human blood she previously collected. It's nearly complete. The water has almost fully separated from the plasma inside the glass contraption her master made. Lara doesn't quite understand how the whole process works. All she knows is that she pours the blood in one chamber and the colorful substance does the rest of the work. She transfers the purified water to a jar and packs it away in her tote.

There is a strong possibility that this whole rescue is some sort of trial, anyway; a plot devised to advance her out of the rut she has been sitting comfortably in for a while now. This wouldn't be the first time her master has done something so ludicrous. At any rate, her purpose is restored.

Lara winces at the first sight of sunlight for the day, even though it is already low in the sky. The air smells different somehow, fresh with exploration. There is one final decision she must make, and it's a hard one to ignore—to bring weapons or not. If this whole operation is a test of some sort, she will assuredly fail if she gets caught using any of her makeshift inventions. On the flip side, if her master needs her help, her inventions might come in handy.

Test or not, Lara decides to grab a weapon that she hasn't had time to finish constructing. Not because she fears anything that her master may have planned. Her reasons are much more selfish than anything. She wants to see if it works.

Dubbed the "quill whip," she shoves the whole project into her tote. She leaves the cleft before she can change her mind about going to her real stash and bringing every weapon she owns.

Lara exhausts the remaining hours of daylight, scouring the perimeter for signs of her master. She doesn't know exactly what she was expecting to find.

With only one lead to go on, Lara makes her way to the very spot where the corpse was taken by the hidden figure.

All of this is a result of her breaking the rules, and here she is doing it again. Maybe the ghost of the forest is punishing her.

"It's practically within our zone, anyway. Master did say that I should clean up her mess...wherever it is," she justifies herself to the dead trees just in case they really are watching her.

Lara's tracks are still visible, which proves that her master never made it out this far. Or maybe she did, and for reasons unknown, she didn't have time to clean up Lara's mess like she intended. There is something else of interest here—the clawed trap that caught the corpse by its leg. She looks back and forth and over her shoulder before snatching it up.

"It would be irresponsible to leave such a dangerous trap about. What if it fell into the wrong hands? I wouldn't want such a thing attached to my foot. No. Better to be safe for safety. I will take it along...just to be sure."

Suddenly Lara's one weapon rule is disregarded. Forgetting her quest momentarily, she sits cross-legged and starts to modify the trap. In its current state, she has no use for it, but after a quick modification... It doesn't take her long to augment the closing trigger by attaching it to the chain. Now she has a wonderful use for the thing in mind. Proud of herself, she throws it over her shoulder.

"Now what?"

The sun is preparing for sleep, and Lara knows that she should make her way back to camp before she finds herself in the same situation as two nights prior—running for her life.

Something out of place catches the corner of her eye. On the surface of the charred soil is a clump of something.

"What do we have here?" Gingerly, she picks it up and watches it crumble between her fingers. There's only one thing it could be...blood. It appears that she didn't drain the human corpse as well as she thought. Even though the thief covered its tracks, traces of the encounter still remain close to the surface. She now has a trail. Crawling on all fours, she sifts through the dirt desperately.

One drop at a time, Lara follows the corpse-thief's path, not caring for her own tracks. Like always, she learned nothing from her master's reprimands.

The blood trail leads her to the mouth of a cave. The outer walls are scorched from sixty-foot-tall flames, from years past. The sun is nearly gone from the horizon. The darkness absorbs all light with its elongated shadows as they creep over everything. Lara isn't sure what to do. Should she venture to the unknown underground or take her chances with the night killers and any other dangers the dark might provide?

After waiting until the very last possible moment to decide, she is left with only one option. Take refuge inside the cave. It seems like the most logical option, anyway. She grips on to her bear trap's chain and enters the pitch-blackness, ready to strike the first thing that moves. Unfortunately, she finds nothing awaiting her fighting stance. After blindly feeling around, she figures out that the cave is far deeper than she surmised. She tests the hardness of the spiky shards that cover every surface.

"They're tough, that's for sure."

Although they're deadly sharp, they're also seemingly indestructible. There is no way for her to scale the cave's jagged slopes without armor of some kind. She carefully places the trap at her back for protection. Night is upon her, and there is no chance for her to go anywhere, not until daybreak.

Sitting at the border of the lightness of the moon and the darkness of the cave, she weaves quills into her whip, making it much longer and much more dangerous. Uninterrupted this time around, she watches the moisture escape the land. The mist groans and rises from the earth in a rippling dance. It is nature's abstract artform, and it's spectacular.

Lara wonders why her master hid such a marvel from her for so long. Was she just greedy? No. Her master was a lot of things, but greedy wasn't one of them. Tough as stone? Relentlessly seeking perfection? Most definitely. She wonders if her master thought she wasn't worthy of its beauty for some reason. Or maybe it was just punishment for insubordination? Her doubts grow with each passing moment in the darkness.

The mist creeps right up to the edge of the cave without entering. The moonlight changes the color of the vapor like a rainbow trapped inside, begging to get out.

Extending her hand out to welcome it, Lara pauses at the notion of disobeying her master yet again.

"Everything I do is a disappointment, anyway. Why not." Before she can change her mind, she reaches out to greet the mist.

The mysterious liquid has a chill to it, but it's also soft and airy. It lightly moistens her arm—feeling refreshing and pure, like water, only magical. Moonlight illuminates her arm as the mist starts to dissolve the soot off her limb. It slowly uncovers her bark-like skin underneath, through the streaking drops. She longs to bath in it and spin around in glee, as if possessed by the spirt of a child.

"Is this what happiness feels like?"

Before she can nod at her own question, her body stands without her willing it to.

"What is happening?"

Her leg tries to step into the moonlit mist on its own.

"No!" She pulls against herself, but her arm is stuck in the moonlight. She feels an immense amount of pain with each tug. Her extended arm starts to harden before her eyes—stiff and unmanageable.

With everything she has, Lara pulls against the unknown force of the mist. She feels her joints pop and crack out of place, but it's no use.

The brazen girl is stuck, and she knows what should be done but doesn't have the right tools.

I need to cut off my arm.

She's caught inside a spider's web, and it's hungry for revenge. While pulling against the misty moonlight, Lara's foot slips out of the cave, getting caught inside the radiance, and likewise held in place. She scrambles and reaches for the chain to her bear trap that's just beyond her grasp.

It's no use, she doesn't have anything sharp enough to sever her extremities with. She has to do something else, something that just might kill her. But what other choice is there?

Lara knows that dying is a possibility. With a shrug of her shoulder, she figures that it isn't that big of a deal, really. *Today is as good as any.* Lara then remembers her master. What if she needs her help after all?

She mulls over her mortality. The way she sees it, death is knocking on the door, and the only question is how will she answer it—slow and reserved, or kicking the thing off its hinges?

Out of options, and almost out of time, Lara plunges her whole body into the misty moonlight. She goes in headfirst, ready for anything, even if it is an instant death. Her master had warned her countless times with life-threatening tales of being outside after dark—plague, excessive bleeding, asphyxiation, to name a few. Her examples were never consistent, and now she is going to find out exactly how far-fetched, or quite accurate, they really are. Though in this moment, she would prefer her master a liar—a compulsive one. In fact, her life depends on it. That thought brings a fighting spirit back to her step.

Within the mist, she feels the moisture engulf her completely—wetting her charcoal camouflage. The dark deception slowly melts off her body, each streak of moisture uncovering her vivacious pigment, which nearly glows in contrast to the drab environment. From inside the vapor, moonlight twinkles magically against the air. She has never been outside showing her true hue, and it feels refreshing. It is not at all like death. More like purity of living.

Whatever force is holding her arm isn't powerful enough to hold her whole body still. She can tell that something is moving all around her, an unseen creature or creatures of some sort. Strange shapes are everywhere, but also nowhere. They're much too swift for her eyes. Whatever it is, it's hidden by the mist. Or *is* it the mist? Then, without a doubt, she realizes that the nature of her predicament isn't mystical at all. It's living, and living things can be killed. They are both members of the same cycle—life, decay, rest. The only question is, what part of the cycle is she currently in?

"Life," she declares to the vapor. Nothing in this domain is ever free, and if the mist wants to devour her flesh, it will not get it without a struggle. Kill to survive, or die so that others may live.

As she moves through the heavy air, she wonders if this is what it feels like to swim. Her feathers flow slowly with the current as if she were falling, though she is standing upright. She is merely waiting, watching and feeling.

Lara arms her quill whip with her mobile hand and thrashes it at her paralyzed arm. Airborne water droplets line up along the quill's trajectory. A hellish noise reverberates the liquid while sending ripples through the air. Whatever was grappling her releases its hold upon her. Lara is free. Some watery air falls to the ground, creating dewdrops at her feet. She is hurting it, whatever "it" may be.

With total control over her limbs, Lara darts

back and forth with graceful form, like an underwater creature.

The mist moves like a collective being. It tries to grab ahold of her again, though now its movements are slow and easy to foresee.

Fighting something so encompassing is a challenge at best and fatal at worst. Being so close to "the one" has Lara in a blissful state. Her eyes shift back and forth without wasting time to blink. She is reluctant to attack, hoping to prolong this feeling as long as possible. With each advance the mist makes, she circles around, matching its movement, like a partner in a dance. She twirls her whip around in an artistic display, cracking and striking, keeping her foe at bay. Her mouth mirrors the music that is pounding through her head in a low hum.

Off in the distance, she notices more mist descending upon her position. It is creeping down the mountainside, blocking her escape.

Lara can't fight too many things at once, and now she's surrounded with enemies.

She spins around, causing one of the quills to fly off the end of the whip like a projectile. Missing a quill slightly shortens the whip's overall reach. However, using the quill whip in this manner is no mistake. She carefully ties each quill loose enough for such versatility. Over and over, she flings quills through the air, creating a comfortable distance between herself and the encroaching menace. Finally, a quill hits something, and another small patch of mist dissipates into heavy liquid. She is quick to turn her assault toward the newly arriving mist, which is keeping her trapped in the moonlight—making her feel divided somehow, as if she is both herself and someone else simultaneously.

"Not so fast." Lara uses her slippery body to slide across the rocks while continuing to hurl a barrage of quills—each one snapping from the finely woven thread.

The mist parts, creating a crater of air.

Lara catches her breath. She has successfully kept the impending doom at bay, if only momentarily. Looking down, she notices that her whip is now half its original length. As great as her weapon is proving, it cannot last forever. Neither can the mist.

"I just have to fight it until sunrise." Hearing her words escape her mouth, she realizes exactly how crazy they sound.

Something is scrambling on the ground

trying to get away. She approaches it while quickly weaving a couple more quills into her ever-shrinking weapon.

Never let your hands go idle, because some-day someone will lob them off and you'll regret wasting how little time you had with them, she recalls her master's morbid warning.

The little creature on the ground is not some strange mist-monster, a scary flying mouth or something equally frightening. It's a dainty nymph with a quill stabbed through his torso. He reminds her of a doll that she read about in a human fable—cute and compact. Lara never had luxuries such as toys or the time to enjoy their purposeless, if she were to even have any playthings. To her, it seems quite wasteful to spend your time not improving your skill.

Still, she's intrigued by the allure of playing with dolls, even though she has long since out-grown such activities. Just the idea of being simple is endearing and sweet. It gives her some amount of comfort, if only briefly.

There is this one unbelievably complicated weapon that she has been stuck on for some time now. As she contemplates where she should stash the little guy, she realizes that this creature and his teeny-tiny hands could operate its mechanical functions just fine. It is a solution that never occurred to her until just now.

"So glad I found you." Lara picks up the nymph by the quill lodged in it. She examines him closely, her device's plans fresh in her mind. Spanning from its arms to ribs are fuzzy wings that look like veiny leaves. They twitch with discomfort. "Are you a night killer?" She bites her lip at the very thought.

"Of course not. We are the people of the clouds. The cloud dancers."

"The clouds? You're a little far from home, little one," Lara says, looking up at the clear, star-speckled sky. A gasp escapes her lips. She is in awe of its dazzling brilliance. "What the..."

"On the contrary, we are exactly where we ought to be. Lifting the world up, or at least trying to." The sprite starts to bleed fluorescent green liquid from his mouth as he speaks. "Hello?" He struggles, trying to dislodge himself from the quill while Lara is mesmerized by the night's freckled light.

"Have you seen this before?" Lara asks, ignoring the dryness coming over her tongue.

"What is it?" The nymph jerks his head sideways to catch a glimpse. "Just turn me a little..."

"Oh, sorry," she says, turning the nymph to

face the sky. "That! Isn't it...? I don't even know."

"Do you mean the stars, the moon, or the blackness in between?"

"All of it. It's so...vast. The expanse is endless," Lara says, removing the quill from his little body with the ease of removing a splinter from a finger. "If you're not a night killer, why are you attacking me?"

"You are our sacrificial gift." He quickly arms himself with a sword roughly the size of a toothpick. Judging by the menacing look on his face, one might think he could cause quite a bit of pain, though due to his size, that seems almost impossible.

"Me? What did I do to you?" Lara is quite surprised by his candor. "We will have none of that." Before he can jab her in the hand and make his way to her eyes, Lara thrusts the quill back at him.

The nymph is no slouch, and he parries it away. "All you bottom feeders ruined everything, thinking you could make peace with them."

Without giving it a second thought, Lara closes her hand, trapping him inside, squeezing until he drops his wee little sword. "A sacrificial gift...like as in a sacrifice?"

"To..."

Lara loosens her grip, allowing him to finish his sentence.

"...take your life and rid the curse of the departed. In order to elevate the trees. To raise the dead."

"So, sacrificing me helps you how? By growing trees?"

"You really don't know anything, do you?" he says with a gleeful undertone. "Your arrogance cost us the wind. Now look at me." He looks down at the ground, defeated.

"I can't be blamed for your misfortune. I wasn't even alive then."

High-pitched chuckles take over his body, causing him to shake uncontrollably.

"What's so funny?"

"You don't even know how stupid you sound right now."

She gives him a look so full of daggers, it stabs right through his gleeful rant. "Would you like to run that by me again?"

"Um, anyway. So, what were we talking about? Right, the clouds. They were so crisp, and fluffy puffs encompassing the sky like a beautiful blanket. That is until the Dark War.

The black smoke came in hot and fought mercilessly. Our barrage of rain showered the endless flame, and we almost soothed the rage of betrayal. That is until the clouds fell out of the sky when your people clipped our wings, killing the forest."

Lara never recalls ever seeing any clouds, fluffy or otherwise, though she has no reason to disbelieve his tale. "We protect the forest, give in to its needs above our own."

"Look around. You're doing a very bad job."

Lara suddenly grows bored with this conversation and no longer wants to play with this thing. She gives him a threatening glance and wiggles her two open palms. "Don't make me applaud you into nothingness."

"If we can resurrect the trees, even partially, then perhaps we will float again. And maybe the sky will no longer reject us."

"I will not be your sacrifice. What will that solve, anyway? I don't see anyone standing around granting wishes in exchange for murder. Believe me, I've done my fair share and seen no such offering. No, I will be your savior." She holds the nymph above her head for all the mist to see. "Go on, fly!"

The sprite takes a leap off her hands and

starts to spin around in circles. His rotation starts out fast but then begins to slow. Green liquid sprays out of him like a party favor. Without enough lift, he drops out of the air like a stone.

Lara is quick to catch him before he hits the ground. The little guy is no longer moving. His expression, lifeless. He expended too much and dies right then and there, cradled inside her delicate palm.

She picks up his little leg and lets it flop back in her hand. In a fleeting moment, she almost misses his righteous conversation. Though brief, this is a new feeling for Lara...remorse.

His little body evaporates towards the rest of the vapor, leaving only his blood behind.

How about that. Master was right. It was spirits after all. Although they're nothing like how she had imagined. A sigh of relief escapes her mouth.

"Here is your sacrifice. Take it." *And let me get on with my life.*

The sprite-filled mist, fallen clouds, or whatever it might be, surrounds her like a pack of hungry wolves. It's closing in around her, tightening with each passing moment.

Looking up, she hopes to see something just

as soft and wonderful as he has described. Though sill beautiful, the sky is clear as day. There is no change in the world around her.

It's for the best. I wouldn't want anything to obstruct that view.

Red colors bloom from the vapor like a raging fire. This catches her attention right quick.

"What else do you want from me?" Lara knows that she has angered the cloud-folk. Being easily distracted, she spies some sprite blood that oozed onto her hand. She quickly wipes it on her leggings. It might be the look of disgust on her face, but the mist is in no mood for conversing. By the time she returns to reality, it is far too late. The mist is at the edge of touching her, patiently awaiting her full attention.

"Sorry he's gone. But now your goal has been met. A sacrifice is what you wanted." Lara counts the quills left on her whip. She doesn't have enough for the mass genocide she is planning. Killing for Lara is a necessity...and sometimes a nuisance. Fighting, on the other hand, is a playful game—one she doesn't like to lose.

"Don't you guys mess up my perfect record. Then I will be forced to haunt you in the afterlife."

The grounded clouds rumble a thunderous sound, which shakes the dead trees out of their rotten roots.

The agile feathered-folk leaps out of the way of a falling sycamore. It almost crushes her into an unmarked grave. "We all want the same thing. The same goal," she reasons, not sure if the words are true or not, or if they're reaching any cognizant being. She is only assuming that there are more nymphs in there. *I wonder what other entities the mist could be? Animated dragon's breath? Time-traveling smoke? The physical manifestation of evil incarnate?*

Electric bolts marble through the fallen clouds and light up the ground. The flash is so intense that the stars disappear momentarily. Echoes of wee laughter is all around her.

Bummer, it's just more nymphs.

The electrified mist cloud covers her like a blanket. There is no escape this time. She is done for.

A Dance, a Debt, and a Deception

Every inch of Lara's body is held in place by tiny cloud-dancer hands. Their sharp, little nails dig into her skin from all angles.

She struggles to reach her quill weapon, which is nearly expended. It's no use. She didn't properly prepare for this onslaught. But it isn't her fault, not this time. She was chasing old information. Last she knew, the only adversaries to contend with belonged to the two sets of tracks. She figured that she would most likely find the owners of them just in time to see her master's fighting prowess. How could anyone expect her to be ready for something that she never knew existed? If only she had gone back to her stash. She has a poison bomb that could exterminate these pests with ease. Instead, she opted for a human-killing device that has proved quite useless on sprites. If it is anyone's fault, it's her master's for omitting the truth about the mist to her. At least this is how she feels on the matter.

In this situation, and many like it, her instincts have proved invaluable. If she had only heeded her master's words, she would have no weapons to bargain with. Currently, her master's logic seems to fail, in her mind. What she really needs is more weapons—to be better equipped.

An image develops in her mind. It's her wearing every weapon she has in her arsenal. Spiked-shells, make-shift swords and other deadly instruments are sticking out every-which way. She stands stoutly, barely able to move—a mobile fortress not to be reckoned with. No one would dare mess with her. Though messing with her is exactly the purpose of the weaponized suit. Despite knowing full well how impractical the fantasy is, a gleeful warmth covers her. The great big smile in her mind transfers over to her face, undeterred by the predicament.

Oh, right, death.

It is amusing to her what trivial things she thinks of in dire situations such as this. She almost has to force her mind to focus on the urgency of the matter. Many times she has been in similar positions, but alas, it never happens. Maybe it is because she always finds a way out, somehow. But what if she doesn't this time? Will she find happiness in the final flickering moments of her life? If so, will the fleeting euphoria be worth the pain and suffering?

Her master says that she cannot give her death away; it has to be earned. It isn't as if she is suicidal or anything. She is just bored, and sometimes she feels that death might be the change she is looking for.

I might as well get on with it. They bested my body, but they haven't bested my mind. Not yet, anyhow.

"I'm out here looking for my master. The Arm of the Forest," Lara says, her voice bubbling as if under water.

A symphony of tiny voices speaks over each other in secession.

"The arm?"

"Is that what she said?"

"Whose arm?"

"It's a feather trick."

"I have to *hand* it to her; it's a clever one."

"This is no time for wisecracks."

"Shock her rotten."

A jolt of lightning heats up the mist, causing Lara to convulse in pain. She tries to speak, but her mouth is clamped shut, tighter than a bear trap's jaws.

Lara has spent countless hours causing herself lots of pain, raising her tolerance for the uncomfortable feeling that can be dreadfully distracting. Nothing that she has done in the past could have prepared her for this feeling. It is crippling. It scrambles her thoughts, blocking her ability to focus on anything but the discomfort until it fades into the background of her consciousness. Once the torture stops, Lara belts out a plea, "Stop! That's not nice at all. That hurts."

"Good. It was supposed to."

"We haven't even begun."

"She thinks she can just order us around?"

"I don't take orders from her."

"You take orders from me."

"Does this look like a restaurant to you?"

"Maybe she needs to learn her place."

"You both do."

"Order up."

"What's on the menu today?"

"Pain, with the crying on the side."

Lara interrupts the pother before the group can agree on another torturous shock...as that seems to be where this whole conversation is heading. "My master protects the forest. She has no hands and a bad disposition."

"The cripple?"

"She is mean."

"Much meaner than you."

"...and stronger, too."

"Is that who she is looking for?"

"The arm is armless?"

"But she's not harmless."

"Is this some kind of joke?"

"She is no friend of yours. She has no friends."

"Lies are rampant with this one."

"Discipline is earned through punishment."

Before Lara can chime in, another jolt of lightning charges through her. This time it electrifies her for twice as long and with twice as much agony.

"AAAAAAre you done?" Lara screams through the pain.

"For the moment, yes."

"No need to get snippy."

"You're not in charge of this execution."

"We need to charge up before charging you with treason."

"Why are we reasoning with it?"

"Can we charge her for wasting our time?"

"Is time even real?"

"She has plenty to suffer for; no need to add time to that list."

"How about killing all the soil for starters?"

"I could go for some soil right about now."

"Shut your trap."

"Will everyone just slow down for a moment? Let me explain," Lara says, her fingers twitching with residual electricity.

"Please, indulge us."

"She is stalling."

"Why won't she spit it out already."

"I think I know why."

"I assuredly know why."

They speak so fast that Lara can't process each voice before the next one starts up. It is both tiresome and maddening.

"Just listen to me and stop jabbering on. My master has gone missing. Yes, the one with no hands. Do you have any information on her whereabouts? This information is quite useful to me at this time."

"Yes, the one with no hands. We saw her."

"How did she lose her fingies?"

"What's the deal with that?"

"Tell us the whole story."

"Tell us and we might help you."

"Might."

"Please?"

"Please?"

"Please?"

Their silence is calming, so much so that Lara takes a full beat before responding. "I can't divulge what I don't know myself. She never told me the whole story. She doesn't tell me a lot of things, but one thing I know for sure is that there was a battle. She lost the match...as well as the obvious."

"Quite scandalous!"

"We know who it was."

"Who? The lord?"

"It couldn't be him."

"Who, then?"

"Maybe she ate them."

"No one could eat them."

"Accidentally, perhaps?"

"My master didn't eat her own fingers.

We're not cannibals, you know," Lara blurts out, trying to stop their tangent from becoming everlasting.

"Oh, really?"

"But you eat humans, don't you?"

"Close enough."

"Juicy, pink flesh."

"Are we making you hungry?"

"Yes, actually. And I'm about to change my diet to cloud marchers, or whatever you call yourselves."

"We are cloud..."

"...dancers."

"We don't go down very easily."

"Speak for yourself. I am quite scrumptious."

"It wouldn't be the first time I've had to cut my way out of a stomach."

"This folk is getting tiresome."

"I agree."

"I third that."

"Let's kill her already."

"Are we still doing that?"

"We can't exactly let her go."

"She must pay for what her kind has done."

Deep in thought, she rids the chaff of incessant chatter, looking for something useful.

There she finds it, in the middle of all their bickering. "The forest. You will never resurrect the forest if you kill me. And before you fry my lights out, allow me to explain why."

Lara remembers seeing her master with illumination salts when she arrived home late the other night. The sun had barely set. Her master didn't need them to see. Could it be that she was using them to ward off the sprites? If true, this would also explain the salt residue that's always prevalent around the garden site. Her master must have been protecting it from them, and now it's Lara's chance to strike a bargain.

"Please do."

"I am intrigued."

"Still bored."

"We are running out of time."

"Get on with it already."

"The garden. There you will find the very thing you're looking for. Clean, fertile and unpolluted soil. Then you can grow whatever you want."

"Nonsense, we've seen no such place."

"I told you she is wasting time."

"The earth is totally scorched through and through."

"Light her up."

"Let me finish. You haven't seen it because its protected by salts." Lara knows that the chemical reaction of the salts emits a smoke. She now has a good hunch of what they're afraid of. "If I can find my master, I will prevent her from creating the barrier and give you the pristine loam." Just divulging the information about the garden leaves Lara feeling sour. It is important to their survival, but not only for the sake of rarity. Cursed soil is all the more prevalent.

"If your master is gone..."

"No one is protecting the spot."

"I know where it is."

"Idiot, we all do."

"Let's go there now."

"What are we waiting for?"

"Maybe you're right, and she is gone, but she always comes back. She always has, ever since the forest went up in a blaze. Not even the loss of her hands has kept her from keeping you guys afeard. She could have even been the one who started it. Who knows what else she is capable of. Especially after mourning the loss of her favorite protégée." Lara lets out a self-assured smile.

"Could she be the pyromancer?"

"That would explain a lot."

"Nonsense, that only produces more questions."

"How can she start a fire without any hands?"

"Either way, let's not anger the folk."

"She has nothing left to lose."

"Now she does."

"It has returned."

"No, it hasn't."

"I saw it with my own peepers."

"What are you going on about now?" Lara interrupts, forgetting her master's rule about interrupting loose lips when they're rambling.

"Oh, nothing."

"Just rumors."

"Yes, rumors."

"If we let you go, will you agree to a truce?"

"We don't want any trouble."

"Give us your word, and your master's?"

"And the sweet, sweet soil."

"Without cause?"

"A bargain."

"With no hard feelings?"

"Or recourse?"

How quickly they've changed their tune.

Giving away the garden is a very difficult decision for Lara. It was all she protected and held dear for so long. Though she also knows that in this heat, the crops will wilt without her daily care, and she was already too distracted to tend to them this morning. She has to give something in return—life for life. Plus, once her master spoke of something bigger...a nursery. This place was the source of soil they used to grow their crops—stolen from an ancient land. The only trouble is that Lara has no idea where it is, or if it truly exists.

"I will agree to your terms, on one condition—you tell everything about my master."

"It has been decided."

"Oh, glorious change, may the wind adhere to our call."

"Thank you."

"I still think we should kill her."

"Shhhh."

"Don't ruin this for us."

"I have a plan."

"Shut up."

"Don't talk to me like that."

"So do we."

"Stop bickering. It's already done."

"Oh, yeah?"

She suddenly has full control over her body as the sounds of a little brawl erupt inside the mist. There is discontent among them and she contemplates using their little spat as a diversion to aid in her killing spree. That would mean going back on her word, but that is exactly what it is...a word. People change words all the time. Brushing off that idea, she chimes in, "Enough. So, where is she?"

"Past the wood rim."

"Yes, beyond the very place the roots reach."

"There you will find what you're looking for."

"Yes, what's coming to you."

"Quite."

"Uh...good fortune. Lots and lots of it."

"Just follow the path."

The mist distorts and churns until it depicts an arrowhead indicating the way.

To Lara this almost seems too easy, though she has nothing else to go on. The cave is not an option, not unless she wants to get all cut up on those spikes.

"Is there anything else you want to tell me?"

The arrow they made quivers, shaking suspiciously back and forth.

Lara thanks them and is off to the next part

of her adventure with less than high hopes.

Once she is out of earshot, the mist starts to ripple with thunderous laughter.

The Edge of the World

Everything is just as miserable as before. Only now, the star-filled sky adds a sparkling gleam to the surface. Mystique and wonderment fill the air. Lara sees the landscape through a different perspective, as if from a new set of eyes—ones that are hopeful and excited to see what the future holds.

No longer hiding from it, she uses the moonlight to guide her along the charred soil. Each step she takes with poise and a bit of bounce. Head held high, she's no longer slinking around hiding inside the shadows. This is the most comfortable she has ever felt in the surface world. Fear has played a big role in keeping her curiosity at bay her entire life; fear of the night killers, the spirit mist, whatever power could have ignited this new land before her, the acidic waters to the east, famine, boredom, and the list goes on and on. Lara fears anything that is out of her realm of control. Fighting and slaughtering humans are pretty much the only things she isn't afraid of, not in the slightest. Relaxed and with an inner sense of peace, she indulges in the crispness of night.

Her master is always warning her to never underestimate the ingenuity and cruelty of humans, but Lara has never seen any behavior short of being pathetic. She constantly bests them with her exceptional fighting ability, cunning tactics, and superior weaponry. If it weren't for her latest blunder, Lara would have had a perfect record for extermination.

"Wait a moment. My record isn't broken; not yet. Those tracks could have been something other than human," she reasons with her wild thoughts.

Braving her fears makes her feel independent and even more powerful. She feels as though there is no feat that can't be bested, if only she can prepare for it appropriately.

Lara still can't wrap her head around why her master would abandon her without sending word. Having a strong disposition, her master always fights problems head-on. Never one to tuck tail and run. Unless she encountered the thing that gave her a handicap. *No, she is too vengeful to flee from anything, especially that.* The truth is that no matter how many years they have spent together, she really doesn't know her master.

Being alone has changed Lara somewhat, though she herself has yet to notice. Her rationale and responsibility are both evolving as she grows emotionally. Just a couple days ago, Lara lived for play, treasure hunting and weapon inventing. Nothing else quite mattered to her—not revenge, providence or even restoring the forest.

She knows of nothing except this "fireplace," as her master calls it. What if the world were worse off before the event? Could the flames have cleansed the bad away? If so, is her master one of those bad things, one overlooked by the purge? That could mean that she is also one of those bad things. No, she came much later. She is an accomplice, if anything. She doesn't feel bad, quite the contrary—more misunderstood and taken for granted, but mostly ignored. Her mind is going around in circles with no escape. Truth is just a lie told from a different perspective.

To her, life never was as bad as her master made it out to be. Dry? Yes. Dirty? Absolutely. But it is all she has—all she has ever had. All her "nothing" expectations are being exceeded ever since she struck out on her own. Who knows what else life has left for her to experience.

The past only lives on through the memories, which perpetuate old feuds and quarrels—inherited pain through old anger and conflicts. Letting go is the only way to move on—to regrow and start anew. Maybe that's why the forest won't grow. It isn't done dying. And her master is part of the problem, not the protector. Guilt twists her stomach as she wishes that everyone who was part of the old ways had burned alive with the trees—her master, the sprites, the humans, everyone. *Maybe then they would all stop crying and moaning about it and leave me to my own life.*

Old wars fought over old scars, where new blood is shed by those too stubborn to put history to bed.

With a crick in her neck, Lara tries to memorize the twinkling patterns as she watches the diamonds in the sky vanish into the violet morning. This starry night may be overlooked by another, but in this single moment in time, Lara logs it down in the history books as one she will not soon forget.

To her master, this would just be another place. Ignorance makes Lara appreciate what she does have—the unknown that is hidden in the aftermath. Blind to the truth, her eyes are wide open, ready to see through the lies.

It has been five straight hours of walking and rigorous contemplation; that is, until she reaches the rim of the forest or what her master refers to as "the end of the world." It is nothing like she expected for such an ill-sounding name. There is clearly stuff beyond the dead forest—rocks, verdant hills and yellow grasses, even life... A small insect is buzzing around just beyond her reach, almost as if it knows about the cursed lands which Lara calls home. Lara watches the bugger closely. "They don't live up to their names at all...'bug.' It's wonderfully busy, and not at all a nuisance." As if hypnotized by its fluttering wings, her eyes follow it intensely, and soon her feet follow, like it's drawing her into its lair. Lara doesn't know or care about its motives; she acts on her feelings of want, alone.

Pausing, she vacillates between staying in the forest and stepping onto that unsoiled dirt, lusciously brown and just outside her reach. Scattered around the rim are dozens of fist-sized pits from some kind a large fruit, though no trees are around to give insight to their source. Reverting to her treasure-hunting side, she wonders what new species might sprout if she were to plant such a pit in the garden. Maybe a tree with one of those juicy fruits she's only read about in books. Perhaps a tall outlook, one that would limit the amount of walking she must do during her daily patrols. Or even a carnivorous tree would be amazing. She can feed it the invading humans almost like a pet—no, exactly like a pet. The possibilities are endless, and she knows deep down that she has to take one, if not all of them.

Something about this place doesn't add up. If unscathed dirt is so hard to come by, how is it that she is currently setting her eyes upon it? *There's life just outside our borders, and we choose to live here in ash and misery?* This place isn't that far, and soil is abundant. This concept is breaking everything she thought she knew. A sharp pain courses through Lara's head, as the fundamental truths of her upbringing come crashing down around her.

The bug buzzes off out of sight. Then something even rarer catches her eye. Off in the distance, thin blades of grass move on their own, like they're swaying back and forth to a gentle song. There is no music to be heard. Instead, the sweet sound of a breeze tickles the grass—calling her to join in on the experience.

Lara holds up her hand. She feels no such gust or sensation the grasslings show. Is she imagining it, or could it be part of a more exclusive party, one that she isn't invited to? There is only one way to find out, but she is hesitant. Breaking this rule might mean sudden death or something far worse—the truth about her master's compulsion to stretch the truth.

After doing some simple calculations, she is now certain that they could have set forth on a journey here at least once a month during the dead season. Five hours here, one hour scooping, and seven hours back, even adding ample rest time for the trip back. There must be some reason why they never ventured out this far. Life doesn't have to be so hard. It is her master's choice. She must be one of the bad ones. Why else would she inflict upon them a life so burdensome and deny her the brilliant night's scene?

Nothing seems to add up. Lara scours her memory for a clue. One thing in particular does stand out. The footprints she was following while dragging that corpulent corpse, they didn't seem right. The weight was all off. They seemed as if they were coming from this direction. No...they were *going* in the other direction. Of course, whoever made those footprints had to have been walking backwards, making it appear as if they were going when they were in fact coming.

The corpse thief was coming towards this place as well. It must have also been fooled by the tactic. It wasn't looking for me at all.

It's a deception her master may not have figured out. This would explain why her master is out here in the first place—providing that what the cloud dancers said is true.

Am I the only one who happened to catch this?

What if her master really did meet her end or found a new adventure outside of this place? Lara wonders what would become of her should she join the other side of the forest...of what she thought was nothingness for so long.

Clearly is not nothing. It is something great and new. Since her master lied about the negative effects of nightfall, who knows what else she is lying about. Maybe a better life is just outside her grasp, taunting her with greenery and abundance. Like at the cave mouth, Lara has a choice to make: Play it safe inside the sheltered life that her master has provided, or lead herself straight toward new, uncharted possibilities? Is this an illusionary spell, placed here to taunt her curiosity? Or were her master's words simply lies told to keep her inside a jail cell?

Feeling like she has nothing to lose and everything to gain, Lara takes her first step off the edge of the world. As her foot starts to bridge the space between life and death, she feels a soft hand grab her shoulder tightly, like a mother cat mouthing a cub by the scruff of its neck. She knows it isn't her master, for obvious reasons.

Frozen in place, Lara's astonishment halts her foot from landing outside the cursed forest. This is the first time she has been successfully snuck up on. The forest always lets her know when an intruder is afoot, but not this time. This is something different.

One Side of a Thought

"Don't finish that step, unless you wish to die again," a breathy voice warns Lara from behind.

She feels a warm exhale beat against her neck with every word. "Again?" Lara asks, balancing on one foot, close to teetering to her end.

"I've been watching you for some time now."

"That isn't at all creepy." Lara wonders how someone could have been watching her without her having any sense of their existence. *If this person got the jump on me now, maybe they could have done it previously.* She soon discounts that idea after reflecting upon her own skill. *Nah, they just got lucky.*

Is it skill or just happenstance? Luck is an

issue that Lara needs to come to grips with. She can plan and plot out fighting stances and moves, overpower her opponents with skill and cunning schemes, but sometimes the world doesn't want her to win, not in the way she would have hoped. Good luck is something that she will never admit to. When things go right, it is skill, and when they go bad, it's a case of bad luck. It is the "luck conundrum" as she calls it.

"I can't believe you're really alive. At first, I had my doubts, but now I'm certain it's you."

"I am me. That's for sure." Lara decides not to pry more into her cryptic intimations, fearing that they are part of some larger deception. *Your mind is your greatest treason; it will deceive you the second you let your guard down,* she recalls her master's words. There is no way of knowing what is apprehending her—maybe a ghost human, or something equally mysterious. Digging in her toes, Lara spins around, releasing herself from the figure's grasp.

The person standing before her is the last thing she ever expected. It's another feathered-folk female—an older one. Looking into her sunken, dark eyes, Lara can't even begin to guess her age, though she appears to be from her master's generation. The folk is dressed in bright colors and free-flowing clothes which fit loosely around her frame. A wooden necklace is draped around her thin neck. Somehow, she has managed to keep herself quite clean in such a filthy, dusty and despicable place. Still in awe, Lara studies the intricate features of her light feathers, giving her a completely unique look and coloring. Each one of the feathers on her crown extends out in all directions, like cactus needles. She has a sweetness to her, despite the burn marks that scar her entire body. There is no mistaking her former beauty, which has all but been burnt away by the past.

Lara thought there were only two of them left. Another of her master's lies manifests. Being face to face with another feathered-folk causes Lara to lose her balance briefly, and she stumbles backwards towards the edge.

The folk's arms swoop under her neck and pull her into a hug, safe from the perimeter she nearly fell into. "I have you now."

"Why did you do that?" Lara asks in a whisper. Chills electrify her skin, sending a surge coursing throughout her body.

"You're so grown," the folk says with an endearing smile.

Lara is lost in the enjoyment of feeling

completely safe for the first time. Her master only makes physical contact with her in a disciplinary manner after a mistake is made. This is nurturing and nice, like a hen resting upon her nest filled with eggs. Feeling caught in a spell, Lara interrupts her own daze. "Why are you following me?"

"She has kept me hidden from you for long enough, but I've found you now," the folk says, stroking the feathers on Lara's crown.

This feels nice, too nice. Nothing gives without taking in return, unless... "Mother?" The words just fall out of her, as preposterous as they might be.

A soft chuckle comes over the woman. "No. Dear me, that would be impossible. Maybe you're not as grown as I had thought."

Lara launches to her feet, dusts herself off, all the while eying the woman curiously. "Who are you, then?"

"I was once the eyes of the forest, the watcher. Now I'm only a witness." The womanly-folk slowly slides her hands by her side like a winding plant.

"The witness of what?"

"The end."

"Look around. It already came and went.

You missed it." Lara kicks some black ash, uncovering more cursed soot underneath.

"Yes, it came, but it hasn't left, not yet anyhow." The folk twinkles her fingers and causes the ash to revert into dirt before Lara's amazement.

"How did you?"

"It is an old trick, a gift granted from years of observation. But like everything in life, it doesn't last."

Once it lands, the brown dirt quickly mixes with the midnight earth, lost as the dead soil devours it.

"Oh." The excitement quickly fades from her eyes.

"I can teach you, if you like."

"I would love... Well, what's the point? Decay is contagious, and it would just make things worse." It all seems too convenient. If this strange folk really is watching her every move, then she knows what sorts of things Lara likes, and she likes learning above all else.

"So is hope, but suit yourself."

"Let me ask you a thing or two. Everything looks much greener outside of the dead forest. Why don't you want me to leave, Enchantress?"

"If one of our kind ever leaves the boundary

of the forest, they will perish to a place of nothingness, never to return."

"You are starting to sound like someone I know," Lara says causally, fighting the frog in her throat.

"There lies the evidence. Fallen comrades who were just as trusting as you," the folk says, pointing at what seems like nothing to Lara.

The truth is sitting in plain sight, though it is hidden to her by ignorance.

"How do I know you're telling me the truth about any of this?" Lara slowly edges herself around the folk, pinning her up against the edge. This is just a precaution; in case The Enchantress becomes hostile, she can simply push her out of the perimeter. If what she says about their kind is true, even in the slightest, it's a good way to find out.

"If you don't believe me, by all means see for yourself. Take the first step."

"Funny, I had the same idea," Lara says, clenching her fists, bridging the gap between them.

"I...didn't mean me."

"I know, but I did." Forcing the folk over the border would be a surefire way to learn the truth about the edge of the world, one way or another.

"I've already seen death. I am already an echo of my own destruction." She gently caresses the wound that covers her face.

"Then what are you waiting for? Take the step beyond."

"Why would I save you, just so that you can kill me a moment later?"

"Maybe you don't want me to leave because then you won't have anyone left to spy on," Lara says, putting up her hands, ready to shove.

"Don't be too hasty with your assumptions. You don't want to develop regrets," the folk says, knowing that Lara more than has it in her to kill her without batting an eye.

"I don't have regrets. I dish them out in abundance."

"I know being bold is imbedded deep within your nature, but please don't make another huge mistake," The Enchantress says, with a serious tone saturating her words. She looks truly scared, certain of what the young folk is capable of.

"What do you mean, 'another huge mistake'? So what, I left a few measly tracks. Why is everyone making such a big deal about this?" Lara puts down her arms and looks at her inquisitively.

"Mmm. Let's go someplace we can talk, before the sun escapes the ridge. It's not safe out here." The Enchantress looks over her shoulder, fear glistening in her eyes.

"I feel safe as can be."

"I'm not talking about you. It isn't safe for me. I'm not a fighter."

"I know. You're the watcher."

"Correct. But it's not only that. No one knows I'm alive, not even your master."

"Then why did you show yourself to me—put yourself at risk?"

"Because you're worth more than you know."

"Worth more than your own life?"

"More than all of our lives."

"Why?"

"Because you can defeat the one who caused all this destruction."

"The Firestarter?"

"No, something far worse. Not until we're all extinct will it be satiated. It stalks me, you, and her."

What could be worse than him? Lara ponders. She has heard of night killers, hideous undead, vicious sicklecats, but no tale comes with higher fear than that of the Firestarter—evidence of its destruction is all around her and impossible to ignore. She draws the aftermath inside her lungs with every breath every day. Every moment, he's on the tip of her mind and won't leave. If there is anyone who might be "the one," the Firestarter is the most eligible bachelor. Except her master says he died long ago from his own burning desire. Another lie of convenience, or for her protection? Lara isn't scared of facing such a monster. She only fears not being prepared enough for the occasion.

"You don't know what you're talking about." Lara decides that it will be easier to just silence this folk instead of trying to comprehend her motives.

"I know where your master is. That's why you're out here, isn't it?" the folk says.

"Finally, you're proving your life has worth. Except, wait, I already know where she is. The sprites told me," Lara says smugly.

"The sprites? They cannot be trusted. They were trying to kill you."

"Then why did they let me go?"

"To get you to kill yourself by leaving the forest, which you almost did. Face it, they outsmarted you."

Echoes of their laughter ring inside her ears. They were all too eager to let her go. But they had a deal, a truce. *No, they were only broken words.*

"And you're going to tell me without malicious intentions?"

"But of course."

"Fine, then. Where is she?"

"She is always looking for trouble, that one is."

"Well, that is vague. In what direction is this trouble?"

"She is tending to some outsider's quest. Some people that don't belong here."

"Humans?"

"It is more than just that. But the simple answer is yes."

"Impossible." This is out of character for many reasons. Lara knows that her master would never help the likes of them. The impetus to her master's rage is centered around her loathing of the humans who won't just leave them alone to die in their ashen graves, although, Lara doesn't share the same hatred towards them. She more feels pity. Still, it is her sworn duty to eliminate the problem. It seems with each year, the humans' numbers increase, and up until today, the feathered-folks' numbers have been the same.

"Let me prove it to you."

"Enlighten me." Lara crosses her arms.

"It isn't here, silly, but it also isn't far."

Lara rolls her eyes. This smells like a trap. "How do I know you're not lying about this or the edge of the forest?"

"You are just going to have to trust me."

Trust? What a foreign concept. Her master claims to put trust in her all the time. But in those cases, they are more like orders to do this or that—to do what she's told, and nothing more or nothing less. That type of trust she breaks all the time. This type of trust involves no actions, just worthless words. In a sense, she trusted the little words of the sprites, but they proved to be garbage.

"I'm not falling for that again. Just like the sprites, you're going to lead me into a deadly trap."

"Trusting them wasn't all for naught. It brought you to me. If you ever want to have friends, you're going to have to learn to put trust in them. That is what friendship is all about."

My master put trust in me all the time, and

I let her down. Was I a friend to her? I never reciprocated. Does that mean I could've had a friend, and I squandered it away? This folk must have really been watching me. That's the only way she would know my desires. Damn, she's good...but I'm better. "Okay. But if you fail to convince me, I won't hesitate to push you over the edge."

"When you talk big, you only hurt your own jaw."

"We'll see," Lara says, following The Enchantress deeper into the undiscovered lands, tarnished with pain.

Frozen in Time

*L*ara and The Enchantress arrive at an ancient place of ritual and peace once known as the Bouquet of the Forest. Magic and flowers have long since left this place of worship. Now, it looks just as lackluster as everything else in these cursed lands.

With waving finger pointing the way, The Enchantress leads her companion into a shallow underground dwelling made out of a tunnel inside an old sinkhole. Inside, everything is perfectly in place without a shred of dust or ash around—meticulous and sweet.

Lara's short attention span is fed by all the neat trinkets The Enchantress has covering every surface—shell art, figurines, furs, pressed flowers, dried foliage, and stuffed birds—each one marvelous in some unique way. Mundane items that have become rare due to their absence from this land. The old remnants that decorate her dwelling give it an other worldly feel—a glimpse of what the past, or possibly future, could hold.

A strange feeling comes over her, one that makes her feel comfortable and relaxed. Somehow, it is like she belongs here, as if she's been here before, although it is far beyond her perimeter. And traveling here would take much more than a day. No, it is something else. Something that is warming her through and through and making her eyelids heavy. It must be a spell of The Enchantress, she surmises. The Enchantress has already shown the ability to alter reality; who's to say she cannot alter emotions or memories, too. I mean, here is Lara showing trust, instead of just torturing her for the information she wants, which is very unusual. Even though her master has taught her many techniques, Lara has always avoided having to squeeze information out of someone through pain. It's a lot of work and doesn't seem at all fun.

Trying out a new experience is like finding the perfect armor set. It takes dozens before you find one that actually fits, and this one feels off somehow—almost too good to be true. The comfort she feels is chafing on her placidity.

"How is it that no one has found you out here? It doesn't seem very hidden."

"You have to know the way to find it."

"It isn't that hard. In fact, it seems pretty straightforward to me."

"That's because I showed you the way. If you don't have the right frame of mind, the right intentions in the pit of your being, you might never find it. Even if you know the correct places to step and turn."

Next to a display of metal rings and necklaces lies a ceramic bowl filled with the same quills she used for her whip, only these are different somehow. Drawn to it, she takes a quill and places it up to her nose. She closes her eyes and breathes in deeply. The sweetness of the air mixes with the oiled wooden trinkets, dried flowers, and old crinkled leaves forming a scent of...innocence. It's as if the fragrance is a ghost haunting her from a time long since passed; a time of growth and life.

"Even if the magic has faded, some of its

effects are still in place," The Enchantress says, with a slight smile.

Jostled out of the artificial sensation, Lara's face hardens. "Okay, so it's time to prove it. Prove to me your worth, why we've come all the way out here, and what you've led me to see."

"We will have time for that in a moment."

Lara lets her shoulders go slack, showing her disappointment. "Are you stalling? It feels a lot like stalling to me." She tosses the quill back in the bowl casually.

"Patience..." The Enchantress disappears into another room without warning.

Of course she had to pick one of Lara's worst virtues—patience.

Any moment left idle means more time for her to escape inside her magical mind. This one is no different. Lara imagines many elaborate plots involving The Enchantress arming herself for an epic ambush. The sound of metal on metal from the other room brings images of large axes and sharpened swords, although they are really just pots and pans.

A moment turns into minutes. She slowly shrugs off the possibility of a fight, for no reason other than she is growing tired of imagining it. Poison seems more like The Enchantress's speed.

Besides the aesthetic appeal of the décor, this place serves as a historic museum of indigenous artifacts. With her hands behind her back, Lara peruses the room once again.

"Where did you find all this stuff? I've come across a lot of interesting things, but nothing like this," Lara shouts, palming a rodent's skull.

"I used to collect these kinds of things when they were in abundance. I had time back then to appreciate the little things that life discards. They might be dead, but they need not be destroyed," she responds, while heating up some tea and crumpets for an afternoon snack.

The young feathered-folk doesn't know how hungry she has become, but spying her companion preparing food brings a rumbling to her stomach. *Yeah, there's poison in that tea for sure.* "What's your name?"

"It has been so long since I've talked to anyone, I'm a little embarrassed to say that I have forgotten it."

"That's a little strange," Lara says under her breath. She wonders how anyone could forget their own name. It's then she realizes that she doesn't know her master's name, either. She only ever referred to her as "master." It's just another example of how her master has kept her at arm's length. It makes sense. The Enchantress and her master seem similar in some way. Maybe because they both came from a traumatic time—something they seem desperate to forget, though every inch of the landscape is a constant reminder. Whereas her master uses revenge to drive away her pain, The Enchantress seems to be using optimism.

The savory aroma of the tea fills the room. Lara's mouth instantly salivates, poisoned or not. "So, if you don't have a name, what do I call you?" Lara is reluctant to ask, but she needs something to distract her from snatching the goodies off the table before it is set.

"Why does anyone need a label? We are all children of the forest. I exist not for vanity but for purpose."

"There is a purpose in having a name. Hey...you...strange girl, watch out for that flaming arrow."

"See, that wasn't so hard. You got your point across without reducing me to a title."

"No, I gave you a temporary one—'strange girl.' Unless you want me to call you that, you better give me something."

"I'm only the witness. You can call me that."

She sets three perfect place settings, complete with plates, matching saucers, cloth napkins and tiny trident-like utensils.

"I like 'The Enchantress' better. I'll call you that instead."

"But I'm not..."

"You have powers. You cannot deny what you did to the dirt back there." Lara feels her excitement return as she recalls the incident.

"A parlor trick. I was going to insist that you call me as everyone else does, but after seeing how your smile lights up your face, I rescind contention. You can call me Enchantress, if you wish."

Lara instinctively covers her mouth with her hand, hiding what unexpectedly got away from her—emotions. *Everyone else? I thought she forgot her name from seclusion...*

"You have a lovely smile. Why cover it up so?" The Enchantress sits sideways on a chair at the table. She looks very formal and elegant.

"If the dead see happiness, they might think you're taunting them with laughter and good fortune," Lara says, taking her seat next to The Enchantress. "Are you expecting someone?" She points at a third empty place setting.

"I always put out an extra plate for my

enemies."

"You don't have a lot of them, do you? Enemies, that is."

"Just one."

Lara takes a small sip of her tea. The moment the liquid coats her tongue, images of a pure, lush forest develop inside her thoughts. It is much more flavorful than any poison she has ever tasted. Scrunching up her nose, she holds her teacup close to her chest with both hands, feeling its warmth against her. "What will you happen to do if your enemy shows up?" she says sarcastically.

"We will eat, drink tea, and talk. Then I will die with a full stomach and a calm demeanor."

"Breaking bread with your enemies doesn't seem like a good idea, unless your food is really spectacular or laced with poison," Lara says, breathing in the steaming hot crumpet that she holds up to her lips. She can almost taste the buttery flavor radiating off of it.

"It is how I wish to go—civilized, without fleeing or fighting. You must be able to look the worst of people in the eyes before they take the light from yours. You can tell if they see you as a living being instead of an obstacle. If they happen to let darkness dictate their actions, your visage will attach itself to their soul. With any hope, they may become changed. And with any luck, they may be merciful to the next person who shows them hospitality."

Wow, this is so tasty. The buttery flavor of the crumpet is light and airy, like how she imagined a butterfly would taste if it were a pastry instead of an insect. Lara happily scarfs it down, barely listening to her host's words.

"What place setting am I eating from, your friend's or enemy's?" Lara asks, dabbing crumbs off the table with her finger, making sure she doesn't leave a single morsel wasted.

"That is entirely up to you." She gives Lara a light smile as she tops off her teacup.

Lara glances over at her belongings in the corner of the room, just in case. They're not exactly within arm's reach, but she wants to make sure she can grab them if things get a little dicey in here. Eyeing the last pastry, Lara looks back and forth between the treat and The Enchantress. "Are you scared?"

"Of death? Of course. Aren't you?"

"I am only scared that you might not offer me the last one of those."

"Oh, please do. I can make more." Before The Enchantress can finish her sentence, the buttery goodness is already in Lara's ravenous mouth, her cheeks puffed out in delight.

With her hand under her chin, Lara starts to talk with her mouth full of hot crumpet, "Death is nothing. What I fear is nothingness. The concept of non-existence."

"That's only because you've experienced it before. We all have. Your mind may have long forgotten, but your soul never will," The Enchantress says, cringing at the young girl's lack of table manners.

"How old are you?" Lara asks before sucking up the crumbs she caught with her hand, through pursed lips. She is hoping to figure out her master's age by comparison.

"To us, time is a concept of passing moons, nothing more. Age comes with experience and wisdom."

"Us?"

"The collective us—as in the feathered-folk. As the moon passes, so does another dream reflecting off its cool light. I've seen many of them go by, more than I can remember. I used to hold on to a promise for safekeeping. A tear escaped my eye each day. Always one. Never more, never less. My sorrow and loneliness were dehydrating this old soul, one drop at a time. Each day, I wondered if I have another drop left in me to carry my burden."

"Did you have enough? Wait, of course you did. You wouldn't be here today if you didn't." Lara shakes her head back and forth, disapproving of her own question.

"Not necessarily," The Enchantress says, wiping under her eye where a tear isn't, though she clearly remembers the feeling.

Prying, despite awkwardness, is the young folk's specialty, but she doesn't want to waste it on The Enchantress's past. Better grill her on things that really matter to her. There is a question Lara fears asking her master but thinks about incessantly. Even though they just met, she feels safe around The Enchantress. "How old am I?"

"Why, I tried to explain before...age is a human concept. You are eternal, but not for long."

"I mean, in moons passing, how many cycles? I need some bit of normalcy to go off of. Am I an adult, a child, or somewhere in between? Sometimes I can't even tell. I try and count the days, but there are too many. I just need..."

The Enchantress places her hand upon Lara's hand, stopping it from blindly feeling around for lost crumbs on the table. The difference between their skin is quite apparent. Lara's is soft and smooth, whereas The Enchantress's is hard and stern. "You are almost fully grown, my dear."

Lara puffs out her chest and pulls her shoulders back proudly.

"But not quite."

Lara quickly pulls her hand away. "What are you saying?"

"As a feathered-folk, we have an interesting relationship with the moon's light. Your mistress has kept you trapped in a state of perpetual adolescence, outside of the realm of human-like time."

"Why would she do that?" Lara slams her hand on the table, knocking over the cup from the extra place setting.

"She must have her reasons. I'm not your master, so I can't answer for her."

Now Lara knows the truth of one of her master's lies. She kept her fearing the night to keep her as a child forever. But why? For what purpose? Spending this night in the moon's rays has unclouded a maturity that has long since been suppressed. She isn't dying like her master described it. She is growing up.

"Why didn't you save me from her? You have a room filled with useless dead things you thought were worth hanging on to, yet you didn't want one of your kind?"

"It was too risky. You know your master better than anyone. What would she do if I were to interfere?"

"She wouldn't just sit around and watch. I can tell you that much."

"No need for placing blame. You are quite lucky to have her guidance. I used to think she had no equal. Even without her hands, I'm no match for her."

"I think you're just scared."

"Perhaps, yes. There is no shame in fear. It's only an emotion, equal to joy or anger."

Lara meets her statement with a shrug while contemplating a bigger matter on her mind. Lara's master always told her that emotions are for the weak. Between her and her master, her master is the more volatile and reactionary one. Using her logic against her, Lara had always secretly thought this made her master the weaker one.

"Let me get you some more crumpets." She walks with a lightness in her step, making it appear as if she is floating on air.

Lara is left alone with her thoughts. Back and forth, up and down she goes through her mind, her life, and everything in between. The more she thinks about it, the heavier her eyelids get.

As The Enchantress returns with a fresh batch of crumpets, Lara is fast asleep.

"Sleep well, child, and dream of your former self."

First and Last

$\mathcal{L}$ ara abruptly awakens, still on her seat at the dinner table, her mouth agape. Lara catches the tail end of a horrendous sawing noise grinding out of her throat. Never has she made such a sound. Yet, she feels quite rested, like an undisturbed corpse. A thick woven blanket is tucked in tight around her. She is warm and amazingly comfortable.

The morning crept up on her without warning. She doesn't remember falling asleep. An instant effect of something even more daunting...magic perhaps? Nor does she dare utter her assumptions aloud for the fear of them coming true.

Upon seeing the defused sunlight pouring through a crack, the young folk launches to her feet. The whole night had been wasted, or avoided—depending on how you look at it. Rubbing her tired eyes, she suspects that she was deceived in some manner. It isn't like her to just pass out, nor to make such a sound. Something untoward is afoot.

"Oh, you're awake," The Enchantress says, while puttering around in the cooking cove.

"You tricked me. Was it the tea or the crumpets? Those delicious crumpets." She finds herself scouring the tablecloth for any castoffs, momentarily forgetting her accusation about them.

"I don't know what you're getting at. You were just exhausted," The Enchantress says, genuinely offended.

"After you lured me into your little nest, you laced my food or drink with something, didn't you? Just admit it." Lara finds her weapons before The Enchantress can answer.

"And that would serve what purpose?"

Lara whips a quill across the table, straight at The Enchantress, shattering a bowl she has in her hand. "That's a warning."

"If I really wanted to hurt you, I had many

opportunities. Though here you are, alive and well rested. I didn't have to give you bedding, might I add."

"Stop playing around and give me some real answers." Lara is getting sick of chasing her master's shadow. All she is uncovering is untruths and deception. She doesn't even know if she needs help or wants to be found. The more Lara searches, the less she desires to find her. "Why have you brought me here?"

The Enchantress's face turns somber. "Very well. It is time. Come, follow me." Her stone shoes crush the bowl shards into smaller pieces as she brushes past Lara.

The young folk's sole reason for coming with The Enchantress was to gain insight or commit murder, but instead she found wasted time and slumber—something she didn't know she needed. No, she wasn't bewitched in some way by The Enchantress; she was merely tired.

With her weapon at the ready, Lara trails behind like smoke from a pipe.

A short hike later, The Enchantress leads them to an outcropping of charred trees. "The guests, they brought something back that has been lost for a very long time."

"How do you know this? Were you spying on

them, too?"

"I couldn't get close enough—not with your master on high alert."

There seems to be a bone of contention between her master and The Enchantress—a past that The Enchantress doesn't want to move past. The broken pieces don't seem to fit the scene somehow. "You mean intruders that made the tracks I was following? The ones my master went after?"

"Hasn't that already been established?" Her facial expression changes so fast, one might believe it to be magic in nature.

"I'm just making sure." Lara wants to further justify her questions with the fact that she just woke up, but she refrains. Besides, she feels great.

"It's very lucky that they slipped by you, or else they might have seen the worse side of that whip you have there. Lucky, indeed."

"I'm not a mindless husk. I can determine if someone deserves to die or not. I would have done the right thing." Never had she laid down the metaphorical sword for an invading force, but who's to say that she wouldn't have this time?

"Who are you trying to convince, me or

you?"

"Don't try and be cute."

"A minute ago, you almost took my life for feeding you and offering you a place to sleep. I would be surprised if you are capable of feeling any compassion."

"For invaders? They're just nuisances."

"They have feelings, like you and me. Well, like me. Though maybe misguided, they deserve life as much as any other being."

"Not on my land, they don't." Lara rolls her eyes to the sky for support.

"There were many species that thrived here before it was 'your land' as you put it. Isn't it equally their land?"

"No. I saw your little collection of corpses. They don't own anything, not anymore. Perhaps if they were alive to challenge me...they still wouldn't have a chance."

"You can't justify your cruelty with ownership. It isn't that simple."

"It isn't cruel to dispose of them before they cause more harm. It's good planning. And life is that simple. You're either living or dead."

"'More harm'?" The Enchantress picks up some cursed soil and lets it fall freely through her fingers. "They didn't do this...the humans.

You know that, right?"

"No, it was a question. Are you living or dying?" Lara's eyes narrow as she furrows her brow.

"Listen to me for a moment. It was a feathered-folk whose selfishness torched us all."

"That's not how I heard it," Lara says, swishing her whip around like an angry cattail. The feathered-folk worship the trees as deities. Lara can't conceive of any of her kind taking to burning one, even selfishly. Humans, on the other hand, they build houses out of the gods' flesh, and make a sweetener out of their blood.

"Well, you were misinformed.'"

"Humans care only for themselves and their own fortunes. The one who caused all this to happen is still at large."

"Which is who?

"A lord of unimaginable power and evil—the Firestarter. It was a human torch that started the fire, but not by human hands. The invaders are always heading in his direction. So, I cut off his connection to the outside by cutting off their heads, figuratively speaking, of course."

Lara thinks about decapitation a lot. She often practices against old remains she finds in the ash. Where a human's skin is soft and squishy, their skeleton more than makes up for it. No wonder they stick around so long. Even with a direct hit, she never possesses enough strength to cleanly cut through their bones. Except for this one time she was practicing against a skeleton that didn't quite make it out of the great blaze. These particular remains were brittle. But that doesn't count, and she knows it.

"Things are not always as simple as that. Do you really believe that a man-made flame could cause this blight? Something more powerful is at play here, that is evident. Nevertheless, there are more complicated questions at hand. Like, what drove it to happen, and how can we ever recover?"

"It doesn't matter. They will all die, and I will be the last one standing. The champion who stands on the mountain gets to keep it. Not my rule, nature's."

"You sound like her."

"Of course I do. Who do you think I've been hanging out with all these years?" Lara says, pointing out the obvious.

"Not your master, someone else…"

"Either say something relevant or keep it to yourself. All this cryptic speak is causing my head to ache," Lara says, hoping to get to the bottom of why The Enchantress brought her here.

"None of the past matters anymore. Good, bad, or indifferent, things are all about to change for us. Maybe a death, or perchance a resurrection. In either case, something is on the horizon. I can sense it."

"Is that why my master is helping the invaders?"

"I would hope so. But I fear it is far more self-serving."

"You said that the invaders brought something with them. What exactly did you mean by that? Is that what she is after?"

"It is an item of illustrious significance—the Pit of the Forest."

"Don't know what that is, but it sounds tasty."

"This is no joke. The pit has ancient power beyond your imagination," The Enchantress scoffs and walks over to a blackened tree which towers high above the others. "It is part of a sacred bond between life, death and the in-between. It is something of great significance. Do you want to know what it is?"

"More destruction?" Lara says with a shrug, not shying away from her condescending tone.

She likes her joke. She is trying to lighten the mood ever so slightly. The Enchantress has been so curt with her ever since she reunited with her weapons.

"Look not with your eyes, but with your feelings."

As if it were a command, Lara clears her mind and complies with The Enchantress's order. The air appears to vibrate softly the closer she gets to the large tree. "Oh, my. It..." catching her tongue, she doesn't dare finish her thought. She places a gentle hand on its bark. It isn't like anything she's ever felt. It feels soft, yet firm and powerful. It's completely black in color, but not from cinder, more by choice. "It didn't burn?"

"That's correct."

"Then I'm not going crazy? It's still alive," she says the thought she didn't dare utter before.

"This is the first tree of the once great forest ridge. The mother of spirits. Its power grows deeper than any fire could penetrate. Though it's in mourning for the loss of all its offspring."

Lara is wrapped up in the splendor of this great discovery. She feels akin to the old wood— hiding in plain sight, using darkness to shade its true nature. And for a moment, Lara swears that she feels a gentle breeze against her skin. It's blissfully perfect. In this moment, all her fears wash away. She is no longer worried about the future or dreading the past. She is merely existing in the present, for the first time.

The young feathered-folk notices what she swears wasn't there a second ago. It's life dangling on a low-hanging branch. A newly grown leaf, electric and stark white. "What is that? What does it mean?"

"The forest is breathing again. It may be faint, but it is very much alive."

Lara presses her face up against the blackened bark. She hears a slight hum from within its trunk. It's talking.

"What is it saying?"

The Enchantress lowers her head with a woebegone look. "'Do not resuscitate.'"

Lara knows without a doubt that The Enchantress's words are true. This is the first and last tree in the forest. It managed to survive the fire, the subsequent freeze and the drought. Dormant and comatose but not dead, gathering enough moisture to keep itself alive—just barely. This discovery is far greater than anything Lara could have imagined. She has a new purpose, a new reason to train. She will protect its bark with all of her everything. "How is this possible?"

"Its roots run far and wide—to the very edges of the forest. It might be the very reason we cannot leave. It is part of us, or we are part of it."

Tears streaming down Lara's face, she looks up at her acquaintance with new eyes—as a friend. Never has she felt so inundated with emotions. She has no words to calm the flood. "I feel its thoughts. It's...frightened." Lara turns to The Enchantress, looking for answers, wiping her emotional embarrassment away with her arm. "What does it have to be afraid of?"

This is much more than the jaded folk had ever expected. The Enchantress has given the young feathered-folk the greatest gift she has ever received—something more powerful than weapons, anger, and revenge all combined. She gave her hope.

Call to Action

*L*ara traces the lines in the tree's bark with her hands, caressing its old skin softly. She glides her hand down to a spot that is missing a large chunk—a scar of some sort. "What is this?" Lara asks, memorizing the grooves of the old wooden wonder.

"A deep wound," The Enchantress says sorrowfully. "Ever since its pieces were taken, the magic of the woods has been fading away, out of existence."

"What happened?" Lara asks. Feeling the old wound makes the tree's branches rustle sharply. She pulls her hand back, as if touching something hot.

"Weaklings. Those who cannot earn esteem or power for themselves, they plunder riches, driven by laziness, instead of earning importance through dedication and patience. Like a parasite who cannot thrive on its own."

"They are cowards."

"As are kings."

"Well, that will never happen again, not on my watch."

"Your watch? This is not your responsibility. It is mine," The Enchantress says, wrapping a cloth covering around the base of the trunk.

"Not anymore. You obviously lack the fighting ability to protect the greatness that is here, let alone yourself. I relieve you of your task and take the burden myself." Lara looks around, already plotting her militaristic perimeter—a booby trap here, some poison gas over there.

"I've been doing just fine without you."

"You can say it all you like, it doesn't make it come true."

"I've kept this tree hidden for many years without conflict."

"That is your mistake. You showed it to me, and I'm taking it from you."

"Now, hold on a second..."

Lara narrows her eyes, ready to take up a challenge.

"Shouldn't you rejoin your master? Remember, there is the business of retrieving the artifact?" The Enchantress's voice hardens, turning almost gritty in tone.

"That isn't my concern. Not anymore. It was more your quest, really. Feel free to go yourself, what with all the extra time you now have on your hands."

"Not I. These are dangerous times. Should they fail, there needs to be a witness to tell the tale. No, the risk is too much." The Enchantress almost looks insulted by the very thought and audacity of suggesting it.

"That is not my fight. I have my own tasks ahead of me now." Lara can't just abandon this discovery. If her master chooses to help some strangers instead of defending the cursed land, so be it. She needs to understand the connection between her kind and the tree. It is much too important.

"Don't you worry about the well-being of your master?"

"It's only been a day and a half. Plus, you said it yourself, she's a great fighter, perfectly capable of fending for herself."

"Don't you want to see the world?" The Enchantress tries to understand why Lara has so suddenly changed her plans.

"I will make this my new home and continue as I always have." *Completely bored.*

With that thought lingering in the ether, The Enchantress bargains, "This place is dreadfully drab. You are young. Go on an adventure." A softness returns to her demeanor.

Lara exhales, letting the words sink in. "No, I have to be more responsible, and that starts now with this ancient thing. It is what my master would want."

"I disagree. Your master would want you to go with her, as backup."

That doesn't sound like her master, not in the slightest. "How do you know my master again?" she asks, turning her head slightly in an inquisitive way.

"We used to be friends. All three of us."

Lara remembers every single day of her cognitive life with great clarity, and she doesn't remember The Enchantress. She read about mind manipulators, and this folk might be trying to put new ideas inside her head and turn them into fact. It would be logical for The Enchantress to use Lara as her personal soldier. "I don't know you. I never met you before yester-day."

"Not in your current state…" Her voice trembles ever so slightly. The Enchantress fears that she is imparting too much information before Lara is ready to accept any of it. As it is, she may have made a huge mistake showing her the tree in the first place.

Lara catches The Enchantress waving her hand in an irritated sort of way as if to silence herself. "Right…" Long ago, she read that living life in solitary can distort fact from fiction. She changes her assertation about the mind manip-ulator theory and decides that this folk is completely insane. When one talks to the voices inside their head, they sometimes believe that they're someone else's and not merely from their own manifestation. Everything she has said thus far has been vague and inconspicu-ous, leaving Lara to fill in the blanks with her wandering mind. It is a trap—one that the an-cient tree has been in for far too long. And Lara has her sights on a jailbreak.

"Welp, I better start making this a safe place. So, you can…you know." Lara flicks her hand, shooing away The Enchantress.

"Aren't you curious as to why I brought you

here?"

"It doesn't matter." Lara finds a large boulder and carries it off to a pile she has already started.

"I was stalling, keeping you here as long as possible." The Enchantress's voice turns sour as it grows into a deeper guttural tone. It is almost as if her voice were a chameleon of sorts, changing and adapting to suit her environment.

Lara drops a second boulder with a low-sounding thud. "What?"

Devious fire ignites in her eyes as she elaborates on her deception, "I witnessed you tracking those steps, and you were almost able to save her. But I interfered, just in time."

"Why? For what purpose? If you wanted to kill me, you had plenty of opportunity to do so while my back was turned, or even better, while I was sleeping."

"It was never my intention to hurt you...it is her I wish to obliterate," The Enchantress says, her sinister voice rife will pure evil.

Lara suspected that she was up to something, and now the truth is starting to show its ugly face. "Why? What do you have to gain?"

"I am keeping you alive. She has you on the path of destruction. I will show you the path of glory and redemption."

"No thank you. How about I decide what is best for me."

"It is too late. By keeping you here, I have already succeeded in my plans. You will never make it to that place in time now."

"What place? Where are they going? You have to tell me!" Lara grabs The Enchantress by her soft robes, tearing the old fabric with the intensity of her grip.

"Shhhh...she has done nothing but shield you from your true calling."

"She has done much more than that. She has done...well...everything for me." Lara releases her intimidating grip and regains her composure.

"No matter. It's much too late. They should be there already, or better yet, dead."

"What about the artifact you spoke so highly of? Just moments ago, you were practically begging me to get it for you."

"It pales in comparison to the power that resides in you, dear girl. You are not like me; you can live forever. Surviving in the shadows like an unseen ghost, while everyone else ages and wastes away, eventually you will get your wish to become the sole survivor. Time is your most deadly weapon. All you need is patience to wield it." Lara notices another sudden shift in her personality. This time, almost stoic.

Now she is sounding like her master, only slightly less vague. "I don't believe you." Yet she fairly does, in a strange sort of way.

"To prove myself, I will divulge what your master wouldn't. Your timelessness relies on the power in the moon's light, or more so, the lack of it. She has been keeping you stunted, so that you may never leave her. It is a selfish act."

Is that the true reason she has kept me sheltered for so long, to avoid the moon? The Enchantress's words go together with Lara's feelings like a verse in a poem, where the last line complements the previous one. One thought enters her mind, *you lost five minutes of your life today.*

"I knew you were tricking me—or thought you were. I am much more clever than you give me credit for."

"You must stay here with me, child, safe and secure, far away from that place of battle and bloodshed. That is the true reason why I brought you here."

The clarity that Lara gained is quickly shattered and replaced by doubt. How could she abandon her master, after everything they've gone through? Although if what The Enchantress says is true, her master does have a lot to answer for.

"Now that I've told you, you must know it to be true. Yes, you believe me. I can see it hidden in your eyes."

"Just give me a moment to think." Embarrassed, she wonders why she flipped her perspective so quickly. *My emotions, they're out of control. Maybe the moonlight did change me, made me more volatile. I have to regain my perspective on everything. I am, everything I want to be,* she deliberates internally. Who will she become if she stays here with the last tree, the new enchantress—a wizen old maid who must rely on trickery to make friends?

The Enchantress raises her hand. Small embers float off her fingertips as power radiates into thin air.

"What are you doing?"

"Keeping you safe. You will thank me later, I promise."

"No. I can't stand by and watch the world burn like you did. I would rather die than suffer the long death."

"You can never leave. I've already started the spell." The Enchantress conjures a dagger with a blue substance dripping off the tip, which is never a good sign.

Without notice, or thinking, Lara knocks the blade into the brightening sky, disarming her inept combatant. "If it's a fight you want..."

"You mustn't," The Enchantress says through gritted teeth.

Lara thrashes at The Enchantress with her short quill whip. A few slashes rip through her robes, showing small cuts underneath. The sting from the quill tips knocks her to the ground.

"That was effortless." The cuts aren't that deep, and Lara judges The Enchantress for her weakness and pain intolerance.

The Enchantress tries to speak, but the disbelief only leaves the sound of her clicking jaw to speak for her.

Once on the ground, Lara is ready to try something out that she has only practiced on painted rocks. "You should have left me alone to decide. I was already committed to staying here with you," Lara says. "You brought this upon yourself."

An expression of horror is all that is left to

respond to the young folk—silent screams behind wide eyes.

With a spiraling motion, she unleashes the
remaining quills. Each one stabs directly into
her opponent's robe, narrowly missing her
body and pinning her to the ground. Ancient
roots are jutting out all around her, almost as if
they're surrounding her in sorrow. But Lara
sees it in a different vein, as if they are hands
holding down the villain that kept her at bay for
so very long.

The Enchantress knows that either she is extremely lucky, or that Lara was intentionally
missing her vitals—playing with her prey.

"Let me ask you one last time. Where did
they go?"

"I...I..."

With the grace of a cat, Lara slinks up to her,
and holds the last remaining quill up to her eye.
"You can't be a watcher without these."

"The...castle ruins...in the eastern lands. But
please don't go. Only death can come of it."

"Look at you. You're already dead."

"Please, I meant no harm."

"Telling me only harmed yourself. You don't
know me—know what I'm capable of. I am sure
you didn't go through all of this just to lie to

me."

"I did it because..." the softness of her voice cracks, "you're spoiled," she hisses, showing her true colors.

"Excuse me?"

"You just kill without remorse, take whatever you desire without respect for those who gave it to you."

"I'm an assassin. What did you expect?"

"Assassins have a code of honor. By definition, they get paid for their services. You kill for nothing, not even for the thrill of the sport. You are no assassin, you are a butcher—mindlessly chopping at flesh to fill up the day."

"I can butcher you right now and end your day." Lara has tolerated the folk's lies and deceptions long enough. What she calls "honor" is simply a lie told by a coward who hid long enough to survive.

"You sit on a fraudulent sense of pride that you didn't earn, yourself. Grow up, and stop thinking you know everything, because you don't.

It ends now. Unable to hold back her emotions any longer, she reacts. With all her might and aggression, she jams the remaining quill up The Enchantress's nose, hitting cartilage. It is much harder than that of a human.

It all happens too fast for Lara to realize exactly what she is doing. She feels as though she's a spectator of the brutality, watching her body move as her training takes over—her muscles straining, complying with the anger she feels. Rapidly, she bangs at the quill with the handle of her whip, using it like a hammer. Each strike drives the needle deeper inside the folk's head. Her trembling lips can't hide her true feelings on the matter, though they are even hidden to herself. Only the ancient tree sees the anguish buried deep inside her.

Each hit feeds her anger. Once the quill reaches her brain, thick liquid gushes out her other nostril and enters inside The Enchantress's agonized mouth.

Before Lara can stop herself, it is over. She has never killed one of her own before. They die a lot differently than humans. With eyes fixated on her victim, she watches as she lets out the last breath she will ever breathe. It's almost beautiful in a necrotic sort of way. A heavy feeling envelops her completely. She is once again alone.

"I'm sorry. I didn't mean to do that." Lara licks the dryness on her lips, gaining control once more. She patiently waits for the folk's eyes to stop convulsing. Recovery from such an injury is not possible, she knows. "You really pushed me too far."

Lara looks back at the last tree with a shameful scowl. It sees her for what she really is, a bringer of death and destruction—or so she thinks.

"I really messed up this time." Lara paces back and forth. She manages to find the spot where she knocked away the enchanted dagger from The Enchantress, but she can't see it anywhere. All she finds is a rotting bird carcass. *What kind of power was she drawing from?* She looks back at what she has done, still feeling uneasy about the whole thing.

She approaches the last tree once more. Only this time it seems different somehow, less alive. Was this also one of The Enchantress's parlor tricks? Was it genuine or just a façade? Like the dagger, will the magic fade from view, revealing another dead tree in an endless sea of decay? *But it felt so real. It had thoughts and emotions.* They had flowed through her like a river of experiences. Now she is left feeling like a dry lakebed of doubt. She can't just sit around waiting for answers to come to her with the wind, because like the tree, the wind is just another lie she would love to believe. Or perhaps she is the lie, told from the lips of a long-lost whisper. Whatever the case may be, there is nothing left for her here.

"What's done cannot be undone." And with that, she collects her belongings, hoists her bear trap over her shoulder and heads east.

Once Lara is out of sight, The Enchantress's extremities begin to wiggle and twitch with short bursts, in a most unnatural way. Like a contagious disease, her movements spread to the rest of her body as the erratic shifting turns into a heavy convulsion. The quill lodged inside her nose is jerked loose. It moves around little by little as if it has a mind of its own. After much exertion, it falls out of her orifice. A larva wiggles out after it, likely the cause. As quickly as it came, it retreats back inside her body. Suddenly, all her shaking stops—matching the stillness of the air.

The Enchantress calmly stands up and wipes under her nose. She appears to be alive and well, if that is what you call it. A baleful smile grows on her face as she looks to the shadows. "The best way to get a child to do something is to tell them they can't. Isn't that right?"

A hooded figure walks out of the shadows. The very same figure who stole the corpse from Lara. He walks up to The Enchantress and stands shoulder to shoulder with her, "Indeed, my dear, indeed."

Eastern Bound

*L*ara is determined to make a heroic rescue, the kind she has only read about in human folklore and fables. Her kind, the feathered-folk, never use paper sheaths to remember their tales—considering what they believe. Instead, they rely on tradition and using their voice to convey the past. This was their way of safeguarding secrets from their enemies. The only problem for Lara is that her master is quite guarded and doesn't share much with her pupil. *Am I really that untrustworthy?* She contemplates her master's lack of forthrightness.

"She's just selfish. Anytime I show interest in something, she takes it away from me."

There's a reason that wizards use their vernacular to cast magical spells. A collection of sounds brought together to birth an idea—a concept of great meaning and importance. Words are only as powerful as the intention behind them, weighing them down with an unbreakable truth, challenging the world for dominance. *Say what you mean, and do what you say, only then will the world obey,* her master says. This concept is lost to liars. Their words are as light as leaves and blow away at the first sign of winter.

What if it isn't that she doesn't trust me? Maybe she doesn't trust my loose jaw. Were her years of insubordination the likely cause? Lara was a lot of things, but a liar was not one of them. She made sure her words were always true. However, she was known for dancing around with lies of omission—leaving out particular details to let assumptions go wild, as they tend to do. It isn't her fault if others come to the wrong conclusion, or so she keeps telling herself.

If her master has any coveted information, she keeps all her secrets close to her chest like a newborn child too weak to fend for itself.

Even though the progeny isn't particularly a

fan of the humans, their culture *is* something to be desired. Tales of metalmen slaying giant griffins and colossus hydras; dark caverns filled to the brim with epic treasure hoards and, most of all, pets...lots and lots of pets. She has never had a pet, let alone seen one. Companionship is scarce in the dead forest, and more than slaying a great beast, she would like to ride, talk, and even care for one. She isn't picky. Just a tiny fairy dragon would do. It wouldn't have to be able to fly or even breathe fire. It can just sit there, adorning her shoulder like a parrot.

Lara stops in her tracks. She looks back and forth, making sure she has privacy for what is about to happen next. When the feeling arises, Lara gives faith to faith. She drops to her knees subserviently. With interlocked hands and closed eyes, she turns her head to the heavens. "Please, human god above, if you can hear me, I will abandon all my druidic ways if you grant me one simple request. One act of kindness and I will be forever yours. You know the nature of my request. I humbly await your decision."

Moments turn into minutes. She eagerly awaits his holy response. As her faith starts to become impatient, she feels something brush up against her shoulder.

"Dragon?" Before her eyes can adjust to the light, she reaches for what isn't there. It doesn't matter how tightly she closes her eyes and wishes for one, the world doesn't work like that. There are no such things as dragons, tiny or otherwise, despite the human fairy tales—or so that is what her master says.

This isn't the first time she has tried to make peace with the human god. Her open mindedness yields her hope for any possibility. Besides, what does she have to lose?

"I know you're getting sick of all my complaining." Lara places a hand on the last twisted tree in the clearing. It topples out of its rotted hole instantly. "I couldn't have said it better myself."

There is a certain amount of conflicting information between texts that makes the possibility of a dragon world seem farfetched. Some say that dragons are lizard-like beasts that are mindless; another author has this theory that dragons have feathers. *Imagine that?* Still, most fables seem to be inspired by the first published text, rife with cliché and a certain amount of predictability.

One book comes up with a new concept, such as dragons playing chess. Then all literary work to follow that book recycles its concept as if it were always so. "Why would anyone want to play a silly game with a dragon. I would take it outside to burn stuff, melt stuff, devour stuff..."

This isn't exclusive to dragons. All kinds of fads and trends pop up with popularity. Then as fast as they come, they're gone. Reading so many adventures about dragons makes them seem almost as common as rats. To be fair, rats aren't even as common as rats in this scorn place.

In the past, she has spent many days gazing at the skies, looking for a flying lizard, but never has anything like that come into view, bird or otherwise. Maybe because they never really existed, further proof that the scripts are indeed works of fiction—a vessel to maintain obedience through fear. Or perhaps the humans really did slay every last one of them. Certainly, there are enough stories to back up that claim. Where is the evidence—bones, scales or even feathers? Something with that level of power, destruction and size doesn't just go unnoticed.

"Where are you hiding?" She looks around the charred landscape and lets out a deep sigh—blowing ash off her shoulder where a dragon wasn't. "Death doesn't just disappear."

Even so, she revels in the inconsistencies in the stories. It is the same satisfaction when one catches someone else in a lie.

True or not, she loves dragons just the same. Because they are comfortable—familiar, and everyone writes about them. On this one point, she is willing to be wrong for a chance to set her eyes on something with the unmatched size and unfathomably powerful features of a dragon.

When indulging in human tales, she always transforms the characters to better suit her liking. In her mind's eye, she changes males into females, boring brown eyes into vibrant purples, blues and pinks, old, crusty maids into beautiful young maidens. Most importantly, she switches all the humans into featheredfolk, like herself. If a line of dialogue doesn't suit her, she crosses it out and writes in her own. Her master always admonishes her for ruining the text. Though, she should talk, what with her ripping all those pages out of them.

It may seem childish to some, but her actions make the stories more appealing. By ameliorating the text, she makes each story seem almost believable. If they are merely works of fiction, what does it matter, anyway?

Often, she gets anxious reaching the dreadful two words "the end." It doesn't just mean the story has come to a close; it means something even more terrifying—back to real life, to a mundane game of survival. Back to the same old routine, devoid of magic and wizards. Just more of the same burnt-out landscape jutting out of cursed soil like gravestones. A world blanketed by a cloudless, dragonless grey sky.

She knows no human could achieve the objectives that are exaggerated on the page. In all of her experience murdering them, never has she met a human who came close to how they portrayed themselves inside the books they write. Could it be that the human's biggest secret is the lies they spin? Just as fake as the dagger she lifted off the intruder?

"Big words leave even bigger disappointments."

Maybe it's their ego, hubris, or delusions of grandeur. Whatever it may be, they're a horrible disappointment. If they held true to legend, she might actually have to try her best from time to time. Necessity breeds greatness. Even though she tries to, she can't completely blame all of her problems on the humans. They're easy targets.

One anxiety that she can't ignore is the end of her own story. Not the act of dying, per se. But that once she peaks, there are no more goals or struggles for her to overcome. That thought keeps her at bay—keeps her from racing to perfection. The more her master pushes her, the more she resists. *If only I was left alone, things would be better.* But now she is alone, and things are worse, much worse...

Stuck with only herself again, Lara tries to think of something a little less real. She wonders what her master is up to at this very moment, creating her own story of fiction to mask her failures.

Bounding through the countryside, her armored steed at her command—lance, shield and sword equipped for a gentleman's invasion—the folk-knightess is no gentleman, or gentlewoman, for that matter. She is the slayer of such fools. This is how she came to acquire such finely crafted accoutrements. Slain metalmen don't need such things in the afterlife. It isn't as if the pilfered equipment did them any good while living; not enough to keep them alive.

When she fights, she doesn't only take their pathetic lives; she takes away the hope, faith, and will of whoever discovers her aftermath. Lara, the humanity slayer, is after life, putting death behind her.

That is a little unfair. They were the best of the best; only the folk knightess is much better.

Princess armless awaits her rescue in the tower of forgotten dreams. And it will be the happiest of endings for the purest of hearts.

Only this isn't make-believe. Lara has no hooved companion to gallivant the untamed wilds with. She only has herself and her imagination as company. It might not seem like much, but it's more than most.

Her mind keeps going back to the encounter with The Enchantress. Something deep inside her is gnawing at her certainty. She wonders if she has made a terrible mistake, the very kind that enchantress warned her about. Death isn't just a tool; it has consequences. Even though they only knew each other for a short amount of time, she felt something strange...she missed her.

"That's not right."

The world really was a bit brighter with The Enchantress in it, even if she was a no-good, dirty liar. Her crumpets and tea gave life to the air with wonderous smells as they hit her senses. No way the world would be better off without those in it.

She has trained so long on efficient disposal of bodies and never once on restraint, or probable cause for execution. Like a sculpture, her master crafted and molded her into what she is—a weapon of redemption. She didn't train on maiming or mercy, only in perfect murder dispensed in abundance. A foolish feeling envelops her, as she has come to this realization so late in life. Lara is dangerous, and up until now, she never thought it to be a detriment—only a skillset.

The Enchantress took her into her home and treated her well—sans all the lies and deceit. Still, she doesn't feel justified. Killing invaders is one thing, they seek to harm, pillage, and destroy.

A labored sigh exits her, letting her shoulders sink. The youngling didn't want to eat at The Enchantress's table setting for enemies. "If you kill all your friends, no one will come over for tea," Lara tells herself, hoping the words will haunt her the next time she is face to face with her rage.

The Enchantress did feel like a friend to her, and Lara didn't return the feeling, not in the slightest. Maybe that is why she missed her so. She never had a friend before—someone who treated her as an equal, not some servant.

Before letting her emotions get the best of her, she lets one sniffle out and clenches her fist. "The past is the past is the past, and this is one regret I will have to harbor." She tries to count how many invaders she's exterminated, but the numbers far exceed her level of math. It doesn't matter, anyway. It's easier to remember the number that she shouldn't have killed, one.

"Having *one* isn't that bad," she says to herself, the human god, or whoever may be listening, hoping to eliminate her actions from wearing on her. Only now, the feeling spreads faster and worse. The Enchantress's proud smile bores into her mind, the smell of the hot crumpets delightfully filling her nose. It's no use. She can't trick herself any more than she can forgive herself for her actions. Guilt tarnishes her soul.

Am I a butcher? Ending The Enchantress over a lie, in turn, made one of her master's lies come true—there are only two feathered-folk left here. She imagines how good it would have felt to throw that lie, among the many others, in her master's righteous face. The edge of the world, the night killers, the cloud dancers, her ageless existence, the Firestarter, and who knows what other truths she will uncover before they're reunited. She starts a list, using a burnt stick as a writing implement, jotting down each one on the back side of the human map she had procured from the intruder. "These landmarks are all outdated anyhow," she reasons, noticing all the trees, roads, lakes and streams on the thing.

She picks up some charcoal and rubs it into the map, making everything black and covered in soot. "That's better," she says with a chuckle.

Learning is embracing your mistakes with an empty eye; filling it with the experience to remedy the future, she recalls as one of her master's teachings. What can she learn from this whole exchange with The Enchantress? *Perhaps, there can be use in keeping someone alive.* Lara decides that she needs to spend more time developing weapons that are a little less efficient in killing. This may give her a moment to think things through. This is ultimately what she lacked with the whole enchantress encounter.

Traveling through fresh terrain gives Lara a sense of how vast the dead forest really is. As far as her vision extends is unrelenting waste-land. It appears as if it goes on forever, and if she hadn't gone to the edge of the forest herself, she might have believed that it continued indefinitely. As it turns out, she only lived in a small fraction of the destruction, a slice her master had carved out of the hidden outskirts. The valley she knew as home made for good protection against higher ground attacks, as it proved more work than it was worth to hike down, especially with there being no source of water or food to greet you at the bottom.

With that on her mind, Lara checks her water skin. It's half empty. She takes a small sip, and licks every drop off her lips, not letting the dry air steal the moisture. There is a slight detour in her travels, as she makes her way closer to home.

A giddy, almost gleeful feeling comes over her as she starts to tread back on familiar ground. Each bounding step fuels her excitement, further driving her stride. She is closing in on her northern stash, located on the outskirts of their perimeter. It is where she plans on restocking, with some of her ingenious supplies.

It is a perfect location. She knows that her

master won't venture outside of the border she created for them both. It is this truth that was the cause of their biggest arguments to date—expanding their perimeter. With the absence of trees in the area, Lara knew that she couldn't hide her travels out this far, not without raising suspicion. So, she dug in her heels. Words flew back and forth between them like poison-tipped arrows. After the dust settled, her master finally agreed to the perimeter increase, but at a hefty price. Lara paid it. The scar on their relationship was the currency. This was one of those "omitting lies." The irony is that she might have been able to handle these invaders if there wasn't so much ground to cover. In turn, the weapons she made for protection left them more vulnerable.

Smile, you got your way. Just like you always do. Her master's words still sting as she recalls the incident.

She scrunches up her face sourly. Guilt is a weapon her master is a master of. But like all weapons, they can be parried. In this case, she knocks away the feeling with misplaced confidence—confidence that her weapons can best any foe and end any war. To her master, however, they are merely distractions—playthings that couldn't possibly match even a human's craftsmanship. The truth, however, isn't quite that cut and dry, black and white, or as much fun as Lara could have hoped.

After the better part of the day, Lara finally arrives outside her hidden supplies cache. It appears to be undiscovered by her master or anyone else. In creating this secret armory, she removed the thick roots of an old, rotted-out bull-bush, which has dangerously sharp spikes. She filed some of the inner points down, yielding her safe passage to the underground hole, which is covered by a rock cloth. From afar, it looks dangerously sharp to the unsuspecting eye.

It has been far too long since she set foot in her hidden place. Thick dust fills the air as evidence of that fact. Years ago, she found this tunnel almost by accident, though somehow she knew it was there—as if something inside her was guiding her to the false wall that held the path's secret. It wasn't at all like the feeling she got when intruders were afoot. This was more like a knowingness. Almost like sleep-walking while completely awake. Since that day, Lara has stored all kinds of contraband at the end of the tunnel, far from her master's judgment.

One day she dreams of making it into a club-house. That is, if she had any friends to join her non-existent society. It could be used for secret meetings and all other orders of business an organized group of girls could ever want. The only problem is that her kind is nearly extinct, which isn't the sort of thing clubs are made of. Still, she coined it as such—the Extinct Club. Contradiction or not, she is a proud member, even if she's the only one.

Broken stone swords, banners of war, and clever traps are among the collection of ingenuity she has scattered around the cave. Not wanting to get caught lugging any of this stuff around, Lara decides to only take a of couple items with her. She paces back and forth with delight as she picks up a turtle-shell shield.

"Too obvious." She tosses the shell aside and makes her way deeper into the cavern. The back of the cave is filled with scavenged treasures from the wasteland. She calls it "me little dragon hoard"—the true treasure of the Extinct Club. Oftentimes, she takes unsanctioned "wyvern naps" during hot, uneventful days. Her master would have a fit if she were to ever catch the youngling napping on the job. Just another good reason to keep the secret stash secret. However, she didn't come here for slumber, she came here for accoutrements for the hunt.

She will not be ill prepared, not this time, not ever again. A true metalman may have shiny armor and a finely crafted sword, but what Lara has is her ingenuity, which is far greater, in her opinion. Untested and unproven, yes, but also underestimated. Countless scripts and technique manuals have gone into great detail on the exact specifics of sword combat. She knows this because she read them all with great fervor. There are only so many ways you can injure a foe with a sword. In her spare time, she has come up with a few new ways, though they are clumsy and require augmentation. One is slapping someone with the face of a flimsy blade after whipping it forward. Another is making a brittle sword that shatters once it hits bone. This one is more of a one-shot kill, where the blade can be released from the hilt and reloaded. Both of these designs are in the theoretical phase, due to the utter lack of materials.

In regard to normal swords, they're predictable. Everyone knows what they're in for in a sword and knife fight—mainly getting cut or stabbed. Some are used for hacking, like broad-swords or the devastating claymores. Others are used for more finesse, like the trusty rapiers and epees. There are a couple techniques where you use the weapon's hilt to knock someone out, but you have to be quite close, which defeats the whole point of having a sword—keeping your enemies at a safe distance. Plus, Lara finds that using such a move involves turning the blade towards yourself, which puts you one duck and riposte away from getting stabbed by your own blade. As exciting as it sounds to go toe to toe against another sword-wielding foe, matching skill against skill, that is not how things often play out. Life isn't fair, and being noble often means a bloody death on the battlefield. In true skirmishes, from start to dead is a matter of seconds. No long dueling, back-and-forth flashing blades, and insults like in all the storybooks. In reality, every combatant does the same thing. They size up their opponent and adjust to give themselves a tactical advantage. The faster the kill, the better. No need to whip out your sabre for an honorable duel when you can shoot your opponent with your hip crossbow from twenty yards.

This is how Lara plans on getting the edge

in any blade fight. All of her inventions are foreign to anyone except herself. Even her master
hasn't been privy to their use and versatility.
The element of surprise doesn't end with her
unveiling herself in a surprise attack; it only
just begins. Each weapon is carefully thought
out and designed for a specific purpose; mostly
to compensate for a fragility she sees within
herself or for exploiting a weakness in a potential foe.

Whenever she reads tales of clashing swords
and shields, at the climax of the battle, she always is pulled out of the moment due to finding
what she describes as "plot craters." *Why
doesn't the protagonist do it this way or that
way? If only they had a simple finger-snipping
contraption, then the crossbowman would be
two fingers away from becoming completely
powerless.* Thoughts like these keep her mind
and hands busy whenever she has a spare moment. And this is how she fills her hoards with
fresh instruments of destruction.

After activating the sole light source—a glow
stone—she starts to rummage through her
stuff. There are piles of poison pouches, sharp
shells, scrap metals, and whatever else she
could get her hands on. Among the weapons

and contraptions is an endless supply of scraps she found, making this armory look more like a junk hole. She kept everything, because she never knew when she would need anything.

Her eagerness escapes through little noises she makes as she snatches up each item, remembering the blissful state she was in when she created it. Every one is a treasure that was made with love and necessity, a puzzle piece to some of the pitfalls she ran across in her training. The answers to her "what if" questions. What if they have a flaming axe? Or better yet, two of them, with great big spikes on them? Often unlikely scenarios. It is better to be overprepared than caught with your pants down. That's her philosophy, anyway. Deep down, she knows that weapon making is more often a business venture, and selling custom weaponry is not very likely. Not when you kill all your potential customers.

Lara laments over the custom fist weapons she made her master. The materials were hard to find, but she perfected the set so that each one could counter any weapon she might be paired up against. "Pain for all occasions," she speaks the name she came up with for the set. They are attachments for her missing limbs, with straps and snaps to keep her from ever becoming disarmed again. One is made from shells and stones ground into points all over the deadly fist. It looks like an artist's hodgepodge rendition of a porcupine.

Another one is made for chopping and thrashing. A year or so ago, she found a broken bronze axe. The blade was cracked. With a lot of determination and hard work, she managed to sever it into two separate pieces and attach them to a fist strap. The third was crude but useful. It was a rugged-edge diamond fist, used for blunt bludgeoning attacks. To her, diamonds are not all that rare. She always finds them scattered in the soot, like pearls in the ocean. At her other stash, she has a pile of medium diamonds she uses as projectiles with her havoc-sling. If she only knew their worth, she wouldn't be so wasteful in using them as ammunition. One this size, however, is one of a kind. She found it at the bottom of the dry lakebed, and it was one of the main incentives that keeps her coming.

She had a fourth design but never managed to finish it. It encompassed the same technique as the quill-whip. In fact, the whip was really just a test that got out of hand. The original design was to make a projectile fist, but now all the quills are gone.

Initially she constructed them as a gift for her master, though she never got the nerve to give them to her. She knows her master's stance all too well on such things, unfortunately. Nevertheless, she shoves them into her hip pack. Just in case.

"Now, something for me."

Against the wall, she spies her rotating, two-pronged pitchfork. "This kills slow, real slow." She wraps it in fur cloth and fastens it to her back. The weapon feels heavy as it pulls on her shoulders. Despite her desires, Lara knows she has to be sparing with the rest of her loot, or else she might become an arsenal with the speed of a statue. The weapon on her back is cumbersome enough on its own.

"Shields, humans like those. I need something that will be good against one of them, nothing crazy," she assures herself, reflecting on the highly improbable idea of running into a foe with a double-spiked shield.

The sound of clinking glass fills the chamber as she rummages through a pile of potions, vials, and elixirs. All of them have been made by combining ingredients that she has found. She has substituted ingredients from some experiments she had read in her chemistry textbook, "Magic for fools."

After going through the pile twice, she finally finds the vial she is looking for. It has a thick, viscous substance inside, which bubbles and froths as she shakes it up. "Still good."

Taking a moment, she ponders what she might encounter on the next leg of her journey. Without hesitation, she begins to shove random vials inside her hip sack until it is nearly bursting at the seams. This may not be necessary, but they're small, and it couldn't hurt.

"What to do about their armor?" She knows that humans love to cover their cowardice with steel. It gives them false courage. Secretly, she would take any sort of courage, fake or otherwise. The folk used to armor themselves with shells. When the ecosystem fell, so did their symbiosis with the shell creatures. This is but one of many ancient traditions that was carried on for thousands of years, only to become lost after the travesty. Gaining your armor set was a rite of passage among the young feathered-folk—a ceremony Lara was robbed of. Without harboring any resentment, she envies her master's shell set. On occasion, she has even tried to fit into it. While the pauldrons seem to be too tight, the cuisses and greaves are laughably loose and fall down constantly. It is just one of the problems with custom-fitted armor. No matter her size, Lara will never fit into them the same way her master does.

Forgetting her purpose, she fondly thumbs objects that are strewn about, imagining putting each one to good use. Time and urgency of the situation escape her as she plays with her things.

She picks up a hollow, cast-iron box she had attached to an old axe handle. This is a great tool she made with the intention of dealing with armor. Its design allows one to fill the box with hot coals, bludgeoning while also heating up a metalman's conductive armor. She calls it the Hot Basher. The box at the end, however, is much too heavy for her to lug around, and without access to any coal, there will be no hot bashing today. With a slight smile, she returns the weapon to its resting place for another day.

"Where has the day gone?" Lara notices the sun is already setting, casting a shadow in the entrance of her tunnel.

The truth is complicated; like a two-headed dog, one side barks while the other bites.

Though her master must have her reasons for keeping her in perpetual adolescence, she believes The Enchantress's words too—that is, before she killed her. Lara doesn't have a real answer to the moonlight dilemma that she is soon to face. There is no denying that she feels different in its cold light—more refined, less immature. Her only hang-up is trying to decide if that is good or bad.

She cannot waste another night by hunkering down and avoiding its rays. She has inadvertently done that her whole life, to no known advantage. Plus, she has already wasted enough time letting the day get away from her. All the adrenaline flowing through her will make it impossible to sleep, anyway. Armed for war, there is no patience for a fighting spirit.

Her creativity is ignited as she rips down the fake-rock covering that hides the entrance to her stash. Holding the covering up to the setting sun, the tightly woven fabric imbedded with rocks and dirt blocks all light from passing through. But will it fare the same against the moon's power? She hopes so. A few alterations later, she has a stone-surface cloak. Scratchy and cumbersome, she uses it to shroud herself. It isn't as stealthy as the charcoal makeup, but it will do the trick.

The only drawback is that her stash is no longer hidden, though there may not be any reason to hide it—what with her master being gone. Even though the make-shift cloak blocks the moon from seeing her, it equally blocks her from seeing outward, and anything at all, for that matter. She quickly develops a solution, though it is not at all practical. She grabs the Hot Basher to use as a guiding stick.

Everything is in place, and she is ready to embark on her first adventure. Filling her lungs with the stagnant air, she holds it in as long as possible. *This is it. My last breath as an apprentice. No more excuses. No more second chances. No more mistakes.*

A blast of hair flows out of her. With her eyes closed, her next breath seems fresh and new—rife with opportunity. Lara doesn't waste a second by lingering. She leaves the moment in the past, where it belongs, for she is on a quest for glory—a future victory.

With her gaze on the ground, the inspired feathered-folk makes her way into the night like a packhorse, slow and heavy-footed. The metal door on her walking-stick box flaps and creaks against the hinges with every step she takes.

Her trek is less than silent.

It doesn't take long before she is outside of her boundary and making strides into the wild unknown.

Who knows what lurks in the shadows when the light vanishes over the mountain ridge. Only time will attest to its dangers.

She uses her stick-on-a-box to feel around like a blind peasant, her shoulders hunched over from the weight of the heavy cloak.

She mentally sketches out what her walking stick feels. Only, in her mind, she replaces the drab reality with the bountiful colors from a time long since passed. As she taps her way through the crumbling ash, she imagines it as colorless leaves, like the one she witnessed on the last surviving tree, expanding over every surface, indicating a fast-approaching winter solstice, though her representation couldn't be farther from the real beauty of this once lush forest. Lara has no way of knowing that leaves come in all sorts of colors—rich greens, deep auburns, and even multicolored combinations. It is a life she never knew and may never know. For now, her mind's image will have to do.

Now that she knows her master is with the invaders, she can rely on her gift to pinpoint their general direction. She rubs her fingers together and dips the tips into the soil. Only now, her guilt from killing The Enchantress is interrupting the alert in the pit of her stomach, resulting in vague directions.

She continues on her path in a new sort of way. There is something freeing about walking without the intent to ever return, without the task of hiding your trail so others can't follow. She used to rely on her careful step to reduce the maintenance later. Now, she walks with a child-like stride rooted in intrigue, almost taunting the people of the future to follow in her very footsteps, to see what she sees, to smell the stagnate air that she exhales. She has spent her life, thus far, following the breadcrumbs of the past and inventing stories to accompany them. Now it is her turn to create her own story for someone else to get wrong. It's the closest feeling to immortality she has ever felt.

After scaling up and over the trail that winds around the ravine she calls her homeland, she is finally on the other side—venturing through the lands that get to indulge in the first light of the sun—not being blocked by the mountainous outlying ridge that keeps her homeland secluded from the rest of the blackened forest.

Her underutilized Hot Basher walking stick clangs loudly against something in the ground. It is hard and not at all indigenous. Tapping around the unknown darkness has led Lara to an extraordinary find, something she has never found in abundance. It is something thought to be a rare discovery, one that her master warned her to leave where it lies and let it bestow its curse upon the next unfortunate traveler. But to Lara, it is more priceless than gold.

A Grave Memory

Without thinking, she pokes her head out of the safety of her rock shroud, letting the soothing light reflect in her eyes. She scrambles to the end of her walking stick to confirm her suspicions. Her excitement mirrors that of a human child ripping through a package concealed with paper during a birth ritual.

"I knew it. Steel metal!" Lara says aloud, letting the world, or any cloud dancers that might be about, hear her claim to it. Dropping her make-shift walking stick, she scoops up the battered helmet. Old dust crumbles out. It has a face covering that swings open like a door, which desperately needs to be oiled. Back and forth, she plays with the hinges making a screeching sound. Time seems to be at a stand-still as she fiddles with the thing. This could go on forever, or until it breaks from overuse.

"The hinges are the weakest part of the thing. What a bad design." Still, she's fascinated with how it is forged. The face mask finally breaks, causing her to move on from playing with it. She touches every surface of the helm with her palms. It is crafted from two pieces of steel fastened together by rivets. A technology, up until now, she never knew. The way the material is bent, heat must have been used to forge the headpiece. The fiction in her head is now becoming a reality. She will be the knightess. This *is* happening.

She slips the helm under her shroud and places it upon her head, face screen or no face screen. It feels cold, hard, and much too big for her. *It must be fitted for a fat-headed male.* Turning her head, the helmet sloshes around freely, though she doesn't care. This is but one part of the dream.

Her mouth agape, Lara looks over the scene that she has stumbled upon. A great battle took place on this very spot, and she's standing in the middle of the ancient tomb. Scattered around her, soft light glistens off metal armor, spear tips, swords, axes, flails, arrowheads, belt buckles, leather studs, and wagon wheels, all of which are slightly tarnished by rust and wear. Still, the sparkling light dazzles in her eyes. Gold coins appear to have been flung everywhere, as if there were a shower of currency. Maybe this is really what the invading humans are after—old war treasure. It is as close to a dragon's lair as she'll ever get. Only there is no dragon, and it is in plain sight. Her hands tremble from overstimulation. There is too much for Lara to take in all at once. Treasure, corpses, armor, weapons, money and an endless supply of materials for new designs.

"It is everywhere. Of course I find this now. It's *not* fair." She spins around looking back at the trail she just scaled.

Then an idea forms in her young mind. It starts with a vision of her wearing a full set of metalman armor. The silver sheen quickly turns gold in hue, like a burning sun. "I can melt it all down. Gold is impervious to rust," she says, suddenly finding a use for the coins, though the logistics of such a task are lost to her in the excitement of the moment. With two cupped hands, she scrambles to pull coins towards her in a pile.

Her master and her current quest are at the back of her mind. "There will be time for that later." She pauses, trying not to get too caught up in the moment so as to overlook the real treasure of this trove—knowledge. This is not just a trading post for her to go shopping in; it's a battleground. *Lives were lost, hundreds of them. But why?*

The night is filled with the faint, agonized whispers of forgotten pain. Lara continues to slither through the darkness, shrouded from the moon's watchful eye, ignoring the omen that tickles at her ears. Cautiously, she approaches a mummified body holding a halberd high above his head. He is taking a valiant striking pose. An expression of pain is still on his ashen face. She wonders what he was fighting, as there is nothing apparent blocking his strike. In fact, all the warriors are like this in their perpetual state of battle—stuck in a moment with no escape. To her, it feels as if she's walking in the middle of a painting—beautiful, rich, with long-lost emotion.

"Maybe death was their only way out." Careful not to disrupt the resting bodies, she scours the battlefield for clues, anything to shed some light on what happened here, before her grubby hands can get to work.

All the warriors share the same crest or house marking. It resembles a silly-looking horse with buck teeth. It seems jovial and out of place in such a tragic scene. Arrows stick out of the ground near withered archers. One soldier is stuck as he drags a wounded comrade out of harm's way while swinging his morning star at an unseen menace. Even the chain is stuck in the air, mid-swing.

"How is that even possible?" She reaches for the chain, but abruptly stops herself. "Keep moving," she tells herself, trying to take it all in before giving in to her greed.

Both women and men are present, fighting equally on the battlefield, equipped with similar weapons and other armaments. This was a desperate war over survival. This truth comes to fruition when she spots a child wielding a slingshot. It is hurling its last stone at the enemy. Ashen tear streaks mark its little face.

It is a grim scene, indeed. To a human, this is a tragic scene, one to be mourned over and prayed at, but to Lara, this is treasure.

Gazing upon the battle has her all fired up with adrenaline. Lara imagines what happened on this battlefield. *The humans fought a ghastly foe, one who rose from unmarked graves in this ancient burial ground. Trespassers of the graveyard were inflicted with something far worse than a swift death, they were haunted from behind their eyelids in the dreams of night. The humans gathered their resources to put an end to the nightly torment, but their weapons were no match for the translucent shades. Pain looks as though it came high as their life was drained from their skin, leaving each human dry and brittle—a husk of their former fleshy selves. Their forms lie as a warning to all of those who set foot upon this wicked scene.*

She mimics the stances of the fallen corpses. A flare of excitement fills her eyes. Her assertion couldn't be farther from the truth, however. Fact is often more brutal than fiction, and in actuality, the evidence of the foe does remain. If only Lara had the knowledge to know what to look for.

The one truth in her fictional tale was the warning—stay away from this dreadful place. Unfortunately, she didn't heed it herself. Instead, a lurking essence looms all around her, slowly creeping towards her.

After surveying the area some more, Lara is certain the entire battle was one-sided. All the donkey men are attacking in the same direction, with nothing opposing them from the other side. *What were they fighting? Could it really have been a shade, or perhaps an invisible foe? Nothing seems to be adding up.*

Then a thought hits her hard, like a punch to the face. She can't help but voice it aloud, "Nothing is burnt. They all died from something else...maybe before? No, it would have to be after. Is that right?"

Forgetting her tact, she touches the halberd from the first victim she came across. Upon impact, the mummified hand crumbles into debris before her, dropping the weapon onto the ground. Dust plumes uproot another figure—one posing as he thrusts his weapon into thin air. In turn, it too crumbles into dust. Instantly she feels horrible, like she ruined some precious work of art.

"Why do I have to touch everything?" As the words leave her lips, she cringes. *Now I'm sounding like her.* "Master...right. What am I doing here?"

There are more pressing issues for her to attend to. As much as she would love to abandon all her responsibilities and loot this place, her master is waiting. Despite what The Enchantress said about her having all the time in the world, she doesn't. Though time may or may not affect her, it does, however, affect everyone else. So, unless she wants to spend the rest of her days alone like The Enchantress, she better hop to it.

"Can't everyone just leave me alone? Myself included?" she says, burying her face in her hands and coming to grips with reality.

After a long beat, Lara decides that she needs to prioritize what she can take with her and what she cannot. Without something or someone strong enough to pull that wagon, she will have to rely on her own body's strength to carry everything. *You have one hour.*

Walking on the tips of her toes, she tries to be more careful with her movements, so as not to disrupt the scene any more than she already has.

Lara faintly hears something moving and quickly turns her head. The oversized helm shifts and covers her eyes. She moves it back, but the sound is gone. Holding her breath, Lara waits for the sound to appear again. The whispers she heard before turn into screeching cries of despair. Something is attacking her with sound, and no amount of pressure from her hands can mask it. She buckles down in pain as the sound increases. Yet again, Lara is not prepared for the unyielding unknown. She only has one option; run and run fast.

What good are rare metals and forgotten battles if you're not around to tell the tale? Lara answers that question with her feet. Darting through the graveyard causes mummies to collapse all around her, which in turn causes a chain reaction, upsetting other surrounding bodies. Debris and human dust remains are everywhere, making visibility nearly impossible. Still holding her breath, Lara doesn't want to breathe any of that stuff in, mostly fearing her own made-up ghost story. Swords fall upon her, as spears graze her fleeing body. Back and forth she leaps and dodges but is still nearly skewered by the crumbling crypt warriors. Their hollow eyes show only death.

Unintentional or not, this place is proving to be extremely poky and quite dangerous. *What have I done?* She shakes her head back and forth at her foolishness. Lara's body begins to slow without the oxygen to keep her agility up.

Her mouth holds in a muffled scream as an

armored skeleton descends upon her. All she can do is jump through its ribs to avoid getting the sharp end of its axe. Its bones shatter much more easily than she would have expected.

This scene is much older than the dying forest. It has to be. Even the torched bones in the forest don't break that easily. All her logic tells her that the warriors are long since dead, but something in the way they're moving is telling her otherwise. They're not just falling apart; they're aiming for her. They must be.

With her cheeks puffed out like balloons, Lara continues her escape. It is no use. The sound follows her, stride for stride, as do the crumbling combatants. The sound is making it hard for her to think, or even exist.

She can't keep this up forever. She needs to breathe. She has to rest. She is going to have to give in to her fears. Lara comes to a screeching stop next to a giant crossbow—a scorpion. She rolls up into a ball, her rock shroud covering her completely.

Debris falls everywhere, as the world comes crashing down around her. The crossbow helps protect her by propping up some of the larger wreckage. She takes a deep breath. The air smells like blood and tastes even worse. She coughs as it enters her lungs, rejecting the plume.

The sound isn't getting worse, because that would be impossible. It's already at the peak of its crescendo.

Pausing for this brief moment has given Lara a thought that she cannot escape. *I know where the loud dissonance is coming from.*

And she knows exactly how to defeat it...

The Leftovers

*L*ittle screaming voices pour out their earsplitting anguish—torturous sounds that feel almost like commands—telling her to do things, unspeakable things. The deafening discord is debilitating. All she can think of is silence. It needs to stop. No cost is too high. No pain is in vain, as long as it ceases the cacophony. Steering away from thoughts of self-harm, she forces her hand to reach for her face.

She puts her hands upon her head and rips off the steel helm she plundered from a corpse. The only good reason she can come up with as to why all this stuff has sat virtually untouched by the hands of man or the breath of wind, is it's cursed by the voices of the dead.

Her suspicious are correct, for the most part. The moment the helm leaves her head, the screams are downgraded to a low whisper. Her ears ring loudly, remembering the incident, like an echo of the pain. Still, she doesn't know the true source of the wrenched noise or its purpose.

Biting her lip, she looks at her hands, which are shaking uncontrollably. She is really feeling the weight of her heavy cloak. It is almost as if it's choking her in a claustrophobic way. First, she removes her fork-like weapon on her back, then the beartrap and anything she has to in order to free herself from the garb.

She drops the fabric and it hits the ground like a stone.

Now that the cloak is no longer restricting her, she is able to regulate her breathing again. The moonlight is upon her once again. She hides in the crossbow's shadow for a beat.

An investigation is in order. Yes, she could just up and leave, in theory, but she needs to further understand how to get revenge on its source. It can't just get away with it. Going in for a closer look, Lara notices something moving around inside the headpiece. Narrowing her eyes, she brings it closer to her face. Not a great idea, but she is determined to see this thing through. It appears to be a bug of some sort, which is the first time she's seen one up close.

"They're supposed to be dead—extinct." Quickly forgetting about the recent event that almost deafened her, Lara puts out her hand hoping to tempt the insect onto her body. For Lara, this is only the second non-humanoid lifeform see has seen, and both within the same week. The last bug got away before she could inspect it. She won't let that happen again. Her master told her that no insects lived within the cursed lands. Of course, it is evidence of another one of her lies to add to the ever-growing list.

The eight-legged creature hesitantly approaches her finger. It seems calm, almost sweet.

Lara encourages it with a clicking sound. "There you go. It's okay." It moves like nothing she has ever seen before, almost unnaturally.

The creature slowly places a skeletal leg on the tip of her finger. It's so light she can't even feel its touch. Tipping her head, she gets a good look at the thing. It resembles the description of a spider, though it has a human skull where its spider-head ought to be. *No human is that small.* There is no doubt about it, this is no living insect. Also, it doesn't appear to be undead but something far worse.

Trying to make sense of what she is looking at, she realizes that its fangs are saber-like, and she mistook one of them for a leg...the very one that is touching her finger.

Before she can flick it away, the thing lets out a loud screech as it pierces her finger and ears once more.

"Fundle!" she yells through the sting of it.

Instantly, it begins to drain her. Each second, with each drop of fluid it consumes, it starts to grow exponentially larger. As its features swell, Lara swears the thing is smiling at her with a wicked skull-grin.

The pain is like nothing she has ever felt before. A low, throbbing sensation permeates from her finger to her toes. It is as if her finger is going to explode from the inside and her body is preparing for the impact.

Kicking and pulling, Lara screams, matching the bugs own pitch and terror, though it keeps on getting bigger and bigger and bigger still. Now she knows that the sound it was making was not from its own lips but from its past victims, as a warning.

With the pulsating pain running deep, her finger feels as though it's going to burst out of her skin. Running out of time, Lara reaches inside her pack, pulls an acid pouch, and smashes it directly on its grotesque face, hoping to melt that wicked grin right off.

The beast's screeching quickly turns to uproarious laughter as its face dissolves into a vapor, which disappears into the sky. She feels as if it's mocking her in some way.

Using all her might, she pushes against the beast. The fang snaps, leaving the end still stuck inside her finger. Standing before her is a headless, six-legged horror that is still very much alive.

Now it has grown to almost half her size. Most of its bulk is in its four-jointed legs. She wonders how large it could have gotten if she hadn't stopped it from feeding off of her.

It jumps and scurries around, thrashing its boney limbs violently with a morbid, burbling chuckle.

Lara ducks and dodges while trying to sort out her own predicament. What to do with this fang that's still imbedded deep inside her finger? Blood is continuing to leak out with no sign of stopping. Something must be done before she bleeds dry.

As it flails toward her, Lara parries a striking limb with her arm. Using this opportunity, she climbs onto the beast and subdues it to the ground. Holding it in place, without fear or remorse, she jams her finger into the frothing, sizzling, faceless beast. The caustic heat burns the end of the fang and her leaking blood. She bites down hard and gnashes her teeth, fighting the searing pain.

Though her work isn't yet done. She keeps it there long enough to make sure nothing remains. Even though the acid is dissolving the tip of her finger, it hurts far less than the bloating pain that the fang produced. She finds comfort in the excruciating relief.

Once she's sure the fang is completely dissolved, she rolls off of the beast. Quickly, she dips her hand in the cursed ground, until the bubbling sound fades from her ears, ignoring the beast that is struggling to get back on its feet.

With half a face, and just one remaining fang, the beast attempts a scuttling retreat. If Lara were a betting man, she would have

wagered everything on the beast sinking another fang in her while she was distracted.
Good news for her, she would have lost her
shirt.

A couple of feet away, Lara grabs the chain
of her bear trap and pries open its jaws. While
tightly clutching the chain, she hurls the trap at
the coward, letting out a guttural "Not today!"
Once the trap collides with the creature, she
gives the chain a tug, triggering a modification
she made to the old device that causes it to
clamp it shut. Bones shatter and legs fold into
the massive jaws.

Hand over hand, she pulls the twitching
thing closer to her. She does a double take upon
seeing the finger on her left hand is now missing. "I guess I'll never be able to fire a crossbow.
Not with this hand anyway." She once had a vision of wielding two crossbows, both connected
to contraptions feeding them a nearly endless
barrage of projectiles. That dream, like many
other plans she had for her digit, is shattered.
She is beyond mad but also disappointed in
herself.

Caught in her snare and unable to move, the
thing hisses and screeches, using its own voice
this time—not as a mere warning, but out of

frustration.

Damn, damn, damn. "To think, I thought you were going to be a positive part of my life. But no, you had to be something truly horrible."

She turns her back to the beast, the chain slung over her shoulder. "Stupid..." With all her might she whips the chain, flinging the creature past her. "...bug!"

It smashes on the ground. The metal jaws gnaw into it, clamping together. Over and over, she smashes it in this manner until it stops twitching altogether.

"Now, every time I point at something, I won't be able to forget your ugly..."

Smash.

"...disturbing..."

Crunch.

"...face."

Thud.

Knowing nothing about the undead, or whatever this thing is, Lara leaves the trap biting down on its corpse, just in case.

"I'll be back to check on your later," she asserts.

After catching her breath, Lara makes her way over to the helm that she cherished so much only moments before. She's not sure if her eyes are playing tricks on her or not, but she could have sworn that there was another creepy crawler in there as she approached. It must have quickly hidden itself as she reached for the helm, she supposes.

"No way. Not again." With perfect form, she kicks the steel helm off into the distance. It flies towards a human husk adorned in a full set of steel armor—the exact style that she imagined herself wearing as a knightess, only slightly rusty at the edges.

With a loud "clang," the soaring helm collides with the human husk, causing the armor to scatter every which way. She raises both her hands above her head. In one respect, it is satisfying to make such a loud ruckus—like she just scored a goal in the game of survival. On the other hand, she really didn't want to damage such a rare set of armor. "It should be fine..." Somewhere deep inside, her mind is still trying to find a way to fully rob this place of its riches.

The ground appears to be rippling like the ocean, as tiny creatures make their way towards her in a tidal wave of horror. They're undoubtably the same creatures that were infesting the helmet. There's no way that they were only infesting the one piece she kicked away. A chorus of tiny legs clack softly like rainfall, getting louder and louder with each step.

This is not a time for debate and thoughtful planning. It is a time for panic, arm flailing, and screaming—lots and lots of screaming.

Onward

With countless tiny creatures at her heels, Lara is in a race for her existence. Having to make a quick getaway, she didn't have time to re-equip her cloak and fasten her weapon to her back. Instead, she holds them in her hands like luggage.

"My Hot Basher..." she says, turning her head as far as it will stretch, looking back for her walking stick. *Oh well, I never should have put it down in the first place. Serves me right.*

One after another, she knocks blackened foliage out of their shallow graves. She is trying to keep her stride as direct as possible. There is no time for things to get in her way, no room for mistakes, and no stopping to ask for directions; only time to move. Her legs burn from giving it her all.

The little creatures are not as fast or agile as the young feathered-folk, but what they lack in speed, they more than make up for with their considerable numbers.

Back and forth, up and down, she skips off boulders, trying to stay nimble and on high ground. Every place she steps is engulfed with the buggers the second after her foot launches off the ground. Occasionally, one glides in the air and she slaps it away before it lands on her body. They are relentless, and so is she.

Never has Lara been so focused. Metaphorically, she's abandoning her past—the folk who she thought she was and everything she has ever known. Most of all, she is fleeing from her naivety. The impending danger is merely inspiring her to get there quicker.

Beautifully darting through the moonlight, she imagines herself as a giant tree person. *A countless army of humans tries to slay the mighty treant-folk for the king's birthday. She doesn't know how many are down there, but she is sure it is all of them. They seek to decapitate her and subsequently mount her head in* the king's royal court as a prize of victory. The fat king isn't here doing his own dirty work, though he will claim her head all the same. Except she won't go down so easily—not without flattening more than a few loyal brigades. Her feet slip and slide on the slick human juice under foot.

"Die, humans!" she roars with a heavy-footed stride, diminishing the severity of the situation.

Even though it's make-believe, she feels powerful and a sense of grandeur, compared to the foe at her toes. A slight smile forms on her face, and she pushes herself past her limit. During these last few days, she has spent more time with life-threatening opponents than the normal run-of-the-mill human encounter. It is exciting to say the least, unpredictable, and a lot less lonely than being cooped up like a prisoner within the boundaries her master had established. She is...having fun.

A week ago, Lara would have never believed that so much life lived inside the dead forest, right under her nose—what with the cloud dancers, corpse stealer, insects, living tree, and now skeleton crawlers. There is much more to this world than she had previously known.

What other gifts will the splendors of time give her? It is almost like a repayment for her years of servitude. She awaits every new experience with open arms, ready to accept its embrace warmly, even if it's hostile—especially if it is.

To some, being deeply entranced in their own imagination would be detrimental, but for Lara, it's a way for her to clear her mind and plan—detaching herself from reality so she can confront the actions she ultimately needs to take. This is how she got through years of murder and mayhem without it affecting her in the slightest. Her empty conscience is a weapon she has at her disposal, because guilt never gets in the way of her actions. It is almost as if she's a witness to her own actions. Her hands may be doing it, but not her. Or so she tells herself, absolving herself of all guilt.

The bone-spider creatures are more intelligent than she anticipated, and before long they are blocking off her exit, leaving her completely surrounded. Could this be it? Are they going to drain her one drop at a time, creating an army of hideously huge monsters?

As they close the gap between her and death, she hears their deafening screeches of despair.

What will become of her if they happen to catch and consume her? Will she become a husk statue like that of the humans on the battlefield, or something far worse? Whatever it is that they have in store for her, she isn't going to let that happen, not when she just barely began to live.

Alas, she was hoping for a swift escape and that it wasn't going to come to this, but she has no other choice. This is her last resort. Reaching into her hip bag, Lara pulls out a nondescript vial filled with a multi-colored mixture.

"Don't let me down, old friend," she says to the vial. With a cringe, she pops the cork. A soul-stealing stench floats out. With a flick of her wrist, the contents spray outward like a fan. The liquid floats to the ground like heavy mist, vaporizing anything organic it touches—burnt trees, human husks, but most importantly, skeleton crawlers. This doesn't stop them all, however. Once the mist fades, the remaining ones launch at her fiercely.

Never slowing her stride, she tosses one bottle after another directly into the closing-in horde. There is no time for her to sort through them and come up with a strategy, only time for randomness.

They explode into a rainbow of prismatic liquids, gases, and solids. Fire, ice and earth ignite, as two incompatible compounds touch each other. Intrigue fills her eyes. If only she knew the formula for that one. Some of these concoctions are experiments she has made. Others are mysterious substances she discovered or lifted off humans. She may be an amateur of alchemy, but she is a professional at havoc.

She lobs more vials and potions, reducing the swarm ahead of her, to the side, and behind her. Anything in the blast radius is destroyed or consumed by the bottles. Random effects are shooting off everywhere. Oils are catching fire, husks are freezing, and armor is shattering. Chaos is everywhere, and her smile is beaming. The multi-colored display could stand up to the finest of firework celebrations.

Pulling out the final bulbous glass container, she flicks it blindly behind herself. She lets out a chortle of joy as it explodes, sending debris flying through the sky.

There is a clear path in the wake of obliterated fiends. Without missing a beat, she takes it. With each step, her woven footwear becomes sticky as she sprints through the residual from the vials.

The heat beneath her feet tells her that something is dissolving her soles. Each step is sticky and slow. Fluorescent pink bubbles start to froth and foam all around her. It is growing faster than the creature did when it attached to her finger. This is not good. She is playing with powers she doesn't understand.

Once Lara is out of the blast radius, she kicks off one shoe, then the other one, only losing a couple steps as a result.

She spins around and marvels at the vibrant stain on the black ground. It worked better than she had ever expected. The rate at which it corroded through materials was phenomenal. Too bad that was all she had in the world. The ingredients were one of a kind, in these parts. It was a one-shot deal—and that shot had already been fired.

She wonders if the foamy pink substance she inadvertently made will ever stop growing. Perhaps it will consume everything and everyone. She ignores the possibility with a shrug. Nothing can be done about it, not at this time.

This graveyard could have been a glorious treasure, only now it's a glorious memory, one she never could have imagined.

***

Even though she has long since left the threat behind, her legs haven't slowed. In fact, they quicken their pace—reaching maximum speed as she enters a flat glade. The ground is firm and stable. Never has she found a clearing so level and easy to stretch out her legs in. She doesn't care about the past blunders. Only the future set before her eyes matters now.

Running through the stagnant air leaves her pretending that the wind has returned, although she is the one moving, not the other way around. Up until now, she felt as if the world had stopped spinning. It just sits there, waiting for the end. With each bounding step, she imagines that she is starting it up again—giving metaphorical mouth-to-mouth to the giant marble.

A sense of freedom comes over her as the air tickles her skin like a lover's caress. Just then, she hears something new but doesn't realize what it is. It's the sound of ancient magic hidden deep inside her—the music of the folk against the air. It is like the soothing sensation of a spring day. Images of fragrant flowers and bright colors excite her mind. Even though she has never experienced such sweet things, her visions are perfectly accurate. All her darkness fades away as she peeks into the doorway of what once was. Maybe it is from the past, from another life, or even another world. It is familiar, despite being the exact opposite of what she has been enduring all these years—She doesn't dwell on this. It is real enough for Lara, and that will just have to do.

Tiredness be damned, she isn't going to stop, not now. The old forest is revealing itself in all its glory, like a ghost haunting her all around. There is much more to this place than what meets the eye.

She reflects on her past deeds with different eyes, starting with The Enchantress. Each one seems a little more tragic than before. New ideas start to bloom within her. One is that humans did care if they died. It was always there, though she never saw it. Maybe she never looked for it before now. It was deep in her victim's eyes, in the wrinkle on the bridge of their nose. Fear is not just an emotion to equate with weakness. It is bravery in disguise. Bravery is being afraid yet resisting the wicked call to run away, or worse, do nothing. Standing your ground when you have something to lose is like eating food when you're starving.

Every human, when they came in contact with her bloodlust, always resisted but to no avail. And that is honorable—a quality she never gave them until today. She figured they were just stupid or ignorant.

Up until now, murder was a chore, and she paid it no mind. To her victim, it was their whole life—their entire existence—coming to an end. She is embarrassed that she can't recall all their faces. Each one blends together in a long line of identical serial killings.

As the tears streak across her cheeks, she imagines leaving her fears behind for the fake wind to carry them away. Cleansing herself from everything and everyone—a new beginning for a newly restored self. It's an artificial notion, though the feeling it births is very much real.

Visions of an alternate world flash before her mind. She doesn't know if it is her own manifestation or if the kinetic air is speaking to her. She wants to attack her own self-image and slay the doubts she has been fighting all along so that she can become something more—like forging a new sword out of the broken blades of fallen warriors. This is part of growing up, the part she never wanted to know. But now that she found it, she won't ever let it go.

When you care about something, whether reality or some false ideology, it becomes alive when you give it merit. Words cannot hurt unless you spit them and infect them with hatred, much like a toothless bite.

Nothing is real unless you allow yourself to be fooled into believing it so. And right now, for the first time in her life, she believes that she's a goodly being, capable of restraint, compassion and making the world a better place. She is not just her master's murdering arms, carrying the weight of her actions with the blood on her hands.

She is a bounding cheetah, taking the world beneath her feet hostage. Squeezing air in and out of her system, with each step pounding out the beat of her soul, she wishes this sprint could go on forever—far past the end of the world and onward to the next level of existence.

Suddenly, she comes to a dead stop. Her chest heaves heavily to try and catch up with the damage her legs have done.

As fast as they came, they were gone—the

visions, the thoughts of self-improvement, the internal bliss she had achieved, the empathy for the humans—all of it.

She stands bewildered at the foot of a large monstrosity—something she only thought existed in fairy tale books but wasn't actually real, like dragons, fairies and magical elves. With a shaking hand, she covers her gaping mouth as she stands dumbfounded at the foot of a mighty medieval castle.

Work or Play

Forgetting to breathe, standing directly in front of the impossible, a drop of drool escapes her open mouth, as though making a suicidal leap to observe the castle for itself. So many questions she wants to ask the air, not with the expectation of receiving an answer, but rather to hear her own voice leap off her lips, just to know that she isn't dreaming. Slack-jawed, not able to voice her thoughts, she is suddenly speechless.

She's faced with a conundrum of great magnitude. As a tourist, she wants nothing more than to gush and coo at the finely crafted stone-work, explore the many tower arches, and open and close the massive drawbridge. The feeling inside her wants none of it. It pulls her in a different direction, urgently. Hoping it's merely hunger pains pulling her in the direction of sustenance gives her pause.

There has to be castle food beyond those walls, and that sounds exquisite. She can almost taste the royal flavors on her lips. Maybe her suspicions are miscalculated. Maybe she is making excuses for herself again.

"But..." She finally manages to squeeze out a word between heavy breaths. "...it's..." She places both her hands on her knees. "...a castle."

Waiting a beat, she doesn't actually think her stomach will reply to her plea. However, if a human god aims to give her a divine sign, she might listen. One eye squints, flirting at the very notion.

No such act of God presents itself to her. No heavenly lightning bolts, or giant hands protruding out of the sky, nor any hellish fissures swaying her one way or another. Instead, she is faced with thoughts of bigotry and blasphemy. "All-knowing, my..." She quickly bites her tongue, scrunching up her nose at the possibility that something, or someone, might be in earshot, omnipotent or otherwise.

While never taking her stare off the master-piece, she paces back and forth like a hungry animal licking its chops at an out-of-reach prey. It is tempting her desire against her duty.

"You're there. You're really there," she says, extending her arm at the building. "Don't look at me like that." She presses her palms against both her cheeks. "What to do? What should I do?"

Closing her eyes, she dips a single digit into the soil, looking for answers. Pushing aside her hunger, she knows without a doubt that her gift wants her to proceed past the magnificent ar-chitecture, on to some unknown land. It wants her to find her master and company, if that's still an option. Days have gone by. A lot can happen in the blink of an eye.

A wishful thought comes to her mind. *What if there is a whole city of castles ahead?* Though even she knows this is unlikely.

Smoke and embers rise out of a chimney, like the end of a cigarette. This lets her know that someone is assuredly home. Who could it be? Some bearded king adorned with a jeweled crown? If she could only meet this king person, perhaps he would offer her a meal and lodging for the night. Again, this conclusion is also un-likely.

"What am I doing?" Having freedom doesn't always mean doing whatever you please with-out recourse. It means looking out for yourself, to the best of your ability, because no one else cares about you like you do. The reverse is also true—no one is ever as hard and cruel to you as you are to yourself.

Remembering her master's warning about the night's sky and the effects of the moonlight, she pulls her rock cover over her head and sulks away towards the gut feeling, dragging her feet.

"I better go before I change my mind again," she says, defeated. Even though she truly be-lieves that her master's words are nothing more than lies told to exhibit control over her, being wrong means death. She isn't ready to be so brash about such a claim.

"On the way home, I'll stop in for tea," she says, trying to cheer herself up.

***

The sun comes up promptly, heating up her rock shroud. While the thick covering insulates her from the coldness of night, it does too good of a job keeping the heat in during the day. Not used to such heavy garments, she pants like a dog. Hoping to replenish the liquid that escaped through her pores, she checks her water pouch. Only a couple of drops remain. She laps them up viciously.

This journey isn't going to last till sunset unless she finds some way to keep herself hydrated. These scorched trees are much taller with thicker trunks than she's used to. They look almost unnatural, foreign. Her eyes trail upward. She notices a large grouping of twigs and branches—charred but still intact. They don't look like they naturally grew in that arrangement. The bundle must be a nest of sorts or possibly a critter home. Curious, she rids herself of the heavy cloak. "It's time for a monkey's errand."

Careful not to uproot the massive tree, she climbs the larger branches. Bark flakes off like dead skin from a sunburn, as she scrambles to keep her footing. A small branch snaps when a little amount of pressure is applied to it. Holding her breath, she watches it fall through the silent air. As if choreographed, she exhales at the same time it crashes to the ground.

"That was close." Lara fills her mind with

light thoughts—the air, a feather, the cloud dancers—as an attempt to keep her climb light-footed.

Her master always told her to not use the dead as her playground, referring to the climbing of trees, although the youngling always justified her actions, as she does today. "Everyone needs to be touched sometimes, even the dead." She leans in to give a thick branch a kiss. Shifting her weight causes the roots to shift and turn. Snaps and cracks ripple through the air. Nothing feels stable, not anymore.

"See what happens when I care?" she says to her master, wherever she may be. Keeping herself still while balancing on one foot allows the tree to re-settle in the earth. With two pats to the bark, Lara comforts it. "Take it easy. You're okay. Sorry I was so forward."

Continuing her climb, Lara makes it up to the second highest branch where the nest is splintering off. With some extra height granted by her tippy-toes, Lara is able to make out what's inside. It's a single egg—as black as the branches and feathers that surround it.

"What a way to go, before you even had a chance to run, slither or fly away."

Each twinkle-step she takes closer to the

nest results in an internal cracking sound. If she isn't careful, this whole tree is going to come tumbling down.

"I wonder what kind of egg it is." She knows what kind of egg she *hopes* it is, dragon.

Inch by inch, she shimmies her way close enough to reach the bottom of the bird's nest. Instead of risking getting any higher, she reaches through the bottom of it. Each twig crumbles into dust upon feeling her touch. Her hand grazes the egg as it falls past her. She kicks her foot out and catches it between her toes and shin. *That was close.*

The sudden shift of balance causes the tree to sway and moan even more than before. She outstretches her arms, gaining the balance she needs to realign the old tree. Steadily, and very slowly, she stretches her foot up to her stomach.

She likes being bendy—a discipline that quickly regresses if not maintained daily. Her leg strains, remembering how she has overlooked these exercises since her master left. Together, her joints and the old tree are creaking to each other as if they're having a conversation in an ancient tongue.

At last, she snatches the large egg off her

foot. Her leg snaps back like a string in a bow. She manages to stop herself from kicking the precarious branch beneath her feet. This is not the time or place for inspecting the egg, and she secures it inside her pack. She needs to get down somehow and hopefully in one piece.

Then, out of nowhere, something catches her off guard and steals her breath away. It's the view. The sun's light causes each dead tree to shimmer like fine jewelry, each sparkle a fragment of their former selves, untouched and as pristine as they were before the blaze took away everything. The shadows they cast create a beautifully haunting contrast to the ashen grey floor— nature's abstract artwork. With the slight movement of the sun, each shadow appears like a ghost dancing in the darkness, showering the ground with emotion and life that has long since passed.

Lara and her master spent years cultivating the ash from their homeland's cursed soil. They managed to collect enough to comprise the small garden they grew their crops from. The cursed soil is rubbish. Only the unaltered ash can become a proper component to support new growth. Death feeds life. It was so long ago that she sifted the soil, that she almost forgot how it used to look. She feels like a child again, before all the killing, before all the training—simple, eager to scoop up dirt as a little game she played. The color of the ash determined how pure it was and how perfect of a job she had done. Any traces of black were removed.

Bringing her hand over her mouth, she remembers smiling more back then, so much so that her face would get sore. Her face starts to remember that kind of happiness, but a forced frown interrupts the moment. Shaking her head back and forth, she denies the feeling.

In the far-off distance, she sees a trail of smoke that she assumes is from the castle. *Wait, I am all turned around. That's somewhere different.* She looks over her shoulder and finds a second smoke line. "That is where I need to go," she says, touching her uneasy stomach while looking ahead.

She might be young, but she is an old soul. And old souls will not be bewitched by the shadows of the past.

Exploring the Tide

Her pace grows slower with each step as the blistering sun beats down upon her moist brow. The smoke she has been following seemed much closer from higher ground.

Rolling her aching shoulder, she recounts the not-so-soft landing she made out of the tree. Tracing the tracks with a stick, Lara knows that there is a much greater human presence than she ever thought existed. Each set of tracks tramples the next, making it nearly impossible to decipher the connection between any of them. If only she had the time to solve this puzzle, one print at a time.

Time. What she once had in abundance is now sacred and pressing. If only she could take a vacation from her endeavor and come up with a really great story for each passing foot. She abandons her inquisitive mind, adding her own footprints in the dark sand. It gives her an almost togetherness feeling, as if she is now part of something bigger than herself. If only a print in dirt, she is here, traveling the world, and no one has time to uncover her hidden marks from that of a human.

Each defeated step brings about a fatigue, which is growing at a rapid rate. It feels as though time is everlasting, like she is part of an endless march leading to her open grave.

Unintentionally, her body is beginning to hunch over the more dried out she becomes—getting closer to the earth as her body prepares to be part of it. Her iron will, however, doesn't give up.

The smell of death is stuck in the air. Not that of a human's demise, but that of the wood turning into ash.

"Hello, Lara. Leaving so soon?" a slow voice says.

Quickly, she turns her head, but nothing appears to be around.

"I'm going batty," she says under her breath.

"You would like to think so, wouldn't you!"

the voice screams at her from all directions.

Ready in her battle stance, Lara turns around looking for what isn't there. A couple of kicks and jabs later, she is still not convinced she is safe. "Show yourself."

She is met by heavy silence.

Her foot slips, and she takes to the floor, collapsing face-down. She wants to stand her ground, but exhaustion is a persuasive mistress. The world seems to be moving all around her. Her heartbeat is slow and consistent, like the crashing of waves. It feels as though she is taking a vacation on a ship. The yaw and pitch movements rock her to sleep like a mother's loving arms.

She closes her eyes and imagines herself swimming through crisp water, following a map's directions. *There it is, in the Ocean of Tears, where The Pirate Queen knew it would be—the sunken treasure. She sank this ship four years ago and risked a battle against the legendary Leviathan. The water was much colder then, and she had much adventure in her eyes. Only now, The Pirate Queen is ready for retirement, either briefly or eternally. For she has caught the shipmate's disease, a sore-breeding illness which is incurable by modern* medicine or magic alike. When the end is in your sights, tying up loose ends is more important than starting anything new. Unfinished business is a spirit's curse. Many moons aboard a ghastly vessel has taught her that there is no joy in sticking around to haunt.

Not getting any healthier, she dives in headfirst, looking to reach the ocean floor before her air runs out. Each stroke pushes bubbles behind her as she heads towards the depths of the endless blue. This has always been a one-way trip, and if it weren't for her blight, she never would have risked the trek.

She is only halfway to her destination when her lungs run out of bubbles to exhaust. An octopus mocks her struggle by changing its color, reflecting her own image on his rubbery skin.

The depiction appears as though she is about to cry. That's not her, not how she is going to finalize her existence. Songs of terror are sung from the lips of land-dwelling kids across the three oceans.

The Pirate Queen takes his insult as a challenge. She swims even harder and faster, right through a shattered cannon hole of the old rotting ship. A couple of twists and turns in the underbelly of the wreckage, she finds the target of her desires. The very thing she gave up on living for—The Chest of a Thousand Kings. This treasure has started many wars throughout the centuries, and now she only gained possession of it by happenstance. It was quite easy to steal from Havo the Destroyer while he was busy destroying his lunch of pheasant with capers.

Once Havo found out he had been robbed by the infamous Pirate Queen, he baited the sea monster of infamy, the Leviathan. He did this by filling his vessel with the corpses of his recently departed crew members, who unwittingly drank the poison he snuck in their wine.

They should have known better. Havo was never generous with his food or drink. As if his pot belly and double chin weren't evidence enough, he was well known for his greedy nature.

The poison had a special condition where you get an endless bloody nose. Well, that isn't entirely true. There was an end. It is called death. Their blood striped the sea with a trail straight to The Pirate Queen.

Before the sea monster could claim two ships to its hungry maw, she undertook an act *of desperation. Leaving nothing to chance, she sank her own ship by pointing a blast cannon down, directly at the hull. Being a loner, and having a crew of one, casualties were strictly sentimental. Her ship was family to her. Only now, like her real family, it was dead—killed by treason.*

After drinking her potion of extreme swimming, she swam to the island of Nore, which only the plank people used to walk off of, acting as the flotation device for her salvation.

But that was then. This is now. She had only one regret—not claiming the prize that resulted in her single defeat. Slaying this regret is crucial for a successful afterlife.

She barely makes it to the heavy iron chest. With no key, she is forced to use her mighty fists to bash open the lock. As her bloody knuckles flavor the water around her for nearby sharks, the lock is successfully broken open by her efforts.

She slowly opens the heavy lid, revealing the contents inside. It is empty—just a bubble holding its shape.

Plunging her face inside the sphere, she takes air into her system. It feels heavenly pure, almost cleansing. How could this be? The most valuable treasure in the world and it's empty? The lock was secure. No one could have stolen it out from under her.

She then realizes the magic that was held deep within the old box is real after all. What would be the most value thing this world has to offer? Is it riches or other shiny things? None of those materialistic things can be taken with you in the afterlife.

The most valuable thing in the world is something that you can never get enough of, and everyone is always trying to rob you of it. It's...life. And deep under the ocean, the chest gave her exactly what she needed, air. As if a sign from an angel.

She glances at her arm. The incurable sore that had been festering away at her body has been resolved and no longer plagues her.

This treasure did not disappoint. It has saved her twice now. The bubble around her head starts to contract with every breath she takes. She knows what she has to do now—she has to live!

Breathing in the rest of the magical bubble, she proceeds to swim upward, following her ship's anchor chain for directions.

Much faster than it took her to reach the

ocean floor, she is topside. A large wave hits her directly in the face and pushes her down again. She takes a gulp of water. It tastes wonderful and quenches her desire to do anything else. She abandons all the air she just acquired and keeps on drinking from the crystal-clear ocean. This will be the end of her, though she is happy to taste life again. This is the dreaded curse of the Ocean of Tears—one small taste and your family will be grieving your demise.

Lara wakes up drinking water off the ground as it trickles into the cracked soil underneath her face. She is not The Pirate Queen. She never was. It was a wonderful dream, and though tragic, she didn't want it to end.

Another huge wave of water splashes upon her head. She scrambles to drink as much as she can before it descends into the ground. It's muddy and chalky and tastes...wonderful.

"Get up, if you can," a raspy voice commands, almost hostile.

The light is blinding. All she can make out is the shadow of a humanoid holding a container she imagines as The Chest of a Thousand Kings—a bucket.

Land of Humans

The cool water is quick to evaporate off Lara's lethargic body. Heat radiating against the moisture in the air creates a haze in her vision. She staggers to her feet, wondering if this is all a mirage or not.

"What are you doing all the way out here, little one?" the scratchy voice says, this time sounding far less threatening.

Swaying back and forth, Lara is busy trying to piece together the blurry shape of the short male standing in front of her. Is he a worthy combatant—a gladiator, or champion of some sort? He doesn't possess the physical form to pose a serious threat, but one should never judge a fight at first glance. The young feathered-folk knows this all too well from her frequent run-ins with invading forces and how they always underestimate her ability.

"Do you understand me?" He cracks his knuckles nervously as he paces back and forth, almost matching her movements. "Can you speak?" Getting no response, he waves his hand across her vision, testing her sight.

Lara flinches at his gesture, shooing it away, annoyed. Her head is pounding, each movement trying her patience. She may be standing, but not everything is exactly awake yet. "Are you a man...a hu-man?" her raspy voice grinds out a dry response.

"Grand. It seems as though you can and do. Look, I am in a pinch of a hurry, and if you're going to be okay on your own, I must bid you farewell."

Puzzled by the lack of interest in her, Lara clears her throat, preparing to indulge her inquisitive mind. Her eyes travel down his side to the object he is holding, "The Bucket of a Thousand Kings."

"I must admit, I don't know anything about that. It sounds...fake. Let me tell you about something real. Back in Scutter's Landing, I saw a toothless tiger, which only tells one truth—it's hungry." The man conceals his laughter behind his hand, but his jiggling shoulders give it away all too well.

Unamused, Lara hobbles over to the man and leans on his shoulder, forgetting her duty to eliminate his race. Even though this is not exactly her domain, it's still the forest, technically. This is not the time to worry about duty. She starts to palm at his clothes, desperately searching for more sustaining liquid. Logic and rationality are lost to her in this moment.

"What are you looking for? I haven't any coinage. You're ripping it," the man says uneasily, forcing her hands off his clothing with a shove.

"Liquid..."

"Oh, you want some more water? Why didn't you just say so? I have plenty."

She looks up at him innocently with lost eyes.

Offering his body as a crutch, the stocky human helps her over to his cart, which is shaped like a boat. It is filled to the brim with crisp, clear liquid. She knows that watercrafts have to be watertight in order to float, but she never imagined someone using the treatment in reverse—to keep water in.

"You can have some. Just be…"

Hand over hand, she shovels it into her mouth, forgetting to breathe. With each scoop, she starts to feel her body become softer, like a sponge taking in moisture. Not until she tasted the cool drink did she realize how parched she really was.

"…sparing," the man concludes, adding a sigh.

Water is splashing and crashing against the inside of the boat, causing it to go everywhere.

"Hey there, slow it down a bit. You just might choke yourself trying to live," the man observes loudly.

Ignoring his warning, she continues slurping out of her palm, one after another after another.

"I really must be on my way. Take some for the road if you must, but do it *quickly*," the man interrupts, shaking her ever so slightly.

He got her attention alright. Her heavy gaze causes him to retract his hand, as if he touched something hot and dangerous. It is quite observant on his part, for she is starting to feel more normal, more like herself. Her look of daggers is more than enough warning to send him creeping backwards, planning an escape.

With a steady stream of water dribbling down her chin, Lara remembers her water pouch and dunks it into the vat, before he has a chance to rescind his offer. Bubbles escape to the surface. She licks her lips, indulging in the life-giving substance.

Her face turns soft and innocent once more. "Thank you for your generosity," she says begrudgingly. It is strange for her to pay tribute to a creature that she thought could only ever help her by dying fast.

"No thanks are necessary. It was my pleasure to share my wares with you. It served a mutual exchange. I should be the one thanking you."

Lara looks at him curiously. "What do you mean by 'mutual exchange'?"

"Before I came across you, I wasn't sure if these water droplets were tainted or not. You seem well enough as any. And now I can sell them at a premium rate. So don't take too much, just enough to get you on your way," the water salesman says offhandedly.

"Are you taunting me?"

"Oh, don't get cross. There wasn't any real danger—not any more than you were already in. If the water was deadly, you would have died with it *or* without it. Lucky for you it wasn't, and now you're alive." The man clasps his hands together in a joyous sort of way; although Lara finds nothing joyful about his statement. It just reaffirms her core beliefs about their race—that they are deceitful, smelly nothings who mess everything up. *If it weren't for a human, I wouldn't be in this mess*, she reasons, hoping to convince herself into a fight. *He is just one more obstacle I have to kill in order to save master—nothing more, nothing less. I doubt he will be too happy about it—dying, that is.*

Lara starts to play devil's advocate against herself. *Well, he should have lied to me about the water. What did he have to gain from telling me that he was trying to kill me? A big "thank you"?*

Back and forth, she debates with herself casually. Not like the stakes are weighing on someone's life or anything.

They take a beat staring each other down. Both are wondering who's going to act first—push the hand of fate that is resting on both of their shoulders. Most importantly, they wait to see who is going to be friendly and who's not.

And for the first time since making her

acquaintance, the man's incessant fidgeting stops cold like a corpse in the calmness of the moment. His eyes cannot hide their nervousness as they dart back and forth.

It's hard for Lara to think of anything other than shoving his scruffy human head under water until his movements become forever still. If he weren't sweating so much from his brow, she might have done just that in the heat of her debate. The thought of souring the taste of his wares seemed reckless.

Recklessness is something that she's working on ridding herself of. Many lectures and arguments have started from such behavior. She takes a moment to reflect upon them fondly. Like the time her master caught her mixing potions in the kitchen, and she melted all of their ceramic pots. Cooking got a lot harder that day, and her ears ring remembering her master's wrath. Though she does appreciate the lack of scolding, she misses her master—judgments and all.

This man, on the other hand, she wouldn't miss him at all if he went missing. His crime is in his intent. He didn't save her out of good intentions or sympathy; he did it as an cruel experiment.

She has never met a human she didn't kill, and letting this one go will assuredly ruin her streak. Not that anyone other than herself is keeping track. Like it or not, principles are principles. If someone is without moral rule or a code of living, havoc runs rampant. Killing him will not keep her up at night. Ending him would mean that she could take his surplus of seemingly not poisoned water. This would ensure that dehydration isn't going to be an issue, though, carrying such a heavy container would slow her down considerably. In turn, she would have to ditch some of her extra weight—which points towards her weapons and inventions... *He did technically save my life, and that deed should not go unnoticed, human or not.*

The streak may already be broken, by letting the invaders get past her. Though technically, she never met them, so it still stands.

Lara is the first to yield, breaking the long silence, "Thanks anyway," she concedes, giving him the one thing she swore she would never give—humanity to a human. She tries her best to hide her disappointment, but the scrunching of her nose is a tell-tale sign.

"Well then, the trail ahead isn't getting any shorter," he says, picking up the handles of his cart.

She raises her hand and opens her mouth, intending to take back her niceties, but nothing comes out. It is as if the air swallows her words before she has a chance to say them.

With a friendly nod and a heavy heave, the man wheels away his boatload of water in the opposite direction she was previously heading. One of the wagon wheels has a flat spot, and she can't help but focus on the rough sound of his retreat.

Lara takes a breather until the man and his sloshy wagon are out of earshot. "What just happened?" She is dumbfounded by the whole encounter. After running through the incident a couple of times in her head, she chalks the whole thing up to bad water. "It must have been tainted after all. I would have killed him if I weren't under its mind-control effects. That's the only reasonable answer. The streak still stands." Her assertation couldn't be farther from the truth. Everything in this world has its place, even lies. Without them, she might have killed the human out of habit alone. Deep beyond her consciousness, she wants something different for herself, something more, and nothing new comes from doing more of the same.

Moments after the water salesman has vanished, Lara realizes that this human had no effect on her internal alarm. The aching feeling didn't get worse or better. It is still directing her onward. She wonders if it isn't as cut and dry as she had believed. Then a daunting thought covers her, like a net trapping a scared animal. What if the feeling has nothing to do with human invaders at all? What if it's merely her destiny beckoning her from inside, guiding her on fate's trail? Or, it could be the human god responding to her hand prayers. Either of these possibilities would mean that she has no control over anything, and this thought scares her more than an infinite number of night killers.

***

Following the trail in the direction from which the water salesman was leaving, Lara figures he came from somewhere, and maybe that place has a spot for her to rest her head before the moonlight comes out to play.

Stepping inside his tracks, she judges the total lack of discretion within his tread, though she capitalizes on this by hiding her own tracks inside his heavy boot prints and long cart tracks. His wide stride is often stopped by a rock or root snagging on the flat part of his wagon wheel. Many frustrated prints tell this tale, over and over again. It could have been avoided, that much Lara knows for sure. She cannot help but wonder "why." Was he too short to get a clear view over the boat? Too dumb to think of a solution? Or maybe too darn lazy to pay close attention? It could be any one of those, though Lara suspects it's a combination of all of them.

"If humans only knew what's good for them, they'd focus on what is in front of them and stop...wait. What's going on?" Lara interrupts herself with human-like attentiveness, in an ironic sort of way.

Even though these parts have been equally burned, there isn't much sign of it. Someone went to great lengths to clean up most of the wreckage. Nothing can be done about the cursed soil, but the presence of ash dust is nowhere to be found. The dead trees, charred shrubs, and singed rock have also been cleared away or cleaned up. The groomed landscape makes Lara feel almost free from the curse that embodies her, free from the decay that reminds her at every glance. It is empowering.

"Who would do such a thing, and why?" It seems like an extraordinary amount of effort without a probable cause. It is hard for her to fathom that just a short jaunt away, the landscape is shaped very differently—like a whole distinct kingdom.

After a good ten minutes admiring the sudden change of scenery, the answer smacks her in the face. It was there the whole time, though she was far too enamored to see it. "Because it's pleasing to the eyes."

One moment, she hates the humans for being lazy and greedy, not to mention smelly. The next, she hates them for being so beautifully stupid, and not at all practical—though still smelly.

The trail meanders into a larger, more traveled road. If it weren't for the heavy load of the cart, she might have lost the tracks and never made it to the crossroads town before her. "Welcome to Strangleweed," Lara reads the sign that greets her. This is her first time entering a town. Lara doesn't know what tactical approach she should take.

She sneaks into town, like a whisper of the wind, choking everything that gets close enough to hear her breath, leaving the rest in the safety of their ignorance. Of course, she could take the town. Killing each person as if she were a ghost—unseen and frightening. This seems like it would take a lot of time and effort to her, and frankly, she doesn't have the energy for it.

She quickly changes fantasy in her head. *The brash soldier-princess walks into this scourge of a human town like she owns the place, taking drink, food, and supplies without permission. Everyone hides their glances at the sight of her sword, which is made from the bones of her victims. A young fool approaches her. He takes his chances with the infamous champion, hoping to earn himself a glorious spot in a fable or a lute song. But just making his appearance known is reason enough for the princess to crush his head in her mighty grip.*

Lara suddenly abandons this fantasy. It feels more like a scene for winter. Today is much too hot for that type of violence. No one is ever scared of a sweaty villain, or hero, for that matter.

Dominance is always effortless. Perspiration is weakness.

The smart move is to ignore this place at all costs, but this young one is much too curious for smart moves. Cautiously she enters the town like a lost soul, not knowing if she will be greeted by the end of a spear or total awe due to the rarity of her race. Maybe they've never even heard of feathered-folk before. The possibilities are numerous, and the knot inside her stomach adds to her anxiety. As a precaution, she shoves her hand into her bag of tricks—ready for a fight or to cause a scene. Neither greeting is awaiting her. Either she is incredibly successful at a stealthy approach, or they have no concern about outsiders. There isn't even a guard patrolling the premise.

The structures seem foreign to her—they're sticking out of the ground for everyone to see. It is a stark contrast to the underground clefts she is so accustomed to, hidden in the earth. Unlike the castle, each building doesn't appear to have the quality or craftsmanship to stand the test of time. Rusty nails hold together rotting wood in a contest of deterioration. The wood seems to be losing the race.

"So, that's a shack. What a waste of effort." Lara can't help but think about how each plank was stolen from a defenseless tree. "And for what, temporary housing?" She is having trouble deciding what is worse, being burnt alive in an instant, agonizing death, or having pieces of your body nailed to each other so that fragile humans can live inside you. "Immolation over humiliation," she decides.

The dilapidated town was once a thriving operation. Empty horse stables and boarded-up shops and houses are evidence of a once larger population. There is even a courtyard where statues have obviously been removed. Just empty platforms remain, without anything worthy to honor or praise. Whatever happened to the forest had taken its toll on the humans as well. At least the ones in Strangleweed.

This must have served as an outpost for travelers. Holding her head up high, she plays the part of someone passing through. *I need supplies for my long journey...home for the human holidays.* Without knowing the purpose of anyone coming out to these parts, she has no idea what would constitute "supplies." *Perhaps a pie will suffice,* she decides, not knowing that it's an edible dessert. With this falsehood on the tip of her mind, she saunters around the town.

People are assuredly home, but she suspects that due to the blistering heat, they're not wandering around. Smoke and laughter escape the tavern adjacent to the supply depot. This must be where the whole town is currently . It must be a human's supper time. "That is where all the action is."

As she makes her way to the tavern, she smells a burning scent that instantly causes her mouth to water. Never has she associated the smell of fire or ash with that of food . The smoke is fresh, with a hint of glorious flavors, which her senses sample. She feels almost guilty for indulging in the aroma, knowing that a flame was certainty the cause.

When half-starved, your mind can perform feats of magic that may bend your moral compass and pride far enough to indulge in the hunger that consumes you, she recalls another one of her master's ramblings, which all of a sudden doesn't seem so far-fetched and actually quite accurate in her present state. She wipes some drool from her chin.

Standing at the wooden door of the tavern, Lara is met with a dilemma, enter with weapons drawn, or let the humans make the first move? She looks at her feet, which are standing on a floor sign. It reads, "Welcome, wayward traveler." She can't help but chuckle at how accurate the sign is, as it speaks to her.

She throws all caution aside and pushes open the heavy wooden door. It is the first time she has touched a tree that was dead but not burnt. It is solid—almost matching that of a soft stone—just like the living tree The Enchantress showed her. For reasons beyond her, she thought it would lose its strength in the afterlife and become brittle and flaky, just like humans did when they perished.

As the door swings wide open, the uproarious chatter from inside hits her like a wave—glasses clinking, outbursts of laughter, teeth ripping flesh from bone, loud slurping. All the while, a man in the corner tries to tune a stringed instrument. It is a competition of sounds that only gets louder by the minute. She covers her ears, taking it all in.

The room is lined with memorabilia of old. Items and artifacts are covering every section of the place, giving it a cluttered look. Old patchwork clothing, metal tools, and hand-drawn surveyor's maps are among some of the things on display. The ceiling displays old war flags with rips and tears from battles both lost and won. Unlike the many treasure rooms Lara has read about in human literature, these pieces are far from cared for, and judging by the rust alone, tossing all of this junk might actually bring this place up in value by allowing for more seating for patrons. In the establishment's defense, this looks to be the whole town, and even still it is only half full. More importantly, the room is filled with more humans than she has ever seen. Every man and woman is outfitted with a soldier's garb—leather mismatched with metal and a house sigil on their overlaying tabard. Even the bartender and waitress are dressed in like manner, although their attire is rife with food and oil stains. This is certainly not a spot for wayward travelers, unless you're traveling with a private army, which clearly this is.

Deep down, she had hoped to see elves and dwarves, maybe even a gnome or two. But this is indeed a human tavern, and she is the only non-human in the joint.

After a quick estimation, Lara knows she's severely outnumbered. Twenty to one, if a fight were to break out. Though the real question is this—could one even be avoided at this point?

Village of Broken Dreams

On instincts alone, Lara whips the two-pronged weapon off her back—ready for anything, though hoping for everything. Taking a defensive stance, her breath steadies, and her muscles are loose. This is the moment she has been training for her whole life; a fight of epic proportions. Except no one seems to care or notice her presence, even after arming herself with the slow-killing weapon.

Judging by the bustling barkeeps and wenches, it appears Lara's assumption is confirmed. This is most definitely a meal-time rush. The tavern staff are focused on serving drinks and collecting payments, and the patrons are too preoccupied with their food, drinks, and jovial conversations to pay her any mind. The customers are focused on consuming as much as they can as fast as they can.

After a beat of observing this circus, a thought comes to her. *Why aren't they checking if I want anything? I could eat some exotic human delicacy.* Lara's shoulders slouch as she peers into her sack for some human currency, of which she has none. She knew she was without, even before looking, but they don't know that. She could have riches beyond their wildest dragon's hoard. They are all just being prejudiced, or so she is convinced.

A bearded man carrying six mugs of drink, three in each hand, nearly bumps into her. Even he didn't notice her just standing there. Maybe she isn't drawing enough attention to herself, or perhaps it's the intoxicated state of the regulars. In either case, not a single set of eyes is upon her. Under normal circumstances, the last thing she would ever want is a human to take notice of her. This is different, however; she is on vacation and exempt from all responsibilities. Most wouldn't consider her quest a trip of luxury, but to her, it is exactly that—a sight-seeing treat, a concoction of business and pleasure, where business is death and pleasure is not dying.

They must not realize that this is a weapon. That's the only reasonable conclusion. This is one unforeseen outcome for her invention. When devising the armament, she only thought of the benefits of its application being unknown, not that there could be a detriment. She wonders how to make it look more menacing—adding decorative spikes, gems, or blades. Her eyes grow wide with excitement.

How does this make me any better than the human who had the flimsy blade? I don't want false glory. I need the real thing. Entrenched in thought, she starts to justify her situation with the excuse that her weapon can actually cause harm, unlike the human's decorative dagger.

Then she changes her changed mind again. *Why does it even matter? Having a discreet weapon could work to my advantage. Stop overthinking everything.*

The distraught folk slowly walks deeper among the humans. Each step smacks against the sticky stone floor. Claustrophobia sets in the farther she moves away from the only noticeable exit. She's like a mouse sneaking into a lion's mouth to steal some food from in between its teeth. Is it going to be worth it in the end? It's too late now. She is already in too deep. Saliva starts to pool inside her mouth as her nerves set in. She doesn't dare swallow. A superstitious notion that doing so will cause pandemonium to ensue at her expense. *Maintain composure. Everything is okay. No one needs to get hurt. You don't actually want to start something with these people. They are not your problem. Not yet, anyhow.*

With an overly exaggerated gesture from its fully drunk owner's hand, Lara almost gets hit with a half-drunk jug of mead. As a reflex, she knocks it to the floor, spilling the contents everywhere. "Hey, watch it!" she protests, looking herself over.

This is not the sort of place that is unknown to spills, but wasting drink is another thing entirely—or so she thinks. After the shock fades, Lara bites her lip and cringes, waiting for the clichéd, all-out human bar brawl to break out. *Here we go.*

Again, her actions go unnoticed. The folk feels like a specter haunting the local establishment, powerless to interact with anyone in a material form. However, the truth is a little more convenient and a little less intentional.

Her mind starts to spin a ghastly tale as she grips the hilt of her weapon tightly. *The ghost bride never got the happy ending her vows had promised, or even to seal them with a kiss. Revenge is the only comfort the spirit has now. In this phantasmal form, she is nothing more than an observer, a baby's breath, a child of silent screams. Her magical day was taken from her, and soon it will be her turn to indulge in the art of taking—one future at a time.*

To avoid another run-in with a belligerent human, Lara steps backwards until she bumps into something much larger than herself. Based on the way it teeters back and forth, it isn't a wall or solid object. Without much debate, she takes action. Spinning around on her heels, she is now face to face with an old grandfather clock.

The concept of keeping time isn't foreign to her, though it seems useless in her way of life. When the light is gone, it's night, and when the light returns, it is time to get to work. Everything in between is just chasing shadows through their day from sunrise to sunset.

The time tracker has beautiful inscriptions

and gears that move independently. *This must be witchcraft.* She looks behind it, thinking a person must be hiding back there somehow. There's nothing there but dirt and dust. Fascinated, she takes in its full design—first looking for the coo-coo bird, which it has none. For a couple of solid minutes, she palms through its hinged doors and parts until she learns its secrets. The magic isn't in the material, it's in the design. The inventor is the real wizard at play here. This sparks up her ingenuity for future creations. It's a real game changer. She only needs some time to process it all.

When the clock strikes the chime once, it will be time for killing. Two chimes, a shower of blood and gore. By the third chime, there will be no more. All the chatter slowly fades into the background as the ghost bride listens to the constant clicking of the pendulum. Until the chime grants her materialism, she must watch the humans only as a guest.

Getting into character, she glides to the end of the bar, as if drawn to it somehow. Each movement is slow and soft as she breezes past the busybodies. To a fly on the wall, it would appear as if she were operating in a different thread of time.

Her eyes follow the endless stacks of empty bottles behind the bar up to a centerpiece grandly displayed above them. It is a set of shell armor, adorned with dark feathers, perched below a pair of stone swords. These treasures are not worthless garbage like the rest of the human junk cluttering up the place. These are finely crafted works of art. These are feathered-folk relics. This discovery snaps her out of her internal story. *Why are they up there? What is the story behind them?*

She grabs the closest person in her vicinity—a moist man whose belly is escaping out of his short studded leather armor, making it utterly useless. "What in the hellscape is this?" she says, hoping that using their word "hell" might help her blend in, although she unknowingly used it incorrectly, letting on to her ruse.

The slob of a man tries to focus his eyes on the young folk. "Hey, how did you get down from there?" he says, pointing at the wall of artifacts, laughing at his own joke, not gauging his audience at all.

With that one interaction, she's back into character as the ghost bride hungry for revenge. *Do you, bride, take this opportunity to unleash your wrath upon this man? To cut and maim, through sickness and health, plundering riches from the weak, as long as they all shall breathe?* "I do," she says, smashing the man in the face with a hit from the hilt of her weapon. He drops to the ground like a stone, knocked out cold. He was a couple drinks away from this outcome, anyway.

The force of the impact causes the two prongs of her weapon to spin independently as she grips it tightly. A high-pitched noise rings out with each revolution. She can't stop it, not now, not when it has only just begun.

Finally, another human takes notice of her and bursts into laughter at the scene he just witnessed. "Jarl got smacked by a feather head!"

Lara can't think of a scenario where that statement isn't an insult. Sure, when you get slapped, you can always turn the other cheek, but that only hides the redness of your pain. Symbolically, this is no different. She imagines throwing her two-pronged fork deep into the funny man's fat, open mouth, ending his laughter forever through the two leaky holes.

She refrains, instead listening to the hum of her weapon. "What's that you say?" Lara whispers to her weapon. *The bride holds up the*

ghostly bouquet that she never got to throw on
that butcher of a day.

"Live longer, kill slower," she says in a hollow voice. Using her weapon as a bat, she swipes at a bottle of fruit wine abandoned on the bar. Her spinning weapon shatters the container into many glass-shard projectiles headed towards the laughing drunkard. Each rotation showers liquid and fragments everywhere. His uproarious laughter quickly turns into the gurgling sound of someone who just started the worst day of his life.

"He'll live...maybe," she says, narrowing her eyes.

This gets her the undivided attention she'd been craving. Like all audiences, they demand entertainment. It would be rude of her to not give them a performance to die for. Closing her eyes, she plays out the moment she created inside her mind. Her emotion feels real and pure. *You may kiss the bride.* Through pursed lips, she blows out a candle on the bar, dimming the windowless establishment.

Imaging herself floating, she slides through the spilled drink and glass towards a man reaching for a hand crossbow. With a swift sliding kick, she knocks the weapon down towards the man's crotch as he pulls the trigger, lodging the bolt deep into his nether regions. His screams are muffled by Lara shoving some of his loose-fitting tabard into his mouth.

"No one screamed when I was butchered. Not even my betrothed," she says still in character, feeling the rage as her own. *The look of horror on his face is the perfect flavor of the vengeance she craves.*

The less tipsy patrons are already making a run for their weaponry after witnessing her impromptu castration—a fate worse than death to some.

The first to act is a quite muscular fellow with his trusty broadsword. Among this overweight and overly intoxicated bunch, this man looks like the most dangerous one of the lot—at least the strongest. His weapon is heavy and huge. Lara can't even imagine dragging the thing, let alone wielding it properly. Secretly, in her dreams, a girl could get used to a weapon of that magnitude. It would be love at first fight.

Mr. Broadsword lifts the massive weapon, using his shoulder to carry the burden. It is apparent her dream is this guy's reality. He is the bravest of the bunch and the first to be made an example of.

Her betrothed stands with a smug grin upon his guilty face. He was priceless to her, though the price of his betrayal had already been paid. Trading true love for coin. What was the going rate for a soulmate these days? The exchange rate for revenge is simple, never vacillating with economic fluctuations—it is death, one for one.

Lara runs parallel to the bar, letting the stone ball at the end of her weapon's hilt rub against the wooden surface. The ball is attached to the inner section of the weapon, causing the prongs on the other end to spin faster with each step she takes. Heat from the friction radiates inside her palm.

The runaway bride runs away from her fears and towards everyone else's.

Along the way, Lara jabs, shoulders, and knocks over a couple of barstools that get in her way. She pushes humans left and right—most of whom are unaware of her presence—all the while, spewing nonsense. Or so this is how they perceive it. "Thank you for coming. No gifts are necessary. Raise your glass for the happy couple," she says while making her maneuvers. She meets the broadsword mid- swing as it soars through the air.

"It's kill o'clock!" she yells. Upon hearing the words leave her lips, she instantly regrets not saying "'till death do us part" or something along those dramatic lines. *If anyone laughs, I'll just have to take their ears.* If she terrorizes anyone who points out her embarrassment, it will give them something far more horrifying to talk about than some cheesy line. That is her logic, anyhow.

Clashing with the broadsword, she positions his blade right between her spinning prongs. This triggers a clutch mechanism, which causes his weapon to jerk hard, snapping all of the bones inside both his wrists with a loud series of cracks.

The heavy broadsword divorces from his grasp and falls to the ground with a large clank. The pitch and tone remind her of a wedding bell after a union of matrimony. The price of retribution is paid. No ring will fit his crippled hands, not ever again.

Silence falls over the room, as everyone stares at her in stilted horror, which she mistakes for glorified awe. They are all starting to feel the same way Lara initially did when she made her entrance—lost, scared and wondering if death is near.

Absentmindedly, her body is swaying back and forth, as if she were under water, being pushed by the current.

"Get it!" some human yells after getting pushed on its back.

"It?" she scoffs when the words finally register. "I am not an object, a thing to wag a finger at. I am *the*."

A man dual-wielding daggers looks at her inquisitively.

Without missing a beat, Lara continues her assault. "*The* one who did this," she says parrying one dagger, knocking it to the ceiling, while kneeing the other dagger into the owner's own chin.

"And...this." Swinging her spinning weapon around, she disarms a couple of men who are prodding at her. The cracking sounds of both bone and wood are hard to differentiate. The pitiful groans are music to her ears.

"I am *the* thing that will keep you awake at night, *the* thing you all whisper about, *the* source of all your fears and failures. I am *the* reason for your downfall," she rants while fighting back the horde of drunken humans.

Their hearts are not really in this fight. They all seem confused by the whole ordeal. By trade, they're soldiers, but they are off duty. It's their vacation time. You see, the humans have a similar attitude toward leisure as Lara does. Though currently, she isn't exactly acting like she is in vacation mode.

"What the..." a shocked man says.

"Exactly," Lara says, slapping a fork out of the dumbfounded man's hand. She then pats him on the back in a friendly sort of way.

"It is a feathered-folk," someone breaks the cold chill of the ominous silence.

Upon hearing those words, she breaks off her attack. Her chest heaves up and down as it tries to catch up with her actions. The spinning weapon slowly rotates, mimicking her exhaustion.

"Nonsense. They all burned," another man says in horror.

"The thing must be a ghost."

Though she knew she was fully immersed in her character, her acting must be even better than she thinks.

Guilt is starting to consume her, as she witnesses all the wounded people grasping at their injuries. Before meeting The Enchantress, this feeling had never really manifested itself before. *I did this? I must be a...* but before she can give in to her own doubt, she answers the voice from the crowd, "No, I'm just a lonely bone collector with a very low inventory." Lara needs a new fantasy to mask her feelings on the matter, and she likes this fantasy much better than the botched wedding.

She runs the ball of her weapon along the length of the fallen broadsword, which is propped up from someone trying to claim it. They're having the same lack-of-strength issue Lara feared she would trying to wield the beast.

Starting up the rotating prongs, the buzzing sound of war fills her ears once again. She laced the inner workings of her weapon with a lubricant that gets slipperier when applied to friction, which her weapon capitalizes on. It's the true magic of its design.

She holds her weapon near another candle, and the wind from its movements quickly blows out the flame.

As though time suddenly started up again, chaos ensues. *Every human in the dimly lit room scatters like a mound of confused ants after being invaded. Some flex their mandibles, looking to become the next hero. Others aim to run back for reinforcements for the queen. It doesn't matter what they plan to do,*

*the collector is going to slowly exterminate
them all. Her customers are depending on her
to.*

With the prongs spinning overhead, she gets
to work. Her weapon has a high impact and
even higher dose of pain. In other words, it hits
hard. The spinning makes it difficult to change
from a vertical to horizontal position, due to the
gyroscopic effect when switching the axis. Her
face is careful to not reveal her struggle. Hours
of practicing with the toy is proving useful in
this fight. The sound it makes lets her know
where in the rotation the prongs are. None of it
is by chance. Its hum is speaking to her through
a tiny diamond stone she embedded inside the
inner workings.

Cornered near the far side of the wall, she is
met with daggers, polearms, axes, maces, and
any other human-made weapons they have at
their disposal. Completely focused, she parries,
blocks, and breaks the hands, blades, and some
weaker-made weapons of every attack that
comes her way. One blade is loose and spins out
of control. She ducks underneath it, feeling its
sharpness give her a slight feather trim. She
never thought someone might let go of their
weapon in lieu of getting their wrist broken.

Not seeing where it went, she hears a yowl from someone behind her. Suddenly, she wishes she had that shell armor on the wall, although it most likely wouldn't fit her small frame.

Some of the humans execute their attacks with trained form, only no training has prepared them for this style of fighting. It is almost like she is taunting them with her toy, a sick game where no one is told the rules. That's because they're in her head, playing out within her fantasy. Entrenched in her own imaginings, she sees them all as skeletons, no longer human. This makes hurting them even easier than the bride story and easier still than the renegade story she created for the invader.

The gleam in her eyes is the scariest part of it all. The vacant look shows how unhinged and detached she is from the brutality unfolding in front of her. She is too young to witness this carnage—or so a bar wench whispers to herself.

A large skeleton man swings its unwieldy polearms clumsily. Lara knows these weapons are not made for close-range attacks and chooses to ignore them altogether, letting each poorly calculated attack land upon one of its less fortunate colleagues. In such a close, confined place, each missed attack means a hit on another unsuspecting human, or skeleton as she now sees them.

Lara couldn't have planned a better scenario for herself, especially how many drinks they had consumed before she got there. Unbeknownst to Lara, today is the last day of the month—a ritual day of rest for humans in these parts. It is a monthly holiday that actually incites much hard work for the days to follow, as they prepare for the next month's festivities and drunken gallivants.

"I can do this myself. I don't need your help," Lara scoffs at their foolery, as another one gets a belly full of his compatriot's spear. "An untrained warrior is worth more dead than making a mockery of honor," she recites a passage from The Manual of Execution. There is some truth in that statement, even if she said it as a taunt. Somewhere deep inside her young mind, she wants to teach them a thing or two about the art of war. Life isn't about winning or losing; it's about going through the motions of battle. Each swing, parry, and lunge is a statement about yourself and your self-worth. Learning is done through experiences, good or bad. You only have to be willing to see the clues and endure the scars that bear witness to your acts. Wounds heal, feelings fade, treasures tarnish, but a legend lives on forever in the minds of admirers and fanatics. But this is not the time or the place, and these are not the pupils for such lessons.

"The thing feels no pain!" an onlooker yells.

"If you really want to get me, you have to stop moving so sluggishly. Is that armor really helping you, or is it hindering your speed?" Lara ask, genuinely wanting an answer as she jams a skeleton's breastplate upward, blinding him temporarily, before she follows it up with a leg sweep.

She moves like the tide brushing up against the sand, back and forth with grace and beauty. They can't catch her any more than they can catch water with an open hand. As each injured combatant goes down, Lara stands triumphantly on them, gaining higher ground for the next pursuer. They are piling up fast in a chorus of groans.

A red-faced man knocks over a barstool, using it as an impromptu shield. He has both hands on the legs, poking and prodding at her without a free hand to arm himself with something sharp.

Lara can't help but think about how this

attack isn't exactly planned out. His act has her perplexed for a moment. *Is this a distraction? A desperate grasp for survival? If he does manage to block my attack, then what? Could it be part of a larger, more sophisticated plan? A trap, maybe?* If so, she couldn't let it go to waste. She believes wholeheartedly that all good traps should be sprung to test their execution—partially out of curiosity, but mostly out of respect for the forethought that went into them.

"Blocking will only delay the outcome. Unless you have a fierce riposte up your sleeves, and I don't see any sleeves." Lara thinks about it for a beat and shrugs. "Let's see what you've got," she says as she jams her spinning terror straight into the wooden seat. Swiping with her other hand against the ball, splinters are flying everywhere.

The weapon drills a hole right through the shield as if it were nothing. Upon seeing the rotating prongs reach the other side of the stool, the human lets go of its shield and abandons the fight.

That was unexpected. Before Lara can educate the shield guy on proper reposts, he is already making his way towards the exit, fleeing for his life. He isn't the only one hopping aboard the retreat train. This proves that he had no course of action beyond blocking her attack, which he utterly failed at.

The plank spins around with the weapon as one. It's almost too heavy for her to hold. Her hands vibrate roughly with the uneven rotation, almost losing her grip on the thing.

Out of nowhere, she spies an axe flying straight for her. Luckily, she uses her newly acquired spinning shield to block the descending weapon, stopping the axe from splitting her head wide open. Wooden bits of the barstool fly through the air and smash against the wall. The debris sounds like rain as it comes down.

She looks up to see who the owner of the renegade axe is, but no one is there. There is only a ducking coward where the axe thrower should be standing.

Then an arrow whizzes across her face, nearly taking off her nose. Looking back, she notices the arrow hit the fleeing shield holder in the shoulder. This is yet another event of fortune that has been bestowed upon Lara in this fight.

The ducking human isn't a coward after all, he is clever—trying not to make an introduction with a loose arrow.

If it weren't for the human ducking, her head wouldn't have been turned down, the shot would have been dead-on, and she might have lost her sense of smell altogether.

Luck is a coincidence that you should pay tribute to out of superstition. Lara is no stranger to this concept and knocks over a mug of bubbly liquid as thanks to the power. True or not, she is in no position to tempt it.

Standing on top of a barstool, the scrawny bowman appears too young to sprout any facial hair. Instead of reloading his next shot, he slams down his fist in frustration. A gesture of inexperience. No one can land all of their hits, even Lara knows this.

A sudden seriousness washes over the feathered-folk as her attention fixates on the human with the bow.

Noticing that she notices him brings a terrified look upon his face.

"Should have practiced your shot more. There is no excuse for laziness. But this is a lesson I am sure you'll never forget—missing by a nose," Lara scoffs at the closeness of his shot.

Living with her master, Lara doesn't think of age as anything special or detrimental like the humans do. This smooth-faced kid is just as capable of killing her as she him. His last shot alone is testament to this fact.

Like a dog, hungry to fetch a treat, the bone collector advances to claim her prize, burying her fears deep inside herself.

As she dodges and weaves through the crowd, the bowman lets loose another arrow. Lara blocks it with her spinning prongs, snapping it clean in half. Now that she's ready for him, he has nothing on her. His life is worth only a few more moments, as she flashes towards him like a vengeful bolt of lightning.

If they were outside, the boy could pull back his bow to its maximum reach and fire a much faster arrow, one that the young feathered-folk assassin couldn't easily block. This is just another advantage, luck or whatever you would call it, that is on her side today.

Without missing a beat, she snatches up another bottle for tribute. She pours out its contents, leaving a trail behind her like a fate harbingering snail.

All the bowman had was the element of surprise, and he blew that when he missed his shot. Now it is her turn, and she hardly ever misses. At least, she never leaves anyone alive to attest to her mistakes, if any have been made.

Even from across the way, she can see the fear in his trembling lips as he frantically pulls a third arrow from his quiver.

Making her way to him, she disarms a barman with a snap of his wrist—catching his skinning knife before it hits the ground. It is not a weapon for killing, unless you plan on killing someone slowly by stealing their skin. Even though Lara is trying to slow this fight down some, this is not what she has in mind.

This time the bowman pulls back as far as he can, knocking a patron in the head with his elbow. He has the same idea Lara came up with and is hoping his next shot will be unblockable and fatal.

"Don't be so predictable. I'm already steps ahead of you," Lara says, with an underhanded toss of the dagger. Anything more than a surreptitious throw would have alerted the bowman and caused him to fire his arrow sooner. A dagger would never win a race with an archer's arrow. But her words distract him just long enough for the knife to reach him in time to cut the bow's string as he releases his final shot.

The top limb of the bow snaps violently in

the air, and the arrow is lost in the kerfuffle, a much wider shot, missing her by a great margin. He loses all balance and falls off the stool. With his hands tangled up with his weapon, he is unable to brace his fall. With a loud crunch, he smashes his face on the way down.

Forgetting about her fantasy, she winces, recovering the ruse. Without missing a beat, she is back within her fantasy.

Images of flying skeleton bones manifest in her mind, covering up the real damage that has transpired. "Don't think, just act. That's what my master always used to say to me," she says, taking advantage of this teachable moment. If only her master were able to hear her.

Yes, her attack was dirty, but it proved to be enough. In the end, death isn't pretty or clean, but it is final.

She moves gracefully, like a dancer, keeping rhythm with the pain that follows her destruction. Most of her attacks are defensive and take advantage of a miscalculated strike or an off-balance assault.

One by one, she disarms each "skeletal warrior," with a broken wrist or a shattered finger, depending on their weapon and the type of grip they use.

The bone collector had to shatter enough marrow to appease her skeleton god. Only by offering a giant's worth of shards will her maker be able to re-manifest. Each snap, crack, or pop brings a euphoric smile to the young cultist's face. Evil cynicism is her game, and currently, she is 15 - 0 in her favor, with only five eligible combatants left.

Despite the fairy tales, humans prove to fancy self-pity and wallowing over heroism. Nearly all of them gave up on the fight once a bone, or four, broke, or after getting stabbed. Lara, on the other hand, doesn't even notice the couple bruises or scrapes that landed on her body. She just keeps on fighting with a frightening level of self-confidence. She is a great warrior, but no one is flawless.

The attacks become less and less, as the pile of humans crying out in pain amassed on the floor grows, until there is only one left—a man leaning against the wall, sharpening his sword. Thinking only of his own victory and not that of the rest of his compatriots, his smug look indicates a level of experience far above the rest of the lot.

"What are you waiting for?" Lara inquires with a smile.

"Just waiting for you to get finished with the riffraff." Unlike the rest of the bar patrons, he knows that there is an advantage to fighting the folk one-on-one and didn't opt to jump in the fray with the rest of the drunkards, to meet his own demise. He saw what happened in that mob. He would most likely get stabbed by one of his own, if he were to be that daring...and stupid.

"Don't you want to help out your friends here?" Lara looks at the pile of groans and cowardice at her feet. Either her math is off, or there are more than a few faking injuries to get out of harm's way.

"Drinking and fighting is a horrible combination. But you already knew that, didn't you?" The man pulls out a bottle of oil and pours it all over his blade.

"I suppose so. Aren't you at all curious as to why I'm here?"

"Nope. It's not my business."

"Then, what is your business, exactly?" Lara asks with genuine curious.

"Murder, mayhem, and revenge, but never my own. I kill for sport, and I bet right about now, these fine people are willing to pay up in abundance for your head."

"Sport? Do you mean like a game? I like games."

"You won't like this one," the man admits, lighting the oil on his blade, causing flames to ignite off of it.

This guy seems quite familiar to her. Under different circumstances, they might actually have a lot in common, what with murdering and all. Could it be destiny—the thing her internal alarm is guiding her to? If she is *the*, could he be *one?* Two verses in the same song? Are they together "The One"? Is this what she has been searching for, or is he just another one?

"What are the rules?" Lara responds to his threat with a gleeful twinkle in her eye.

"The last one to die, wins."

"Oh, I *do* know this one. It's my favorite."

A Fight to the Death

Smoke from the human's flaming sword fills the room. Tension rises as the injured cough and hack, still too worthless to even try to escape.

This human is different than the rest. This one might prove to be worthy of a swift death, though she is gauging his skill solely on his arrogance, which oozes off of him like an aura turned viscous.

Her bark-like skin has much less moisture inside it, giving each feathered-folk almost a natural armor. It is not without its downfall, though. Fire, smoke, and flames in general have a huge advantage against the feathered-folk. Lara and the man are both aware of this fact.

The smoke causes her eyes to burn and water. The burning smell is nauseating. She feels disoriented, and the room feels as though it is spinning. This situation is no longer ideal for her. This must be how the drunkards felt fighting against her, and it isn't fair or legendary. All she can do is crouch down low to avoid the thick cloud overhead.

"What's the matter? You don't look very good," her opponent says.

Lara tries to engage in pre-fight banter but ends up coughing instead. He has been studying her every move, and most likely her weapon is going to be quite useless against him—especially now that the prongs are almost completely bent to bits. Its rotation is off balance, and it wants to jar loose from her hand. *Do you have one last attack left in you, friend?* With a respectful nod, she tosses it at the sole window, giving the smoke an escape route.

"Go right ahead, try and squeeze through there," the challenger scoffs.

It isn't her intention to flee, but observing the shards surrounding the hole gives her the idea of jamming his fat head through that little hole.

Crouching low, she cannot help but look at

the aftermath of her actions. The floor is riddled with weapons—some broken, some merely damaged. She briefly gives them a once-over, but Lara ultimately decides to go along with her master's rule. An unarmed attack seems appropriate for this situation. In such a confined space, having a weapon is cumbersome, and the unarmed approach gives her the freedom to use her hands for other things.

Using the cloth from a table as a filter from the smoke, she wraps it around her like a scarf. Lara clenches her fists while racing toward him, trampling everything and everyone in her path to close the gap between them.

The man's swift, flaming swipes keep her at bay, but she remains right outside the reach of his weapon. "You're testing me. Very good," he comments. The mad grin on his face tells a tale of delight and excitement. He is enjoying this way too much.

Launching into the air, Lara grabs on to the elk horn chandelier. Holding her breath, she swings over his fiery blade and lands right next to him.

"If this is a test, you're a bad teacher," Lara taunts, but her muffled words fall on deaf ears.

He won't be distracted, as he is trying to be

the one who distracts. With a swift maneuver, he passes his gauntlet across his weapon's blade. It too is now on fire as he reaches for her.

"Oh, oops. What have I done? It seems that I've caught myself on fire."

This is no mistake. He has done this attack before. It is all part of his deception—lure her in and flame-punch or at least set her on fire.

She doesn't know why this plan aggravates her so. It was clever, that's for sure. A retreat is her only move. She rolls back beyond his sword's reach.

He snuffs out his hand before continuing the assault. Each flaming swipe comes at her faster than the last.

Suddenly all the patrons seem to be scattering to the corners of the room. *What a bunch of fakers,* she thinks to herself, almost letting the words escape her lips.

"Get back here!" the attacker demands, getting ready for his next strike as she makes another pass on the chandelier.

He nearly chops her down with his flaming blade, but she swings out of reach. If only genetics had made him a couple inches taller, he might have cut her down. With his weapon's flame lighting up his maniacal sheer, he starts to yell and carry on. He douses his weapon with more oil and holds it as high as he can, making the flame grow right into her.

Lara uses all her might to pull down on the chandelier, ripping it out of the ceiling. It crashes down on top of him, with her right behind it.

The antlers of the chandelier are quick to ignite.

The nimble folk tumbles on top of him, keeping some distance between her and the brutal flame.

One of the elk horns is stuck in his shoulder, and his hot, flaming sword is wedged between the chandelier and his armor, causing the armor to heat up quite fast.

"Aaaahhhhhh!"

Lara holds the antlers in place, unfazed by his screams of agony and kicking feet as the flaming sword heats up his armor like a cooking pan. Soon, his tabard, clothes and hair all catch on fire, but Lara holds her position. He is burning alive, and she stays with him the whole time. No fantasies this time, no crutches.

There are many moments in one's life where one does something and instantly regrets it, where obligation trumps all rational thought, and by the time you realize what is happening, it is too late. For Lara, this is one of those times. How did it come to this? Was it all really worth it? Were they so bad as to deserve her wrath? She never had to think about it before. It was always just what it was—part of life. As long as she can remember, she's been playing this game, never asking herself if her opponents were willing to play with her—or even if they were worth asking.

Something has changed in her since The Enchantress. It must be a spell or something far worse. Whatever the case, it makes her feel. And that hurts most of all.

It takes all of her strength to keep from going to that magical place inside her head. This is not fun anymore. Maybe it never was. Lara stares directly into his eyes until they turn cold and lifeless in front of her.

"You're right, I don't like this game," Lara says, wiping something from under her eye.

After a beat, she lets the moment fade. "Take everything and leave nothing in return," she quotes her master. She is no longer emotional. It's as if nothing just transpired.

"Damn it." Lara realizes that she may have cheated in the way in which she won this fight.

She wasn't exactly unarmed. She uses the chandelier as an improvised weapon. It was a necessity, she knows, but her master wouldn't have approved. She tries to rationalize with herself that it wasn't a weapon but more her way of using the surroundings to her advantage.

Right or wrong, intentional or not, it is quite important to her to sort it out. Going back and forth within her mind, she finally concedes that she had used the chandelier as a weapon, and it wasn't a fair way to end his life. "Why do I keep doing this? Stupid. Stupid."

Not that her master is watching her every move, though she dreads having to explain each fight in great detail, once things go back to normal.

"It's like, why can't she fight her own battles and not have to hound me for every excruciating detail. And if I leave anything out, I'm a liar and a deceiver," she says, suddenly realizing who she is complaining to—a room filled with slowly sobering humans.

This isn't what she had planned to do. In just a short while, she has destroyed this establishment, along with a handful of humans. The saddest part is that it wasn't even particularly difficult. From the get-go, she was toying with them, and the worst part is that she doesn't know why. Was it just for attention, or to prove that she could? Whatever the case, it wasn't worth it.

She leaves the attacker to smolder in his own weaponry.

Even as a victor, her master would have found fault with her methods. She could have torched the whole place, barricading everyone inside. "Well, I didn't think of that until now," she says to a cowering human.

Not being one for torture, she picks up from the ground a sobbing human, hoping he will sing like a bard. "You. What are you doing here?"

"Don't hurt me. Don't hurt me." Both hands protect his face completely.

"No one *has* hurt you," Lara says, noticing his unwounded state.

"I just want to enjoy the day, that's all."

He smells like alcohol and tears. Nothing is more sobering than life-and-death situations. "I won't hurt you, as long as you answer my questions to the best of your ability." Lara tries to pull him to his feet, but with his armor, he is much too heavy. "Can you just...manage to stand on your own?" she asks through frustrated teeth.

"Yes. Yes, I can do this." His eyes dance around the floor, never meeting hers.

"Okay, here is my first question. Are you ready?"

The blubbering man nods his head quickly, not wanting to anger the girl after seeing the carnage that just unfolded.

"Why is the town empty?"

He looks at her with a baffled expression.

"Besides this tavern…"

"This…um…is the day of respite. At the end of the month, all soldiers drink for free on this day as a reward for staying alive."

"Oh, great. I just ruined a bingeing holiday." Lara feels horrible that she interrupted the party with the very thing they are getting a break from. She truly is the fundle in this situation. "Now, for my next question. Who does this sigil belong to?" Lara asks, pulling at the image of an ugly-looking horse from his tabard.

"You mean, you don't know?"

"Would I be asking you if I did?"

"Sorry…sorry. I just thought if you were sent here for…slaughter, or something, you might know. That is all. No harm in thinking that."

The man starts sweating profusely.

"No. This is all a misunderstanding that I'm trying to clear up. Just answer the question...please." She forces out a pleasantry to try and hurry things along. His fear is really getting in the way at this juncture.

"It's the house of the duke. The donkey is his house's sigil. It represents his dumb luck. He employs us to make sure his trade shipments make their way to him safely."

"Where is he now?"

"At The Deep, of course. Uh...Castle Deep, if you're not from these parts."

"That castle down the way? Is that the one?"

"Yes. It's the only one in these parts—the only one I've seen outside the ten."

"The what? You know what, never mind. How did he put it there?" Lara asks pointing at the donkey sigil.

"I don't...understand."

"I am saying words that you don't understand?" She looks at him, confused.

Another human submissively chimes in, "When the forest burnt, the old lord was forced to sell off all his worldly belongings, including the castle. The old lord is the one who put it there, if that is what you're asking."

"I heard that its construction was a huge undertaking. That's how I heard the tale, anyway,"
another man says, grabbing a half-empty bottle
of mead and chugging it down, as if hoping to
gain some much needed courage.

"Why not? I guess we're all having a little
chat now," Lara says just under her breath.
"Why was he forced to sell? Debts?" Though
never having used money, or other human bar-
ter systems, she has read about them in her
books. If history is proof of their behavior,
every argument in human history stems from
either a woman or monetary gain of some fashion.

"I believe the old lord was in the logging in-
dustry. You cannot sell burnt trees; there just
ain't no market for it," another chimes in.

"I heard that their competitors did it," a
sweet voice says.

"That is absurd," the crowd responds.

More and more humans are coming out of
the woodwork and casually joining the conversation. It is surreal but also quite natural in a
strange sort of way.

"Now, let me ask you guys a more serious
question. Why does this establishment display
articles of folk?" Lara asks, pointing at the

items that first put her in a foul mood. "Is it some kind of joke? Or is it an omen or warning?"

"No, no, nothing like that. Those are just more items that the duke acquired through the auction of the estate. He displays this stuff to show respect for capitalizing on a dumb-luck situation. You should see the inside of the Deep. No disrespect, I assure you," the barkeep says from out of nowhere.

"I found it quite offensive. And...that is why I attacked. Yes."

All at once, the group of people sympathize with the folk's claim, even if it is clearly a lie. She doesn't want their sympathy. It only makes them seem less deserving of her punishment.

Lara climbs on top of the bar and gets a closer look at the folk armor display. There are no signs of contempt, other than parading their feathers like a headless deer—like some trophy. Maybe the man is telling the truth, and it is more a case of ignorance than disrespect.

"I'm taking these. Does anyone have a problem with that?" She reclaims the two curved stone swords from their mounts without waiting for a reply. They feel heavy in her hands as they fall to her sides.

She is met with silence and assumes that they are happy for her to take whatever will ensure her quick departure.

"One more thing. Has anyone seen my friend?"

The man she was previously interrogating shakes his head back and forth then quickly takes his spot hiding with the rest of the humans, hoping his answer doesn't displease her.

A quiet argument starts between two men in the corner of the tavern. Lara makes her way to them, with both swords drawn. "Am I interrupting something?"

"Go on, tell her what you told me," the stout one says.

"I told you that in confidence," the other retorts.

"Tell me what?" Lara demands, pointing one sword at each of them.

"Well, the other day, I saw someone who might be the person you're looking for."

"How can you be so sure? I haven't even described what they look like," Lara sharply replies, holding the edge of the stone blade to his neck.

"I don't mean to offend, but we don't get a lot of folk around these parts. Not since...you know…and well, I spotted two of them traveling with a third person."

"Two of them, like me? And a third what?"

"The girl and boy were both feathered-folk, and the third person they were traveling with was most likely a human male."

Lara doesn't realize she is scowling at him.

"At least I think he was. He seemed very odd, but I am sure of it. They looked to be friends, or at least companions."

Lara figures this to be a trap or a lie—possibly both. If there are more of her kind, she would have known about it. Although she didn't know about The Enchantress, but that was a fluke, she justifies. "Give me a reason not to kill you for lying to me. Choose your words wisely, because they may be your last."

The human gulps, the sword still pressed against his neck, "Hands. The girl folk was missing a hand." His eyes cringe as he awaits her response.

"One hand, or both hands?"

"Yes, yes. Both hands, you helped jog my memory some. A little too much drinking for me. That is all. Not lying or withholding any information or nothing."

That *was* her master. But why was she

traveling with a human? All Lara's life, she has been taught to distrust humans, in a more than just a mean sort of way. No one despised humans more than her master, and never in a hundred years would she travel with one, let alone help one out. Even though his tale sounds far-fetched, there is no denying that it was her master, because of her signature injury.

"I believe you, and you may live." Lara retracts her blade away from his body, giving him room to breathe and swallow. "In fact, I am feeling very generous. You all may live."

The crowd cheers and people start reaching for drinks. This is unreal. The place is still in shambles, but you wouldn't know it based on their cheerful responses.

"Wait. Wait. Hold on. It is not the time to celebrate yet," she yells to the crowd, preparing to ask her final question. "When exactly was this?"

"The other day...I mean, yesterday. Yes, I am sure of it."

"Where were they heading?"

"We didn't engage with them, but we chased them far to the northeast, out of this region and onward to the caverns."

"What kind of soldiers are you guys?"

"The low-paid kind?" a voice squeaks from the crowd, hoping she will take pity on them.

"Hmmm," Lara carefully makes her way to the exit, making sure she doesn't step on any more humans. Despite all her faults, she is a much better soldier than everyone in this entire room combined. If only her master could see the competition, then maybe, just maybe, she would appreciate her work for once. She killed slowly, got some information, and met a few reasonable people in the end—drunk, yes, but reasonable nevertheless. Then she remembers the antler chandelier incident, and her face turns sour for a moment. *Useless.*

Whereas the young folk is great at fighting, she's quite the opposite at diplomacy. She stands there in the doorway, wondering what to say to these people. Whatever is said will be remembered. There is a possibility that her words could be handed down for generations to come. Does she thank them for the information, or apologize for all the sprains and broken bones? Or should she keep the fear stoked like fire?

She pauses and turns over her shoulder, "Tell the donkey man that I will pay him a visit, soon enough...as a guest, not at all in the way of all this," Lara says observing the huge mess she has created from a mere misunderstanding.

When you're raised with war and fighting as the main topic of study, one might become a smidge of an overachiever, when it comes to the subject.

She is merely a day behind, Lara is determined to leave this crossroads town at once, though the fast-approaching darkness has another idea entirely.

Today has been a day of learning. First, she has a newly restored perspective on humans. They might not be as insignificant as insects, though they are still just as weak as them. Part of her regrets causing them any pain whatsoever. It's not really fair in a sportsmanly sort of way. The other part of her feels bad not disposing of them completely—sparing them from their miserable lives. It is her old ways competing with her new self. What is real? What should she believe? One thing is for sure, her eyes tell no lies. And even though it started out bad, something good happened in the tavern today. Something that she will need to make amends for and repay. But that is for another day. For tomorrow, she is going to find her master!

Reunion

After taking shelter from the moonlight for the night, Lara wakes up inside a closed-down building. Dust and dishevelment have taken over everything.

Awake and ready to continue her journey onward through the unfamiliar, she knows there's a lot of ground to cover if she plans on reaching her master during the daylight hours. Mentally she's ready to continue her journey, yet Lara's body is resisting her will.

"Why does everything hurt so much?" Stretching her stiff joints, something in her neck pops back in place with a snap.

What was exciting in the heat of battle seems unfortunate by the fresh air of morning. During the fight in the tavern, she was so entrenched in her fantastical glory that she didn't notice getting scratched, let alone injured. She's in much worse shape than she felt. Every muscle in her body aches, as if she had been placed on a torture rack. She may have overexerted herself a little.

It doesn't end there. Her wrists are swollen from holding the heavy stone blades, and both her hands feel tender from getting singed from the fire.

It is quite understandable. Holding someone down in a blazing inferno will do that sometimes. It was a first for her, however. Flames aren't something she is used to dealing with. Next time she will know to keep her distance.

Giving herself a once-over, there is something lodged in her side. Using a spare quill that she finds in the bottom of her sack, Lara digs at the hole in her skin—opening it up more to get whatever is inside...out. She deals with the immeasurable pain by going to a place inside her mind.

The folk mother peers down at the innocent

eyes that soothe her soul. Kindness is inherent in the young, while hatred is taught through ignorance and fear. To be brave is to let your guard down and face yourself. No assassination hurts quite as much as the one you do internally.

Without warning, a stranger barges into the cleft, unannounced, his mouth slack-jawed upon seeing the bare-breasted mother. Based on his expression alone, something isn't right, either before or after he entered the dwelling. Or possibly both. The fearless mother rises to her feet, careful not to disturb the sleeping child in her arms. Slowly she makes her way to the table, paying the intruder little mind.

Realizing his mistake, the folk turns on his heels, making a swift retreat.

Keeping the babe level, the mother uses her foot to hurl a stone longsword that is leaning against the table towards him. End over end it flies until it squarely pierces his back. He falls to the ground with a thud, and a gurgle of agony.

The babe stirs slightly, the mother looking down adoringly, petting its soft cheeks. With closed eyes, the baby flashes her a smile, and she returns the loving look.

With a sword lodged in his back, clawing and kicking, the man crawls at a snail's pace towards freedom. The mother is only slightly gaining on him, rocking her bundle back and forth.

She's light-footed and silent. With a swift kick, she steps on the wounded man's lower back and gingerly removes the blade cushioned between her elbow and side.

Stepping aside, she utilizes her chin to hold the hilt while she repositions herself so that she can wield the blade properly.

Rolling over, the folk is bleeding from this end as well. The sword went in deep.

He puts up his hands in defiance, scrambling to find his words. This is not how he envisioned meeting his end. It never was. But there is nothing more vicious than someone getting between a mother and her babe.

By any normal means, the mother looks so calm and happy, in contrast to her merciless actions. With a doe-eyed expression, she puts a silent finger up to her lips. "Shhhh."

The folk isn't sure if she is talking to him or the baby.

Then, while looking at her child and humming a soothing tune, she cleanly and quietly *hacks the intruder into pieces, without a peep out of the sleeping bundle in her arms.*

Lara falls out of her fantasy when her fingers discover what was embedded in her side—it's a tip of an arrow. She doesn't recall getting hit, where the rest of the projectile went, or how the shaft could have broken...none of it.

The evidence, however, is apparent. It did happen, and even if she doesn't remember, there's no excuse for it. She got hurt, and that was foolish. "Master dislikes fools. Oh, right, master."

Lara bandages up the hole with cactus skin. The needles hold the skin together like stitches. There are so many bruises covering her body, one might think that she has a rare disease.

Being around all these humans has really confused the feelings inside her. She can no longer pinpoint which direction she should be heading in. There is no rhyme or reason for it, but she must accept it as it is. There is so much that she doesn't understand. All the rules she once went by have been twisted upside down, as of late.

With a longing stare, she leaves the cross-roads during blacklit, the hour where neither moonlight nor sunlight are present.

On her way out, she hears the sounds of laughter and merriment coming from the tavern. "Injured or not, they really don't mess around when it comes to free booze."

Making her way into the deep blackness, she's trying to figure out what exactly to say to her master, knowing now that she's still alive. At least, as of a day ago, she was. Although, in the back of her mind, Lara never really doubted her master's safety. In all her years of training, she never saw her master fail at anything, especially a fight. Her armless predicament was the only evidence of any failure. So, it was possible.

She has so many questions about the lies her master has told her, that she is not sure where to start. Will she be upset with Lara for some unseen reason? The variables are too numerous to wrap her head around. She knows that if she overthinks it, her conversation will turn out awkward and not at all organic. However, it is hard to turn off your mind when you have nothing else to distract you.

An idea comes to her. The stone swords are much too heavy for her to wield effectively. Her sore wrists are a testament to that. Both swords have circular hilts, and if they were lighter, she might actually be able to twirl them around with some flourish. Judging by how they were crafted, she figures the weight is used to hack through bone. Though if she is unable to even strike someone with it, how can she expect to sever a limb?

To pass the time while traveling, she uses the edge of each blade to chip away at the other—making them both much slimmer. All this extra weight is unnecessary. Really, only one side of the once double-sided blade needs to remain sharp.

The idea of severing bone does excite Lara, however. After many different designs, she comes up with an alternative solution by boring a rectangular hole in one hilt, while carving out a square peg in the other.

She scrapes, chisels, and shapes the weapons until the fit in her hands is comfortable and secure. Pleased with herself, the young folk continues onward, pretending she is battling many imaginary enemies hiding inside her shadow as she walks—sound effects and all.

These are going to kill fast and hard. And she can't wait.

***

After walking more than half a day out of town, the young folk finds a couple sets of tracks out of nowhere. Much to her amazement, one set is irrefutably her master's. This is a huge break-through, mostly due to the fact that it is unlike her master to leave any traces of her comings or goings. It never happens, unless it's done for the purpose of being found. Which begs the question, why does she want Lara to find them? And if she does, it would mean that her appren-tice is making the right decision by going after her. But most importantly, it means she is get-ting close!

Excitement energizes Lara's feet as she takes off into a full-on sprint. She misses her master dreadfully, and her joyous smile and glassy eyes tell her secret.

Following the tracks, she makes her way to a cavern. It smells familiar, like the cave she hid out in, days earlier, with the wind dancers. This one, however, doesn't have any steep cliffs. In-stead, most of the stalactites and stalagmites have had their pointy ends filed off, giving the mouth of the cave a toothy look. It's easily walk-able for her, or anyone with two legs, for that matter. There is evidence that this place is well traveled. Once Lara enters the cave, her master's tracks blend in with years of traffic. Judging by the number of tracks alone, the cave must have existed even before the catastrophic events topside.

"This has to be it," Lara says, taking in a deep breath, "The end of the road, the final leg in the race." Her master is in there. She has to be.

With that thought rattling around in her mind, she hastily scales through the cavern, darting and bouncing back and forth through the moist tunnels with great agility. She only stops at intersections to leave an item from her stash in order to make sure that she isn't going in circles, or at least help guide her to get out of this place in a hurry—if the moment arises for such things. At first, she left broken quills or shards of the stone swords that she has saved. Now she's reduced to leaving things of more importance like empty vials and rock bits from her cloak. Moisture lines the walls making them slick and slimy, but where is it coming from?

She opens her sack and grabs two glow crystals. Rubbing them together illuminates a small area. These were once part of a larger stone, but through years of use, they've gotten smaller and smaller until they cracked into shards. She keeps them tucked in her palms to shelter the light from giving away her position. Opening her fingers slightly allows a beam of light to shine outward, helping guide her further into the underground depths. In a couple of intersections, she might be forced to travel in the dark once again and leave her light source as a marker.

Deeper in the cave, the air grows humid and feels thick. This doesn't slow her—nothing could. Her Master is holding on to all the truths, and she is the key to getting the answers to the questions that have been plaguing Lara for days.

Before this journey, Lara would accept her master's empty answers without any question. Even though it has only been a couple days, she has come so far since then—with herself, her confidence, and her wants.

Before having to sacrifice her other shoe to the intersection gods, the cave opens up to an underground lake, the source of all the moisture. Mouth agape, Lara stares into the rippling surface. This is worth more than if the cave were filled with precious gems. The dark water splashes and sloshes against the rock edge, echoing throughout the open hall.

This must be some kind of underwater spring, Lara gathers. Out of the hard stone, grey roots break through tiny cracks and dip into the lake for a taste. They look like withered old hands, straining to absorb all they can. Thicker roots splinter off into smaller offshoots and so on and so forth. Flashing her light source, Lara can see that the bottom of the lake is covered with the roots, giving the water the texture of a stone—or at least that's how it looks in the shallower areas.

Following the water's edge, Lara finds herself at a rickety, old dock. There are no signs of boats or anything of use, only old, rusty hooks and tangled twine strewn around. Standing on the floating wood gives her the feeling of freedom, as she finds the swaying motion soothing, coming from a land of perpetually stale air and motionless sand. She takes a moment to enjoy the simple pleasure, forgetting about her task at hand.

Watching the undulations of the water's surface makes her feel dizzy—bracing her hands on her knees. Never has she seen anything alive with so much movement. It is hypnotic. Part of her wonders if this is how the forest moved against the wind's guiding hand.

Snapping out of her daze, she kneels down to refill her empty water pouch, then recalls something the waterman said, "Poisonous water…" It was a new concept that she had never even thought of before the encounter. Squinting one eye, she leans in close, her nose almost touching a ripple of a wave. With a deep breath, she takes in the vapor from the surface into her lungs. Straightaway, she knows that there's something off about it. The scent is…sweet. As scrumptious as it smells, inside her gut Lara knows that this water is tainted somehow. It might be for the sole purpose of intensifying its flavor; that seems like a human thing to do. Most of the sweetest things this world has to offer often have the most brutal bite, herself included.

Information gleaned should never be taken for granted, she remembers another lesson. Before meeting the water salesman, she never thought water to be anything but pure and refreshing. In her defense, Lara rarely came across the stuff unless her master filtered it or Lara plundered it off a corpse. In either case, it was not in a natural state like this when it was found. It is a possibility that natural springs carry a different aroma and taste. She can't be too sure on this point, though.

However, there is never any uncertainty when something is made by your own hands—just another benefit to being a recluse and trusting no one.

Wiping sweat from her brow, she decides to leave the lake be. The risk far outweighs the reward. "It isn't going anywhere," Lara says, slightly louder than she anticipated. The end of her sentence speaks back to her, as it reflects off the surface walls and across the lake. Arming both her swords, her gaze darts between the bouncing sounds. Years of being a silent killer has robbed her of being able to play with echoes. The concept doesn't escape her; it's just a new experience for her.

"Hello?" she says, hoping to hear only her own voice speaking back to her. "Boo," she says slightly louder this time, intrigued with the effect. "Ba!" An innocent smile spreads across her face as she throws her voice to the air.

Moments later, the sound of an object smashing echoes back at her, almost like a reply.

That wasn't her doing. Someone is down here with her. Her face turns stone cold.

Leaving the dock and making her way over the embankment, she spies ash from torches lining the promenade—more signs of occupants.

Around the bend, she spots a rope bridge with wooden slats leading to a hole in the wall above the subterranean lake. She follows it slowly, step by step, as it sways back and forth reacting to her motion.

"Thank you for supporting me in your death," she says to the wood underneath her feet.

Lara climbs up into the hole. Inside, it branches out into smaller sections that appear to be rooms not naturally carved out by erosion. They are chiseled, square-shaped cavities. This is not the work of her people. They would never make nature bend to their own aims and desires. That's a human's way, or possibly a dwarf's.

Water marks indicate that this was once an underground river before being hollowed out. It must have fed into the lake below, though it appears to have long since dried up.

Keeping her back against the cavern wall, Lara makes her way deeper into the sections, fearing unstable ground or traps that might be strewn around. Soft yellow light pours out of an excavated opening. Entering a room, she spies a dozen or so metal cages. A vile stench radiates off of every surface, though it doesn't waft very far. It's an old smell from an ancient time of decay. It resembles defecation and rotting flesh.

The first cage she approaches is inhabited by a human-looking corpse. Something, or someone, must have put that person inside there, and in this moment, Lara hates that person with all her being. What a waste of meat, resources, and air—just rotting and wasting away. Without scavengers to clean up the mess, it may rot there indefinitely.

"Whoever said that the dead can't hurt you hasn't spent any time around corpses." The scent of decay wafts into her face as she passes by the putrid cage and on to the next. Instantly she regrets opening her mouth to speak. She pinches her nose and holds her breath until she is far enough away to feel that it's safe.

A couple empty cages later, she discovers a heaping pile of bones—some animal, some not. Judging by the freshness of the remains on top, this is obviously a storage area that has been visited recently.

There hasn't been a real animal sighting in the forgotten forest for longer than Lara can remember. They had to have been imported from elsewhere. That, or the pile might be much older than she will ever know.

Directly across from the mound of bones is a smaller crate. The crate's lid has been pried open, exposing rusty nails, and it is filled with circular fruit pits of some kind. They are about the size of her fists and all have a distinctive color to them. Casually, she picks one up and suddenly her internal alarm is back in full swing. She knows exactly which way she needs to go, because she is already here!

Out of the corner of her eye, Lara spies another room with small pieces of shredded fabric scattered on the ground. Creeping closer, she sees a figure slumped against the far wall. Based on the unique shadow it casts from the torchlight, Lara recognizes it immediately. It is none other than her master.

About Time

Without hesitation, Lara runs over to her fallen master, cradling her under her floppy neck. Based on the rise and fall of her chest, she is still breathing—just barely. Her master is in bad shape.

People live long but die fast. One minute they are there before you, then in an instant, they are gone forever—no more words left to be exchanged. Everything ever said is stuck as history, never to be queried, questioned, or clarified for better understanding. More importantly, whatever final words are spoken will remain a whisper you'll take with you into the afterlife—a memento to remember this life by. So, they better be worth every single syllable.

That is what Lara believes, anyway.

All of her animosity vanishes from this world, along with the questions she has rehearsed to grill her master on. Nothing matters anymore—not pride, not being right or wrong, or even the past. All that remains is life and living.

"Master, are you hurt?" she asks with her sweetest little voice, though the answer is obvious to her. Fiddling and fidgeting with her fingers, she eagerly waits to see if her master is up to the task of talking.

Her master's limp body doesn't respond. Scratches, cuts, and holes cover her. Rips all over her clothes and cracks throughout her armor reveal more injuries hidden than at first glance. Something has beaten her in battle, and that is a nearly impossible feat.

Lara force-feeds her master the remaining droplets of water she has in her pouch, not caring if it is the very last of it, more reckless behavior her master would undoubtedly scold her for. At least, this is what she is hoping for, anyway.

Seeing her master in such a poor state draws a lonely tear from her eye—liquid she can't afford to waste. Her wiping becomes constant now. What if her master sees her blubbering on like this? She needs to be strong, if not for herself, then for her master.

Upon tasting the water, her master's eyes flutter open slightly.

"What happened to you, Master? Who did this?"

"Keep...your weakness...hidden, dear child," her master manages to spit out the words, noticing Lara's grief.

This is no time for a lecture, but never before has Lara been so happy to hear one. "You're okay! I'm so sorry. It's all my fault. I..."

Her master raises her stump arm to Lara's lips. "Oh, my, you're not a child anymore. Look how grown you've become." She flashes a weak smile at her pupil.

Lara can't help but give herself a once-over. She gives a coy smile as if to say, "You mean me?"

Before now, Lara didn't feel any older, but briefly reflecting upon her adventure, she starts to believe that observation. It feels like a year's worth of experiences have been crammed into a couple of days, and it shows—enough for her master to take notice, anyway. "I've been through a lot, changed in so many ways. I wish

I could tell you everything. But...are you mad at me?"

"Everything is...okay. I knew you would clean up my mess. And here you are, just like I taught you."

"I'm not here to clean. I am here to save. You're going to live. Tell me who did this to you."

Her master's eyes start to doze off.

"Who? Just tell me." Lara gently taps her master's cheek, bringing her back to the present.

"The Lord of Cuts," she manages to get the words out.

"But, Master, your skill is unmatched. You cannot be bested by a single combatant. He must have cheated or tricked you somehow," Lara says, trying to bolster her confidence. Somehow, a naivety embodies her whenever she's around her role model. Old habits die hard.

Her master coughs out a fair bit of laughter. "I forgot how funny you are. He isn't the only one to ever get the better of me." She holds up both her stump arms and shrugs her shoulders weakly. "But with each failure, there is the gift of education. You remember that, sweet thing."

"Stop acting so nice to me. I messed up. I know that. You're mad at me! You have to give me a punishment so that I can make it all better, and I can't do that with you acting this way."

"I'm only hard on you because I care about you, not to motivate. It's what you would have wanted."

"I need motivation. I'm telling you what I want." A feud starts to brew inside her, but she presses it down. "I'm sorry, I'm…"

"I don't have enough words in me to explain it all to you. But…if you do as I say for once, it will all become clear—everything you ever wanted to know."

I want to know now… Lara's mouth lingers open as the endless questions hang on her lips.

"I shouldn't have come here, nor should you have. But what's done cannot be undone. We just have to make the best of it."

"Just give me direction. Tell me what to do."

Her master's breathing becomes slow and labored. "I don't want you to avenge me. There is a more important task I must ask of you."

"What else have I come all this way for but to fight?"

"To save us all." Her master swallows hard

before continuing. "The lord is immortal. He can be hurt...but not killed. Pain is useless without an end. Many great warriors have tried to put him to rest," her master says, giving Lara a grimace, "...and all have failed, including me." A thought forms inside her master's mind, which she finds humorous, and a quiet chuckle breaks loose.

In all the years they've spent together, Lara has never seen this side of her master. Either she was great at hiding it, or she's found euphoria this close to death's door. No matter the reason, it makes her feel uneasy. "What's so funny?"

An eerie smile forms on her master's face. "You're im...im...immortal too, in your own right. It is so simple."

"What do you mean, immortal? You never even told me how old I am. How can I be immortal?"

"Age? Now I know you've been...hanging out with humans. For our kind, age is nothing more than a feeling. So...ask yourself how old you feel, and that's your answer. To tell the truth, I, myself, feel quite ancient right now."

"Don't waste your words on me. Just tell me your plan."

"You're right. I've missed you." A burst of energy comes over her master, first lighting up her eyes and then continuing throughout her body. "There is a reason I hid you...from the night. It was to keep you as an adolescent. As long as you stay out of the moon's aging rays, you are immortal, in a sense. Ageless, as the humans would think of it—forever young and pure."

"Why? For what purpose?"

"To be the greatest weapon...to ever exist. In your child-like state, your mind is the perfect implement for learning complex routines with ease. This is when all folk peak, and I've kept you training at this level for more than eighteen years. I, too, was trained in this manner for just two years. That's my secret. I'm not a dedicated fighter...just groomed. You have surpassed me in every way, if you would only utilize yourself once in a while. This has been my plan all along, but you must continue to better yourself, if you can, until the world is yours for the taking. That is my gift to you."

Speechless, Lara tries to take it all in. This is a big piece of the puzzle. Her master invested so much into her success, sacrificing everything for the greatest weapon, as she put it, ever to live. Her protégé. Her bringer of death. Her daughter.

"Then let me take care of him for you. I promise, I won't let you down."

"The only promise I want...is that you won't fight the snop."

Tears of laughter well up in Lara's eyes upon hearing her master use an obscenity, though she blinks away the feeling. "Curses are a lazy way to wield your words," Lara quotes her master back to her. Secretly, she loves hearing her master curse. It is a moment she always wanted to share with her mentor, to laugh about life together as equals, as friends, and perhaps family, instead of the normal master and student. "Why else have you been training me, if not to fight this bully? I can win. You know I can. You said it yourself."

"Some battles are won by walking away. As long as I live, I forbid you to engage with him."

"But..."

"You have your whole life ahead of you. His is all behind him now—almost forgotten completely."

Lara can't help but clench her fist in frustration. "Okay, I promise." She doesn't want to pick a fight while her master is mortally wounded. It isn't fair, though nothing in life is. You take from others before they take from you first. And right now, it is taking everything she has to not break down. Strength is what she must exude in this moment.

"The lord is already old, and one day...he will die on his own. Patience will be your victory. It is the one thing you have that he doesn't...time."

"He must pay for what he did, though."

"Oh, but he does...with every moment he breathes, he does. Suffering in his own self. Judgment and death are a merciful end. One he doesn't deserve."

There is no way for her to respond to such a harsh truth. Her master's ploy goes far deeper than she had ever imagined. Not only is patience a weakness she struggles with, but she might have prematurely ruined her master's legacy. How much had the moonlight forced her to evolve? Was it too late for her to continue what was started? She can't simply ask her master to go into more detail without giving away her insolence. But if she had been more careful, she wouldn't have gotten here in the nick of time. "I won't let you down."

"You must..." Her master's head goes limp

and bumps against the hard stone wall—eyes rolling back in her head, showing the whites of them.

Lara slaps her mentor's cheeks, not as softly as before, but in a "you better wake up" sort of way—hoping to bring life back to her wrecked body. "Stay with me. Come on."

Without opening her eyes, her master manages a couple more words, "Help...my two companions escape with their...precious cargo. Don't...engage with them...or even share a glance. It's...important to be out of sight at all costs. Can you...do this last thing for me?"

"Why? Tell me, please?"

"Must you always...be so defiant?"

This is the master she remembers, so she still has some fight left in her. Lara knows that she just has to give her something to live for, something to fight for. Maybe she should tell her about her insubordination, but she quickly discounts the notion. *I haven't the time for games.* "Sorry, Master. I will heed your words to the letter."

Her master lets out a sigh and rests her head against the stone cutout behind her. That was a lot for her to explain in a short amount of time. "I am pr..."

"I'll be back. You can finish that thought in a bit." Lara rushes forward through the darkness.

How can she help someone without them knowing she's doing anything? It is a selfless act, and a near impossible feat of stealth. Especially down here, where it's a game of alcoves and shadows. But her master must have her reasons. And, like always, Lara isn't privy to them.

Walking deeper into the underground cemetery, it starts to turn into a maze of seemingly endless twist and turns. Her only map is internal, and it steers her true.

There is no way that Lara cannot overanalyze what her master has revealed. Immortal? Forever young? Some super weapon? It is hard to wrap her head around, but it also makes perfect sense. These revelations are the missing puzzle pieces that now revealing the big picture of her life. How old does she feel? That, in itself, is a doozy of a question. To accurately answer that, she might have to line up a bunch of human girls and point out whichever one looks like how she "feels."

Groping her way around the total darkness, she hears a shuffling sound in the distance as it echoes off the cold, hard walls. Words and whispers reverberate off surfaces, turning into an inaudible hum.

On the tips of her toes, she quickly moves in to eavesdrop on the action.

"It's no use. I can see your every move. It's only a matter of time," a raspy voice says, raw, like fingernails ripping through fabric.

With a voice like that, he must be the immortal, Lara deduces. She follows his echo instead of the feeling inside her, which is going haywire.

"I really thought, after hearing your friend's screams, you would have tried to rescue her. You are more of a coward than I thought," he taunts.

Hearing his words angers Lara to the point of full-on rage. *No revenge,* she repeats internally. Her master is resilient, and screaming is out of character. If true, he would have had to have caused immeasurable amounts of torture to make her react in such a way. It could be a lie, but he has no reason to. Whomever he is talking to was witness to it. They would know if he was.

If ever there was a moment for Lara to follow her master's will, this is it. No matter how hard it is for her to keep to the plan, she holds it together—proving that her age isn't the only part of her that has changed.

Bright light shining through the cavern ahead, Lara is almost upon them. No more lurking in the shadows, she has to face this threat head-on, but also from the back.

"I got you now," the immortal says eagerly.

Peeking around the corner, Lara sees a man hunched over, wearing tattered rags. White, stringy hair is sticking out in all directions. He drags a leg behind him and ambles around like some sort of undead thing. Light reflects brightly off his tattered cloak.

She hears a whisper from the other direction. "We're trapped."

"I know. What should we do?"

"This is the end. I'm going to face him."

"No, please."

Looking for something to throw, Lara is out of options and time. It's now or never. She opts for now, as always. Jumping out of the shadows, Lara makes her introduction to the immortal man.

The Immortal

"Over here, you gross piece of fundle snop!" Lara yells, voicing her true feelings aloud.

A wretched face turns to meet her with a hiss. It's the immortal, alright. It has to be.

The decrepit thing is wearing a cracked white mask. What's not hidden by the face covering is hideous and horrendous. She wishes the mask covered more, maybe even his whole body. He may be immortal, but he's not without wear and tear. If pain and evil have ever merged and manifested in a material form, it is standing before her now.

"No wonder you live in a cave. You're the worst-looking thing I've ever seen," Lara says brashly, not actually meaning it as a taunt.

The feeling in her stomach heightens as she sets eyes on him. She holds her gut, stopping herself from wrenching over. Really, she knows the feeling in her stomach isn't from a place of disgust, but she plays it off like it is, just the same. However her senses are guiding her, it doesn't like this guy, for good reason.

"And who might this baby be?" the immortal spits, shuffling closer to her. There is an eerie swagger to his stride—as if his torso is resting on top of independent legs.

"The keeper of beautiful things, and that means putting an end to whatever is wrong with you, which I am guessing is everything." *The keeper of beautiful things. I like that.* She starts to imagine herself as the goddess of the lake, then quickly she snaps herself out of it. *No, this is not a game. Not this time.*

"Oh, the youth always think themselves clever. As if they're the first to invent an insult before. I hate to dampen your spirits, but I've heard it all. Insults lose their sting when you accept them as truth. I know how I must look."

"And you don't care?"

"I don't."

"You really should. It's bad."

"Let's cut to the chase. Why are you here? Did I kill your parents or something? Oh, that's right, I killed all of your everything. If it had little leaves or feathers, that was my doing." He rolls his hand towards her with a slight bow.

Bridging the gap between them, he continues, "Mothers. Fathers. Friends. Neighbors. Chieftains."

She catches an aroma permeating off the immortal. It matches his look perfectly. It is the very stench that was covering the room of bones before. And here she thought it was the decay of the pile of bones, not the decay of this living person.

"...that about covers it, I think. Oh, and children." Without warning, he slashes at her with a concealed thin sword, built for finesse and skewering.

Lara dodges, but not completely out of its long reach. The tip grazes her. Grabbing at the stinging wound he left on her arm, she flashes him a wry smile.

Based on his slow moments, there was no way for Lara to predict his swiftness. Maybe he was conserving everything he had for that attack.

Would encouraging him to attack her more

drain whatever is keeping him alive? *I am not here for that. It is a rescue operation now.*

Going against her master's wishes, and in a sense herself, Lara pulls out her twin stone swords. Stepping backwards, she draws him in closer with the threat of a fight.

"Oh, you want to dance, little girl?"

"I never learned. Please teach me." Alternating wrists, she twirls the light stone swords with ease. From reading armory books, she knows his weapon all too well. Her blade will never match the light frame of his epee.

"I will do more than that." He slashes at her with three consecutive strikes. She almost doesn't see the first one coming, but manages to block all of them with a sweeping arc of her stone swords. It was sloppy but effective.

He is extremely fast and exact with his moves. Each one aimed to kill her in a single precise strike.

"Normally, I toy with my victims a little by slowing my blade's speed. Letting them think they have a chance. Unfortunately for you, I don't have time or the patience for such things."

"Great. I don't play games," she lies. Her hands are shaking for some reason. This has never happened before. Is it a pang of fear or dread? Whatever the case, it throws her off her game a bit. He might be able to kill her. He might be able to kill everyone.

"You fared well enough, a little lucky, but well. I figured you for a 'dead in one strike,' type but you lived through three. Congratulations."

"You haven't seen anything yet." Lara meets him with an array of attacks of her own.

Even against twice the number of blades, his defense is perfection.

She is in awe of his talent and technique—a masterful work of art, beautiful and clean. The exact opposite of his...everything else.

"Interesting." The immortal's frayed tongue sticks out of the corner of his mouth as he concentrates intently.

"I am sorry to interrupt, but do you know where the rest of your mask went? I am a little distracted."

"Now you're just flirting. You seem familiar to me. Have we met before?"

"I am afraid not. You have one of those un-forgettable qualities that sticks with you," *every night in your nightmares,* Lara says, leaving the last part in her thoughts.

Sparks light up the room from their clashing blades.

With each swing, the feathered-folk's muscles grow tired, whereas the immortal seems to gain momentum, like a rock rolling down a hill.

For all the killing she has done, she has finally met her match, and these two stone swords aren't going to be enough. She knows it, and so does he. So much for killing slowly.

"I don't stick with you, I stick *in* you." He finds a slight opening and takes it, skewering a hole through her rock cape.

Taking advantage of her opponent's sluggish bottom half, Lara distances herself from the fight in order to catch her breath. *I am too slow.* With a roll of her shoulder, she drops her cape to the ground.

"Is it nap time, sweetie?" the immortal chides.

Stabbing both her weapons in the ground, she bends down and touches her toes. "I just don't want to pull anything."

His slow stride quickens to a hobble as his thirst for pain grows exponentially. "Don't think that I don't know exactly what you're doing. Leading me away from your friends. It is predictable. The same move that cripple tried, and look where it left her. I can only assume you saw what I did to her, and what I will do to you."

The disgust she feels in this moment is hard to hide, but she manages. "You have to catch me first," Lara says, leading him down a dark corridor.

"I always win, one way or another."

"Not this time," Lara says, dancing slightly.

"I pine for your screams."

Where the immortal's hands are lightning fast, his walking is slow, and his witty retorts fall somewhere in between.

"You may be on a winning streak, but so am I. One of us is going to have to yield and accept a broken record." He starts to jam a different, thicker sword into the ground—using it like a walking stick, pulling himself closer to Lara.

This is unexpected. She has no idea where he got this new sword, but there it is, working its magic on the ground.

Her arrogance gets the better of her, and she strikes at him, thinking his downed blade has left him defenseless for the moment. Her blade stabs directly into his chest, straight through his heart.

Fundle. The one thing her master didn't want her to do, and she has done it without thinking. Her plan was only to taunt him away, not actually fight the icky thing. Before she can get too bent out of shape about her actions, she sees his true defense. He shows his blackened smile, seemingly unharmed by her attack.

Now it's his turn.

Luckily, she manages to intercept his riposte with his first sword. Or is it the new weapon, just different somehow? Everything is happening so fast, it's hard to discern what is up and what is down. It was a trap he set for her, and she fell right into it. Her block doesn't go without taking a bit of her, leaving a gash across her cheek.

"My cuts are contagious. Soon they will plague your whole body."

Those few thoughts were almost her undoing.

"Just a scratch," she says, wiping away a bead of blood.

He has feigned letting his guard down before. He does it like second nature. Faking injuries or not, he really might be immortal.

Lara pulls out her blade out of him just in time to miss his grabby hand. If he can't be hurt, grabbing her blade is a smart move on his part.

"Ha! I nearly had you there," he boasts.

He wasn't lying. That was a crucial mistake,

one she won't be making again. With a racing heart, Lara flees, faster this time, and without looking back.

The sound of his sinister glee is trailing behind her at every step.

They are both getting what they want. She is succeeding in leading him away from her master's companions, and he is striking the fear of a smiteful human God inside her.

Twisting and turning in the dark has currently gotten Lara lost inside this twisted maze. This time, she was too distracted to pay close attention to her steps.

She no longer hears her pursuer behind her. What if he found the two that she swore to her master she would protect? Either he was too slow, or she was too fast. If only she had kept a closer eye on him, as hard as it was.

Doubling back loudly, she tries to get him back on her trail, but he is nowhere to be seen. Her desperation grows with each passing moment. "Immortally hideous monster!" She calls out to him as a last-ditch effort to draw him in. "You're not a very good dance teacher." Step by step, she wanders through the darkness, but he is gone.

Distracted, she almost walks straight at the

owners of the hushed voices whom she saved. Hastily, she takes cover in an alcove. *Don't engage. Not even a glance.* She reminds herself of the importance of stealth.

"Who was that?" one voice whispers.

"I don't know, but they couldn't have come at a better time."

They weren't far. Lara can almost feel their breath as they pass by.

"I thought it was La..."

"Shhh. Did you hear that?"

"..."

"Let's go this way."

After a moment, they are gone.

That was close. Lara wonders what all that was about and if her master was exaggerating about letting them see her. It is possible they have some incurable disease. If that is the case, she may have caught it already, being so close to them as they brushed past her.

Her master never wants witnesses. She operates like a ghost, out of sight and definitely out of the bard's songs of glory. This is where they differ. Lara wants nothing more than to be revered by everyone for epic tales of heroism.

The companions aren't what you would call a stealthy bunch. Following them shouldn't be a hard task. If the immortal is following them, he will have to get past her first.

After a couple of minutes waiting to ambush him, she realizes that he isn't coming. She continues on in the opposite direction double time.

Without any idea as to where the immortal went, she manages to make her way back to the chamber where she left her master. This wasn't her target destination, but here she is, just the same. She looks over her shoulder, giving thought to the idea of going back into the labyrinth.

"Master, we have to leave right away. I did what you asked...sort of. I mean, they got away."

"I can't leave. It too late for me."

"What?" Lara is struggling to catch her breath. "What about the sacred place? We can make it there in time. So we can heal your wounds. I can bring you there straightaway. Let's go right now." She is referring to a secret garden where they would often go to recover from almost any injury.

Although her master used the site to heal her severed hands, it didn't make them grow back. Making it that far is a long shot, but it's the only shot she has left.

"I am sorry to say, it has all been used up."

"How? By whom?"

"I gifted it to the half folk...half human."

"The what? Are you serious? It was mine as much as it was yours. We worked so hard on that place. It was supposed to be used only in emergencies."

"It was...you would have wanted it this way. I promise you." Her master turns, exposing a large hole in her chest that Lara must have overlooked before. That isn't the only thing that is new. She's now sitting inside a pool of her own blood.

This is bad, much worse than before. The injuries Lara saw previously were treatable. This one is not.

"Don't make me any more promises. You can say the words, but their meaning has to be executed to become true." Lara clenches her fists in frustration while clenching her jaw as hard as she can. There is no easy way out of here. "You promised to teach me all you know!"

"I *have* taught you all I know. You must take care of yourself. I know you'll do fine...even without the sacred..."

"No! There is so much more I need you for. I have questions, you know. I even wrote them down... There is so much more I need to learn."

"Nonsense. You've...exceeded my expectations." Her master's breathing gets deeper and slower with each fleeting moment.

Her master is a fighter. Lara has to get her angry and keep her fighting to survive. That is the only way.

"You are selfish. You only taught me to hate and kill. You never taught me to love." She lets her weakness show in an endless stream across her cheeks.

Her master's face seems as if it is radiating with soft light from an unknown force.

"If you could only see yourself, you would know that I have." With those words lingering on her lips, her master's body falls back like a stiff statue—slowly turning dull and flaky. There is no doubt about it, she is gone.

"I am not done fighting with you! You never back down, and you never lose, even when you should have let me win. You hear me? I want to fight with you...just a little longer." She feels horrible saying such a thing to her mentor who gave her so many years of her life.

There is so much more Lara wants to say to her dearest friend, but it is too late. She wasted her last moments on an attempt to make her fight just a little longer. Gripping on to her teacher, her family, her world, Lara loses all her composure. "You can't leave me like this! It's not fair!" Her master's form starts to crumble inside her young hands. She cannot hold on to the moment any longer. It is gone, never to return.

In this fraction of time, her master is the only care she has. Years and years of training instantly undone as she breaks to the ground, trying to take back every error she has ever made. "I have things to get off my chest. Please come back to me. I am sorry for everything. I want to take it back, take it all back." Her words are tied up with painful sobs, occasionally causing her to gasp for air between hysterics.

All the other mess is gone—fate, destiny, the whole lot.

Lara embraces what is left of her master's husk, though it falls into pieces within her hugging arms. "I need you, more now than ever," she says with a trembling whisper.

Never will she hear those dreadful lectures again. All because she wanted to have a little fun with the renegade human. There is nothing fun about this now. Why can't she take it back? Why can't it be a mistake she learns from and fixes? The forward motion of time is a stubborn stickler for the rules.

In the empty space in her embrace, something hard falls to the ground. It is a circular pit, exactly like the ones she saw in the storage room. If that fell out of her, what does that say about the crate full of them? There is so much about her race that Lara doesn't understand. Life and death are very much on that list. *Is this all that's left of her? A token, a memento?*

She holds her master's pit to her chest tenderly as she sniffles softly. She has never felt so small and insignificant. Out of her control, emotions cycle through her—anger, defeat, dismay, regret, respect, to name a few. They are changing so quickly, it is hard for her to grasp anything tangible, or express herself in a proper manner. She breaks down, buckling to her knees. Physical pain is something she can handle in abundance. However, she has never felt emotional strife such as this. It is wrecking her, making her unable to control her shaking body.

"I will do all my training and never talk back or defy you," Lara continues to plead to the pit of her master, to no avail.

It is unbearable. She can't take the pain of living any longer. Her master taught her to detach from herself, to do what needed to be done without her feelings or emotions getting involved. This gave her to ability to kill without remorse or guilt. The only flaw is that she was attached to her master, and the trick isn't working, not this time.

All the guilt comes crashing down upon her at once, and it isn't what you call a "safe landing."

Once anger passes through her, she holds on to it, trying to stop herself from grieving any longer.

Death is a major part of life, but she never thought she could feel so much sentiment when someone transitioned. How many humans has she ended in her lifetime? Hundreds? Maybe a thousand? Was there someone close to each of them that felt the same as she does right now—like they have lost someone irreplaceable?

That's the missing piece to the human stories that she has been looking for and her master censored for so long. It was endearing, likable qualities and, most of all, love. Yes, love, the devastating feeling that makes someone a folk, or even a human. They are more similar than she once believed. If they can breed together, like this *thing* her master spoke of, that means that they are no different, human and folk.

Her master, always a teacher until her dying breath. And Lara doesn't doubt there are more lessons to be learned, even in the afterlife.

What is so special with these particular invaders that her master would trade her life to help them? This is the burning question that is clawing at her mind. What is this cargo, and what is its significance? It has to be important, that much is apparent.

"I don't want to protect a world without you in it," Lara admits.

"I can help you with that request," the immortal says from out of the shadows. In the corner of the room, darkness changes into light as he turns his illuminating cloak, which was inside out, right side in. The immortal was there this whole time, hiding inside the darkness his cloak cast. He must have been the one who finished off her master while he had the chance. He hit Lara where it hurts, in her weak spot—her master.

This is her fault. She failed again at a simple task, failed at keeping him distracted. Guilt punches her in the gut, hard. Why did she have to run so fast? Why does everything always go south when she has the upper hand? Why didn't her master warn her, or at least say anything? Instead, she wasted her words on compliments? These questions and more plague her young mind.

This is something she doesn't have time to dwell on. There will be many years of emotional trauma, leaving Lara time to pour over these events, leaving no detail unturned.

"You're right. I don't have to fight him." Wiping away a final tear, she gingerly places her master's pit down. Lara reaches inside her pack, pulling out the three fist weapons she had made for her master. She holds each one up to what is left of her master, showing them off proudly. "I made these for you, so that you can feel complete again. I knew you would never use them, but I made them anyway because that is what I do," she lets out tearful laugh. "I didn't mean to disobey you. I made them because I care about you. It's a funny way of showing it, but it's my way, I guess. I just wanted you to feel how you make me feel on a daily basis—complete." Lara attaches the clawed glove to her elbow, tightening down the straps.

"Isn't that touching..." The immortal swipes

at her, now that he's in reach, but she circles out of the way.

With a child-like expression on her face, she attaches the blunt knuckles to her knee. "This one is for heavy armor. You can crush your foe internally with this hammer hand. I remember the stories you told me about your battles with the metalmen." Lara lets a sorrowful smile escape as she bites her lip.

"You know she can't hear you, right? Why? Because I killed her. She is dead. The long forever."

Ignoring the immortal, she walks around the length of the room, pulling out the third, and final, arm attachment. It is the one meant for chopping. She adjusts the strap all the way and wears it on her other elbow. "This one is for cutting guys down and severing limbs."

"Oh, I know that all too well," the immortal admits with a chuckle, trying to lay claim to her master's missing limbs.

"I know it wasn't you. Your sword couldn't cut anything without making hundreds of tiny holes first," she corrects him, instantly regretting the engagement.

Having made her final strap adjustments, Lara is now ready—repurposing the gifts she made for her master. Never having been brave enough to give them to her, now she is brave enough to use them herself. She lets her master's fighting style encompass her soul. "I see clearly now."

The immortal comes at her with unmatched speed and precision.

She blocks and parries each strike with the help of her two swords and three fist attachments. This is giving her the upper hand, or hands. She needs to keep him at bay. It is like five against one.

The immortal goes on the defensive and adjusts accordingly, as if he is being attacked by a mob.

Fighting this close to him, Lara notices something peculiar with the mask he wears. Based on its yellow glow, she believes it has some magical properties. It isn't just to cover up hideousness. Though he really is hideous.

Inside the mask's eye, she sees a different scene playing out. It's a human man. He appears to be collecting the pits she discovered next to the pile of bones. This has to be the cargo that she was supposed to help them acquire.

If they *are* the same objects that came out of

her master, that would mean that they are all that remain of the feathered-folk of the forest. This is where they all went, hidden deep in a cave. Lara knows very little of her heritage and the significance of rescuing the pits, or what to do with them once they are liberated. They must be worth dying for, or so her master thought. The immortal surely does, enough to keep them for all these years. That is a good enough reason, because whatever he wants, Lara is going to make sure he doesn't get it. Not anymore. Not ever again.

Based on his twisted facial features and how he seems to be drifting in the direction of the storage room, the immortal also seems concerned with the companions' actions. He could be watching their every move through some magical means.

She can no longer obey her master's request to not kill this beast of a man, even if she wanted to. Letting the likes of him live only taints the air everyone else has to share. Cleansing him from this world is the only way. Promises are made to be broken—so are hearts and dreams. Life is pain, and you have to just live with it as long as you can bear.

Thinking back, her master did say while she

was alive. A loophole of semantics that Lara will exploit. Truth be told, nothing could stop her from dealing with this bully. Not because she wants to; there is just no other choice. Right here, right now, someone is going to perish.

The figures in the mask are not ready to leave this place, and she is their only hope of getting out alive. In the off chance that she fails, she must not and kill him or die too fast. They will need to dance a little, to bide some time.

Defining moments don't define anything if you escape them. This will be one of those very moments, and she plans on showing off as if her master were watching her as she transitions to the next life.

Lara comes at him with heart and focus, occasionally landing a slice or slash, though it seems to do nothing but bolster his ego.

Immortal or not, she fights back with all that she has left, everything she has ever had. Exhaling through each attack, inhaling with each parry. Each move she makes is fought with passion and respect, leaving the last of her youth behind. This is growing up—facing what you need without ever getting what you want.

He keeps attempting to disarm her, but like a juggler, she simply catches her weapon with her other hand, switching hands in succession. She doesn't even blink, to avoid giving him an opening in her routine—staring him down with a devilish gaze. This fight isn't to win; it's only a distraction. By that logic alone, she is winning. She just needs to keep him busy enough for the two companions to do their task.

The immortal lord has never seen such a relentless opponent. "Just give up, already. You cannot win because, as you know, I cannot die."

She doesn't give him the satisfaction of her banter. She looks at him plainly and continues the onslaught of attacks, watching the companions in the mask's socket. With all the weapons at her disposal, she manages to push him back against the wall.

"Your strikes lack any power behind them. You may have talent, but you're weak. How do you think you're going to hurt me, pitiful child?" He kicks her in the gut with his heavy boot. This answers her question those feet are actually a part of him or not.

After a swift parry, with a downward motion, she uses the chopping blade on her elbow to slice into his mask, cutting it straight off his face.

He drops and scrounges around the floor

like a man looking for a fallen monocle. "What have you done? My face..."

His spider-like hair is standing on end, and the full extent of his grotesque features is exposed for her to see. The section where the mask was is now exposed tissue and bone. It must have been on his face for so long that his skin fused into it, and when the mask went, so did half his face.

His horrendous visage knows no equal—decrepit, withered, and contorted from disease, curse or fire, or maybe a combination of the three. She cannot bear to look at it any longer, but endures. He is everything that is wrong with the world, wrapped up in a single being.

"The show's over. You don't get to watch any longer," Lara says with disgust in her voice.

Holding his epee with both hands, it begins to crystalize and become stiff as stone, losing its once flexible finesse. "Well, you don't get to live anymore."

The immortal comes at her with all his hatred and power embodied in a vile scream. Each strike knocks her off balance and pushes her backwards. His rage powers each strike, giving him the upper hand.

No matter what she does, she's too small to

not be overpowered by his strikes. Losing ground, she tries to flee out of his reach and re-group, but he stabs the ground like before, pulling himself closer to her, matching her stride.

"I unleash upon you one thousand years of pain and torture!"

The young assassin is slow to anticipate his moves, but it doesn't matter. The pace of the fight is no longer up to her. She decides to not let that happen, not any longer, and looks fear directly in its hideous face. She drops one blade and matches his stance, holding just one of her stone swords with both hands. Preparing for a powerful strike of her own, she screams through the maneuver.

The immortal readies a lunge at her throat.

She doesn't flinch. Instead, she comes at him with unwavering conviction.

Both attacks move toward each other as they trade blows. The moment slows down. Sweat glistens off her body like an angelic glow. He is straining, blood and gore dripping from his rotten face.

At the very last second, she manages to block his attack with her clawed elbow attach-ment. Her sword chops into the crook of his neck, with all her might behind it. It hits his spinal cord and stops dead in its tracks—not going all the way through—thwarting her decapitation.

This is what he was anticipating and pulls back, already prepared to take another quick stab at her. "Ahhh, haha. It may hurt so good, but it doesn't stop me in the least. Nothing ever will," he gurgles through his open neck hole.

He finishes his lunge, and Lara ducks underneath it at the very last moment. His weapon is much slower and heavier, now that it is crystalized.

Grabbing the sword she dropped on the ground, she swipes at the underbelly of his wrist guard—knocking the blade out of his hand and taking along a couple of fingers. The mangled hand hangs like an object.

Ignoring everything but her task, she quickly places the hole in her stone sword over the peg on the stone sword still lodged in his neck—connecting them. "You see, you don't need strength when you have ingenuity." Using both blades as a giant pair of scissors, she pulls the hilts together, using leverage to her advantage. Her muscles strain and stretch as the blades pinch closed.

A cringe-worthy popping and crunching sound rings throughout the hall as she cuts and tears the immortal's head clean off—in a unique diagonal angle.

Both parts of him fall to the ground independently. Trading blows isn't really fair when you cannot die, and she knew he wouldn't play fair.

Both pieces of his body twitch, a little life still remaining, despite the life-ending move. Launching in the air, she bashes his skull with the blunt fist attached to her knee, using her weight to her advantage. Still, she is too light.

Picking up a boulder for added weight, she jumps on him over and over until he stops moving altogether and his head begins to crack and leak.

She is covered in splatters of him. Is he dead or mortally wounded? Is death even an option at this point? No matter the outcome, the strange feeling inside her is suddenly at peace, and it's serene.

"For your sake, I hope you really aren't immortal. But just for good measure, I'm taking these and leaving your body to rot forever."

Lara isn't going to take any chances. With a couple of quick snips, she severs both his hands, using the same method as the crude de-capitation. Even if he comes back from the dead, he won't be nearly as deadly.

Without hesitation, she shoves both of his bloody limbs inside her pack...just in case.

Parting Ways

Countless times Lara has killed, but this is the first time her victim truly deserved it. A crippling pang of sorrow fills her when she thinks about all the humans she has slaughtered in the name of survival. It may take the rest of her lifetime to complete, but her debt must be paid, and that starts today.

There was no other option than fighting that thing. Her master must have known that reverse psychology works wonders on her protégée. It is all clear now. A smile forms on her face just thinking about her master's tactics. *She did and said what I needed to hear to complete the task. That is all.* Except her master promised her answers, and now she is left more confused than ever.

After defeating the immortal, Lara abides her master's instructions, leaving the companions to their task—never asking why or how.

But then something strange happens. She is drawn to the immortal's mask. It's beckoning her in a language without words.

Her feet move independently as she inches closer to it. There she stands, looming over the thing. The inside is still laced with the human's gore.

"Put me on!" the object demands of her through sheer conceptualization.

Reluctantly she reaches for it.

It feels rife with energy as it fits perfectly inside her palms.

Upon touching it, images flash before her eyes—people, places, and things she recognizes but never set eyes on. All the fantasies she hid in her head are becoming a reality.

She is here, then on a peak riding a mighty stead, hearing the howling wind against her heavy armor. It is as if her eyes are tuning into another place in time.

Then she is back, feeling ripped right out of reality again. Both places seem no more real than the other. Living in different times, yet at the same time.

She holds the mask away from her face, slowly bringing it closer. If touching it brings such a feeling, she wonders what it would feel like to put it on—if only for a moment.

Everything is coming at her all at once, and it is overwhelming to comprehend.

Now she is in a dense forest petting a friendly beast with long claws. In this instance, all her previous knowledge is gone. She isn't just witnessing this place; she is there. This is the present. It feels peaceful and safe.

Like before, as fast as it came, it violently leaves.

Now with the mask only inches from her face, it all starts to make perfect sense—just as her master had promised. Nothing is as it seems—the concept of forever and never seem to meet somewhere in the middle. Life isn't that precious, nor is death that final.

Elbowing the mask with her clawed attachment, it breaks into two smaller pieces of albino wood.

Lara knows who she is, who she was, and who she is going to be. She is the bearer of many names, many titles. She is special—the first of her tribe of feathered-folk. The connection with the mask unlocked all of her lives through the forest's magic.

The image of each life is vague with conflicting details, where the more her mind reaches for it, the more distant it becomes. It's like she had all the answers one second and now they're suddenly slipping away.

Like the seed of a fruit-bearing tree, the pit of a feathered-folk lives on through each planting. Each life evolves into something new and even more sentient.

All future, past, and present incarnations and reincarnations of herself were simultaneously unlocked. The places she went inside the mask weren't just fantasies. They were echoes of other existences she has had, or is going to have.

Time is different for the magically infused. She has and will live from the dusk to the dawn of time—sometimes dormant, other lifetimes being quite active, like this one. It doesn't end here with her, nor does it start.

When she would delve into her imagination, she was just using the experiences from these other lives, as if tearing a page out of two different books and reading them together as one. Her fantasies were just as real as they were fake. An amalgamation of truth and lies, where the lines are only blurred by a simple feeling.

Like all feathered-folk, as long as their pits survive, there is hope for them and the forest where they live.

She looks down at her master's pit and wonders what would become of it if it were to stay with her. The young feathered-folk imagines herself as an old maid, a hermit, talking to her master as her only companion, like some spindly lady talking to her taxidermized cats.

This is not Lara's fate, or else she would have seen it unfold while holding the mask. No, she will become the best that ever lived, like something out of a human epic saga.

As for her master, she never enjoyed Lara's ramblings, anyway. Why would the afterlife prove any different? This is not her master's burden, not any longer. She alone will be the guardian of the forest and restore peace among everything.

Lara claims the immortal's light/dark cloak and pulls it over herself. Turning the cloak one side exudes darkness, and the other, light. Folding it equally between the two causes it to negate both effects, giving it a simple tattered look.

Making her way back to the room with the mind-numbing smell, bones, and pits, she approaches a human and a figure that resembles a feathered-folk, but different somehow.

They both freeze at the sight of her.

"You forgot one," Lara says, extending out her hand, offering her master's pit. "This one deserves a vacation."

"Oh...why thank you," the human says, gently grabbing the pit from her clutches, adding it to their pile. "Who are you?"

"Just someone doing the right thing."

"You sound familiar. Do I know you from somewhere?" the feathered-one asks.

Lara pulls her cloak tighter, hiding herself even more. "No, I get that a lot," Lara says, in a lower voice, trying to disguise herself. Before awkwardness can set in, she turns her back to them, and quickly makes her exit.

"Thank you," they both yell out to her in unison.

"For what?" Lara asks, pausing slightly.

"For saving me...I mean us. I don't know why I said 'me.'"

"Oh..."

"That was you, right?"

With a reluctant nod, she turns the corner

out of sight, and nearly out of breath. Her body is perspiring. She feels weak in the knees. She doesn't understand why that was so hard for her.

It takes everything she has to not look back. But nature is nature, and Lara can't change who she is any more than she could pretend to not care about her master, who was everything to her.

She catches a glance of the two who have loaded up a cart with all the pits. One is a short human, weak and stout. The other is a male feathered-folk. Upon looking at him she feels complete somehow, almost pure, like a restful sense of peace. Majestic light glows from the crown of her head. Something is different.

At first she thinks it's the cloak's power, but it is a different kind of light—soft and gentle. She touches the spot from where the light is emanating. There are dainty flowers blooming on top of her feathery head. This is something unexpected, something new, something quite grand...

This trait has long been lost among her people. Ever since the humans had come to the forest, greed had overtaken their kind nature, uprooting the symbiosis of nature's design. As a result, the forest started to die, alongside their love and compassion.

The flowers on her head shine so brightly, giving her solace in time of goodbyes. There is something about that feathered one that unlocks a feeling that has been jailed inside her soul—kindness.

As long as she is happy, those flowers will rest upon her head, like her ancestors before her, and those before them. Which is also to say that the opposite would be true, if they were ever to wilt and die. They symbolize a beacon of hope, a contagious glow that will inspire the hearts of many.

And now she knows her purpose in this world is...

...to keep them forever blooming.

Epilogue

One month later...

A long-lost sound blows through the forest, lifting up ash from the ground and taking it to far-away reaches.

Upon hearing this miraculous sound, The Enchantress rushes to the albino tree just in time to see that its bark has been restored in the place where it was once stolen. Ethereal and tranquil, it shifts and moves like quicksand until the spot is almost unnoticeable. It has been a long time coming, but something is different.

"The curse...it's reversing. She must have done it!"

The Enchantress looks all around, hoping to catch a glimpse of a fleeing shadow—anything to shed light as to how or why.

Delicate leaves quickly sprout on the albino tree's old branches, as if they're catching up for lost time.

This is how The Enchantress remembered the tree, as it was when she was a child. Things are going back to the way they were, as if time is reversing, for the better. Glee fills The Enchantress as she spins and twirls around, singing a song of reprieve. This goes on until her legs go weak, and she falls to the ground on top of her flowy skirt. She feels young again—full of life.

"There is but one thing left to do before life will be complete—find the stolen fruit..."

The End

Make sure you check out the next release in the *Tarnished Lands* world:
The Mad Wizard!

As a new author, it's extremely difficult to get started without the support of a marketing team and publisher. The make break point for self-published authors is honest reviews.

If you could take a couple of minutes to leave a review on Amazon and/or Goodreads, (even a line or two) it would be greatly appreciated.

Thank you so much!
-PA

ABOUT THE AUTHOR

After surviving an almost fatal car accident directly in front of a bookstore, P.A. Wikoff decided not to ignore the sign and proceeded to self-publish his work. Mr. Wikoff kick-started his writing career by releasing the epic fantasy novel "Feylin Lore: Reflections." When P.A. is not writing, he spends all of his free time with his beautiful wife and two fabulous kids who inspire him every single day.

A Dark Fantasy Novella

The
Harrowed
Half-Breed

P.A. Wikoff

Magic has been slowly fading from the enchanted forest ever since the greedy humans invaded. The native feathered-folk were kind in sharing their homeland, but peace couldn't last forever. Conflict stirs while Barne, half human/half native, is stuck in the middle. Trapped between two worlds he must try and find himself before choosing a side. In a world where he never really belongs, Barne searches to find his smile through all means necessary. But there's a dark secret that holds his happiness hostage...

Review: *Hot damn, this was an awesome book. I wouldn't call this a "horror" book, but more of a dark fantasy. P.A. Wikoff builds a grisly world with all sorts of creatures you've never thought of. It's violent, gritty and dark. It has a strong plot and you gotta have a stomach for it. Hang around and this will tell you a story like never before. I am blown away.*

A Fantasy/Romance Novel

·FEYLIN LORE·
REFLECTIONS

P.A. WIKOFF

Talia is a mysterious woman with a complicated past. She is a fighter who keeps her thoughts and feelings well guarded. While fulfilling her destiny, she meets Hark—a man whom she is inexplicably drawn to. Little does she know, her life will play out before his eyes during the very moment he intends to destroy her. Hark develops a deeper understanding of Talia's past as her secrets are revealed to him. Will Hark choose his feelings over the fate of the world, or is it much too late?

Review: *This is a great fantasy book! I absolutely loved this story! You can't imagine the world this story brings to life. The narration was superb and gave that extra flair to the story. It will keep you entertained. This was my first book by this author but definitely will not be my last. I will be reading any books that are released in this series (can't wait).*

A Single-Author Collection

ANTHOLOGY OF SCROLLS

P.A. WIKOFF

Magical libraries, ego-eccentric gravity experts, O.C.D. people, scary stage shows, dirt-poor romance, spirit guides, calming yourself down, moment stealing harpies, corrupt elections, gluttonous cake eaters, evil doppelgangers, drunken incoherence, circles, cross dressing witches and warlocks, catching up with the past, antiquated technology, treasures in the trash, brain surgery, irreplaceable loss, gang-bangers and their dogs, comic books that contain bats and/or wolves, the murder of relatives, revengeful ex-girlfriends, changing fact into fiction, magical smartphones, facing your unfiltered fears, severed lizards and dangerous Christmas gifts. 28 shorter works accompanied by photographs P.A. Wikoff took to add a visual aid to each literary piece.

Review: *I'm not a big fan of short stories or poetry, but I enjoyed this ebook. My favorites are The Librarian's Story and Pockets Void of Green. I read The Librarian's Story out loud to my husband and it had us both laughing at the Crazy Girl. The Pockets Void of Green is a very deep poem that leaves you thinking long after reading it. Each little narrative has a deep meaning.*

www.ingramcontent.com/pod-product-compliance
Lightning Source LLC
Chambersburg PA
CBHW072159130726
47910CB00011B/1638